Juan Antonio Masoliver was born in Barcelona in 1939. He lives in London and teaches Spanish and Latin American Literature at the University of Westminster. He is the translator of Robert Coover, Vladimir Nabokov and Djuna Barnes amongst others; literary critic for *La Vanguardia* of Barcelona; novelist (*Retiro lo escrito*, *Beatriz Miami*) and poet (*El jardín aciago*, *La casa de la maleza*).

The Origins of Desire

Modern Spanish Short Stories

Edited by Juan Antonio Masoliver

Library of Congress Catalog Card No: 92-83759

A catalogue record for this book is available from
the British Library on request

First published 1993 by Serpent's Tail, 4 Blackstock
Mews, London N4, and
401 West Broadway #1, New York, NY 10012

Typeset in 10/12½ Times Roman by
Contour Typesetters, Southall, London
Printed in Great Britain by Cox & Wyman Ltd.,
of Reading, Berkshire

Contents

To Nissa Torrents, *in memoriam*

Introduction

The short story is the literary genre which has more obdurately resisted attempts at definition, and at the same time it has been the one genre more dependent on other genres to find a definition. Whether common traits are sought with the novel (tension of the narrative or of the storyline) or with poetry (the tension of the language), such relationship has been seen as one of dependency, turning the short story into a sub-genre. Literary theory has made a substantial contribution to disentangling this misunderstanding, and in this sense Vladimir Propp's *The Morphology of the Folktale* (1928) is an unavoidable reference.

The practitioners of the genre themselves have been able to define it through their own experience – suffice it to mention Chekhov or Poe, the Latin American writers Horacio Quiroga, Julio Cortázar, Enrique Anderson Imbert or Augusto Monterroso, or Spaniards such as Emilia Pardo Bazán, Clarín, Azorín or Francisco Ayala. The relative and perhaps transitory discredit of the nineteenth-century type of novel, as well as the blurring of the rigid division between literary genres, allows for the rejection of the dependency notion and of the historically even more valid one of interdependency, rescuing the short story from its predicament as poor relation or inferior genre. All these factors have inevitably left their mark in the fertile development of the contemporary Spanish short story, which will nevertheless encounter, as we shall see, serious obstacles.

The short story is, moreover, the genre that throughout time has gone through more convulsions and has struggled more to remain faithful to its origins, to enlarge its range of expressiveness and to affirm its independence of the novella and of the novel itself. The short story was born as a form of artistic expression of the oral tradition, linking in a close relationship narrator and listener – which explains the fact that even today the first-person narration is dominant – and of the need to entertain, teach or moralize (usually all three simultaneously) as is still evident in the *Panchatantra*, *Arabian Nights* or, in the fourteenth century in Don Juan Manuel's *Conde Lucanor*, or Boccaccio's *Decameron*.

With the spread of the printed word it was inevitable that this oral tradition would become but a rhetorical device, and as such it has survived the centuries. Yet the short story was threatened by the birth of the novel as a genre. In the sixteenth century *Lazarillo de Tormes* aspired to be a novel (a sole character as protagonist, a unity of purpose, a stressed relationship among the different parts of the book, etc.) without rejecting the vibrant presence of the story. Each chapter or 'treatise' stands on its own, just as a short story would; the main character has a clear vocation as a narrator (shared, to a certain extent, with the blind man and the pardoner) and the author reveals an intimate knowledge of the traditional short story as well as a remarkable ability to adapt it to the demands of his own narrative. In the seventeenth century, even though *Don Quixote* represents the absolute and conscious triumph of the novel as we know it today, the other genres – albeit wholly integrated with the architecture of the novel – are never in a subordinate position: rather, they have a life of their own. And there are many characters with the vocation to be narrators, not to mention those with the vocation to listen. We should remember that the first contact that school children have with *Don Quixote* is through its episodes, that is to say, it is read like a storybook. In all probability they will never read it as a book, because for most people *Don Quixote* does not have an independent existence as a novel. Thus, it is not surprising that for contemporary story writers (and *Don Quixote* is nearer to us than to the nineteenth century just as, for instance, Sterne is closer than Dickens or

Pérez Galdos) who have never written novels (Borges or Monterroso are a case in point), *Don Quixote* is the model *par excellence*.

Paradoxically, in Spain the short story began to be considered a sub-genre in the nineteenth century, the same time when it became an independent genre, and began to compete with the novel and enjoy its popularity. This was also the time when it definitively shed its oral tradition of medieval origin to address – like the novel – not a listener or somebody who needed to imagine the narrator's voice to make the story credible, but someone who is solely *a reader*. However, writers have not invented this hierarchy, since many of them wrote in both genres indistinctly: names that come to mind are Alarcón, Pereda, Clarín, Pardo Bazán or Palacio Valdés. Nor was it a creation of the public, because both the novel and the short story became enormously popular in Spain through newspapers and magazines, a popularity that lasted all along the first two decades of the twentieth century, especially in *El Cuento Semanal* (1901–20) where Azorín, Ramón Pérez de Ayala, Gabriel Miró, Wenceslao Fernández Flores and Ramón Gómez de la Serna, among others, were published. The proliferation of periodicals (*El Libro Popular*, *La Novela Semanal*, *La Novela del Domingo*, *Los Contemporáneos*, *El Cuento del Sábado*, *El Cuento Azul*, etc.), was an indication of the apogee of the novella and the short story, but it turned into a mixed blessing: on the one hand those publications contributed to its diffusion, but on the other they produced a saturation that soon turned into boredom. Popularity became the paramount consideration to the detriment of artistic quality, and they ended up as vehicles for the promotion of writers – a practice much favoured until very recently. In this way the short story began to be considered a sub-genre not only by critics but also by publishers, readers and writers themselves. The demise of *El Cuento Semanal* in 1920 coincided with the beginning of a crisis that would reach its lowest point at the time of the Spanish Civil War of 1936–9. And it is against this adverse backdrop that the contemporary short story will emerge.

In order to understand the dynamics of the contemporary short story, and by contemporary I mean the fifty years since the end of the Civil War, it is also necessary to understand the political dynamics of the period. It would be a mistake to believe that the thirty-six years of Francoist dictatorship made no impact on the arts, especially in cinema and in literature. On the contrary, every decade had the imprint of profound changes, both political and literary. The forties were dominated by repression, by the isolation of Spain, poverty, and the hegemony of Fascist ideology through the *Falange*; censorship was widespread and strong, and a majority of writers had to go into exile. The short story was in crisis: the quality was mediocre, there were very few publications, and publishing houses shied away from it. In the fifties Francoism endeavoured to overcome its isolation with the support of the Catholic Church and the United States. The power of *Falange* weakened, and this ideological feebleness ran parallel to a greater social awareness in a new generation of Spaniards who only knew the Civil War as a childhood experience.

This was the generation known in literature as the generation of 1950. Rarely before had a group of writers shared to such an extent a task and an aesthetic, that is to say, the denunciation of injustice by means of social realism, although in many stories the Civil War – or rather memories of it – was present in an elegiac tone that helped to correct the excesses typical of a *littérature engagée*. The fact that this type of writing has today gone out of fashion should not lead us to the false conclusion that it was a negative era: on the contrary, there was a new flourishing of the short story and of the novel, as revealed by the writings of Ignacio Aldecoa, Carmen Martín Gaite, Ana María Matute, Juan Goytisolo, Medardo Fraile, Jesús Fernández Santos, Rafael Sánchez Ferlosio, Juan García Hortelano and Daniel Sueiro, to mention only the most prominent. These names illustrate the fact that simplistic dogmatism was rare, and that common preoccupations drew a wide aesthetic framework.

The problem, if there was one, lay in the fact that most of those writers did not know how to – or did not want to – adapt to the remarkable changes of the 1960s. In the field of political transformations, the economic development encouraged by a government of technocrats represented the beginning of the end of Francoism, and social concerns were largely overtaken by the defence of civil liberties, an urge for personal development and freedom also found in literature. Some writers, such as Juan Goytisolo or Luis Martín-Santos, destroyed the realist novel from within realism itself; others – and Luis Goytisolo is a case in point, a writer representative of the demands of the times – tried to avoid traditional realism altogether. But these new approaches did not occur in the realm of the short story, which went into a period of stagnation.

This marked the end of the first stage of the Spanish contemporary short story, embodied in the work of those writers who experienced the Civil War and immediate aftermath as adults (Rafael Sánchez Mazas, Samuel Ros, Edgar Neville, Miguel Mihura, Alvaro Cunqueiro or Camilo José Cela) and the generation of 1950. This period is best represented in *Cuento Español de Posguerra* by one of the most notable experts in the field, Medardo Fraile.

In the same way that the writers of the first period were all born before the Civil War, started to write during its aftermath and experienced the evolution of Francoism throughout three decades, those included in this anthology were born – Javier Tomeo and Esther Tusquets excepted – after the war, started writing during Francoism's fading years, and experienced the extraordinary changes that led from the struggle for freedom to a 'habit of freedom' more typical of democratic societies. At the beginning of the 1970s Francoism was already an anachronism. Its true agony had begun in 1973 when General Franco remained Head of State while naming as Head of Government (and 'heir apparent') Admiral Carrero Blanco, who represented those who favoured a 'liberal' path after Franco's death. Carrero's killing accelerated the pace of Francoism's decadence. Franco's death in 1975 was followed by a period of uncertainty brought about, to a certain extent, by those who, under Arias Navarro's presidency, refused to accept the inevitability of the regime's disappearance. The *novísimos* emerged in literature in the first five years of that era and the name was taken from

Josep Maria Castellet's anthology of poetry, the *Nueve novísimos* (1970). The *novísimos* suggested new cultural models far removed from the Spanish tradition, but at the same time they sought to recover what was most valuable in what Vázquez Montalbán has described as the 'sentimental education' they underwent under Francoism. And just as the previous generation had looked back on the tragic years of the Civil War and its immediate aftermath, the present one found its inspiration in the more dismal years of Francoism. There was still a strong ethical component in the new group of writers, but humour, creative freedom and cosmopolitanism left their mark. A majority were poets, or poets and fiction writers, and only occasionally did they write short stories – and thus Félix de Azúa and Vicente Molina Foix are not included in the present anthology. However, Manuel Vázquez Montalbán and Ana María Moix represent accurately the spirit of the *novísimos*. Perhaps I should add Esther Tusquets, so close to Ana María Moix, who only published her first book in 1978. Lastly, Javier Marías has many things in common with the group, but we identify him more readily with the following generation, of which he is forerunner and a clear influence.

The year 1976 signalled another key date in the political and cultural evolution of Spain: Adolfo Suárez was appointed President of the Government and on 15 December of that year a referendum showed a majority in favour of a new constitution, which was to become one of the most liberal in Europe. We are now in times of *desencanto* (a disenchantment enhanced by the economic crisis) and of the *movida*, two apparently opposed attitudes but expressive of a similar indifference towards the conflicts and ethical quandries of previous generations, as well as a disquieting and amoral attitude towards life. Although it is true that there were signs of widespread frivolity, the truth is that literature benefited considerably from the vitality surging from this new sense of freedom, opening up an enormous range of possibilities. Taken together with the dynamic culture backed by official institutions, and the emergence or consolidation of publishing houses such as Anagrama, Tusquets or Quaderns Crema, where literary criteria influenced strictly commercial ones, the picture was one of an unprecedented development of the short story. This development extended well into the 1980s, a decade which, with the 1982 electoral victory of Felipe González, the Socialist candidate, marked the end of the transition period. The acceptance of socialism by the army and the more conservative sectors of Spanish society meant the definitive institutionalization of democracy. Literature could now devote itself to problems that were neither exclusively political nor social, and penetrated freely the (up to then) forbidden labyrinths of the imagination.

This is not the place to offer a literary analysis of all the authors included in this anthology. My intention is to draw a picture in which the reader will be better able to appreciate, among other things, the artistic quality, the originality and the maturity achieved by the short story throughout the last twenty years. The new writers do not rebel against those of previous generations; rather – with the exception of Juan Benet, a true inspiration for many – they ignore them: there is a need to break with the past and make a fresh start. The post-Civil War writers drew their inspiration from national sources, and more often from novelists than from short-story writers. Even in the 1960s, with the arrival in Spain of the new Latin American narrative (the so-called 'boom') there was an almost exclusive fascination with the novels of writers such as Mario Vargas Llosa, Julio Cortázar, Gabriel García Márquez or Carlos Fuentes, when most of them were in fact excellent short-story writers. The end of Francoism saw the demise of the 'boom'. The end of censorship heralded a new dynamic in publishing, a result of which would be the proliferation of translations. Story writers gained a new awareness of the genre (of its history, its technical aspects and its theoretical approaches), making them more demanding not only in their own writing, but also in what they were reading: Chekhov, Maupassant, Poe, Kafka or Joyce were no longer mere references, but living presences in fiction writing. And the same applied to the great Latin American short-story writers: Horacio Quiroga, Felisberto Hernández, Jorge Luis Borges, Juan Rulfo, Adolfo Bioy Casares, Juan

Carlos Onetti, Augusto Monterroso or Juan José Arreola. While for the story writers of the first period Cesare Pavese embodied the Italian model (and once again, his novels were more influential than his short stories or his novella, *The Beach*), today the model would be Italo Calvino.

The distance separating the short story of the last two decades from the different forms that realism took in the two previous ones, is now established. Practically all current fiction (and the short story more so than the novel) is imbued with fantastical elements in the shape of dreams, terror, mystery, omens, or supernatural phenomena, erasing the boundaries between everyday reality and imagination. Although predominantly urban in character, places are seldom identified or they reveal exotic locations, to highlight the cosmopolitan nature of the narration. Humour has lost the aggressiveness and grotesque distortion of the Spanish realist tradition, to become ridiculous or ironic. Eroticism is everywhere in evidence, but sex as guilt and as the expression of a repressive morality has disappeared. There is an urge for originality and for avoiding the commonplace (typical of the realist story), while straining for effect and making a brilliant use of smile. Moreover, if on the one hand there is a textual consciousness typical of the story in the literary tradition, on the other there is true joy in telling a story, in recounting, inventing and astonishing within the oral tradition to which I referred at the beginning of this introduction. In a majority of the stories ancestral fear, solitude or the inability to communicate, the passing of time (nostalgia for childhood, ageing, death) are dominant. Having established its distance from nineteeth-century realism as well as from experimentalism – the Spanish short story of the last two decades, and of the one that has only just begun, does not look for freedom in denunciation or experimentation. It lives within that freedom.

Finally, a few words to explain the criteria followed in selecting the stories included in this anthology. And I say explain, and not justify, as is usually the case with editors of anthologies, because I believe that with a transparent criterion and a degree of eclecticism that will impede the exclusion of aesthetic paths which the editor does not necessarily find congenial, it is possible to present a reasonably objective anthology. At the time of making a decision I have considered the quality of the story, the extent to which it is representative of an author's work as a whole, and how far it represents the spirit of the new writing: in all the writers included in this anthology there is something new that identifies them with the other writers of the period and separates them from the previous one (the period represented in Medardo Fraile's anthology, an essential reference). This explains the inclusion of story-writers in the rural tradition, such as Luis Mateo Díez or José María Merino; or 'decadent' ones, as may be the case of Pedro García Montalvo. The length, of course, bears no relation with either the quality or the interest of the story. In few instances was I forced to leave out a story that exceeded either the nature or the limits of the anthology, and replace it by another story, equally representative, of the same author. These criteria cannot, of course, be applied to writers such as Ana María Moix or Esther Tusquets, who only write long stories, just as Javier Tomeo is a master of the very short story, and as such he is represented here.

In all anthologies every inclusion is self-explanatory. Exclusions, on the contrary, demand a justification. Although this is an anthology of the Spanish short story, and not just of the short story in Spanish, not all the languages in the Spanish national territory are represented in the same proportion. I have only included writers who have published books of short stories or who publish them regularly in journals or newspapers and can thus be regarded as short-story writers. I have similarly excluded those writers who have published a book of stories as a platform to the publication of novels, and who are known as novelists. Nor have I included writers who have been living and publishing in Spain for a long time, but who continue to identify with the writing of their country of origin.

A distinguishing feature of the new Spanish fiction is the importance given to the plot, complex, sophisticated, and sometimes astonishing, but also its awareness of language, something seldom found in previous generations. Their break with the tradition of realism and the role of imagination has offered the writer the possibility of choosing his/her own path. Thus, and in contrast with other anthologies, the task of translating has received special consideration, as has that of editing and coordination. The variety of translators is not arbitrary: there as a conscious effort to seek an identification between writer and translator, since it is not the same to translate García Montalvo's eminently artistic prose, Paloma Díaz-Mas' lexical one, José María Merino's fantastical and poetical writing, García Sánchez's pragmatic one, or Vázquez Montalbán's irony. Fortunately, just as we witness the rebirth of the Spanish short story, we are also witnessing the emergence of a considerable number of translators of Spanish.

A final note: many people have contributed with their suggestions to the wisdom of this anthology, among them, Pere Gimferrer, Jorge Herralde, Mercedes Monmany and, very specially, Fernando Valls who has made valuable suggestions even though he was preparing his own anthology for a Spanish publisher. My thanks also to Celia Szusterman for her help in the selection of the translators and coordination of the translations. Of the shortcomings let us not blame anybody: they were all unintended and merit the tolerant understanding of the reader.

This anthology is dedicated to the memory of Nissa Torrents, whose passion for literature was only surpassed by her passion for life.

Juan Antonio Masoliver
London, December 1992

(*Translated by Celia Szusterman*)

Robert Saladrigas

Child Rodolfo

That summer I returned for the second time to Santillana del Mar and, just as I feared, nothing had changed. There wasn't even any variation in their answers when I asked what had become of the child Rodolfo.

Santillana is always the same. Attentive to the sea's muted hum echoing in Ubiarco, Santillana came to a stop years ago, as if hypnotized by the harmonious sound of the heartbeat of history. It drowsed, sprawled on its damp grassy mattress, dreaming forevermore of the rupestrian bison, goat and horse that survived in outline on the granite ceilings of the Altamira caves. It is the rosy daydream of a solitary maid, beautiful Arcadia, daughter of a nobility petrified in time and the salpetrous air of the Cantabrican coast.

Three years before, I had walked around the mediaeval alleys of Santillana, never imagining that I would fall in love with the town, that I would always remember it. Now it was recaptured more than ever in this mirror without doors because I had the strangest experience here, which I preserve intact in memory.

I had arrived in Santillana intending to visit it at leisure, walking and walking through streets and alleys, contemplating the marvellous houses one by one. Everything about Santillana attracted me: the coppery sky with its bloom of a Nordic autumn, the embossing of great balconies steeped in the drizzle of centuries, severe towers patched with verdigris, stone arches, scarcely eroded as if trying to deny the savage impact of time. It dragged at famished eyes. Minute drops of water fell from above. My vision of Santillana was emotionally intemporal.

On the other side of the Santander road, just at the Berreda crossroads and facing away from the walls of the Regina Coeli convent, he appeared, a boy of about twelve, an alert face, hair black as octopus ink, eyes like mercury exposed to high temperatures. Without preamable he proposed himself as my guide. I would never find one better informed. *Try me, sir*, he said in a dignified tone. In return for his services he asked only what I wanted to pay.

'If you're happy, give me what you think I deserve. If not, nothing.'

He spoke a very precise Castilian, not in keeping with his age. I accepted. He thanked me with a smile. The lesser bells of Regina Coeli announced the Angelus. I asked where he came from and he replied that he was born and raised in Santillana. 'I've never been away from here. I haven't even seen the sea and yet it's almost within touching distance. It must be beautiful when the sky and the water turn into one.' I remarked that one day he'd see it. 'I don't think so at all,' he said turning his head away. His voice was sombre. He quickly changed the subject, however. He told me his name was Rodolfo, that people in the town knew him as *child Rodolfo*. He added nothing more, and nor did I prod him because in the meantime we had climbed the street of Juan Infante and were beginning the guided tour.

I quickly realized that Rodolfo was a magnificent guide. He spoke confidently of the style of each of the splendid Santillana houses of which he knew the details and even the histories of most of the families that were or had been their owners. I must confess that Rodolfo's knowledge had me highly intrigued. I recall how totally naturally and in few words he related the vicissitudes of the Tower of Don Borja, a XVth century palace which seems to have been passed on from the Barreda to the Güell family, who sold it to Doña Paz de Borbón, Princess of Bavaria and daughter of Isabel II, and how it finally came into the hands of Mercedes of Bavaria, Princess of Bragation.

'Typical mess-ups of the great families,' Rodolfo commented, shaking his head as an old man in the mid-winter of life might have done.

It must be said that Rodolfo didn't tell me the story of the

Tower of Don Borja as I have reproduced it here, deliberately condensed. Rodolfo took pleasure in bringing together the different passages of the story, and I listened to him, trying to imagine how and why he knew all he knew.

A fine rain was wetting us through but neither of us quickened the pace. I wasn't aware of the chill of the soaking. The water misted over my glasses, slid down my cheeks. Some more presumptuous drops rolled down my back making me shiver. I took off my glasses. It didn't occur to me that we could interrupt our itinerary and seek shelter until the rain eased off. Rodolfo gave no sign of discomfort. His voice convincing and meticulous as ever, he informed me about the histories of the great houses, of the Villa family, of the Gómez Estrada, the Pereda, the Cuevas y de Bustamante, the Velarde and the Valdivieso families, until at about two o'clock I invited him to lunch hoping to probe him a little more. My curiosity was becoming increasingly irksome.

We ordered onion soup and two plates of *churrasco*[1]. While we sipped at the scalding soup, Rodolfo showed no surprise when I asked for details of his life. I'm convinced he was expecting it. His full name was Rodolfo de la Borgolla y de Collados, and his forbears, aristocrats of *la Montaña*[2], had been the constructors and owners of one of the oldest stone houses still standing in Santillana.

As I listened, I made a mental effort to reconstruct the façade of the palace. He had shown it to me not long before but without revealing that it was connected with his family. I *saw* it again, immediately. The doorjambs at the entrance were plated, the balconies of wrought iron, and right at the top was the flourish of an impressive family shield. Against a vaguely gilded background, a sable-black eagle grasped a lily-stalk, crowned by a helmet decorated with mantling, scroll-work and enamelling, and as an emblem, the crest was a blazing golden phoenix, with the legend *Ut Vincat*. While we were standing there at the

---

[1] Grilled meat (Castilian in the original text).
[2] The mountain country behind Santander (Castilian in the original text).

house, Rodolfo had told me that it held one of the finest collections of paintings in the country and the library contained real bibliographic gems.

At the beginning of this century, Rodolfo's grandfather sold the palace to the Duke of G., stipulating only that the third floor, a kind of attic, should remain thereafter at the disposal of any member of the family wishing to inhabit it. And it was precisely there, right at the top under a free-stone and slate roof, that Rodolfo lived with his mother, a haughty, fusty woman who had hardly gone out onto the street in I don't know how many years, whose skin was smudged with a stubborn nostalgia that held her spellbound by the moth-eaten glories of her family, and permanently humiliated in seeing how her only child earned a pittance in tips as a guide for strangers.

Rodolfo suffered too, but his tribulations were of a different kind. He'd had to leave school at the age of nine because his mother said that it wasn't proper for an *hidalgo*[1] to have the same education, and in the same surroundings, as the riff-raff. Rodolfo's mercurial eyes shone like two beacons awash in the waves of a tempest. I don't know whether they were letting fly sparks of distress or flashing with anger. Rodolfo had taken refuge in the books of the family library, and all he knew he had imbibed from them. But his greatest ambition was to get to the sea.

'Now I'm putting aside all the money I can and when I've got enough, I'll be off to Santander. Once I'm there, I won't just see the sea, but I'm getting on a boat and I'm going to sail all the seas in the world. I know from the books, that there's no such thing as closed horizons, and when you start travelling you can travel all your life and never come up against any wall that tells you you've come to the end, that you can't go any further because there isn't anything on the other side. I assure you that the moment I start running, nothing and nobody is going to stop me because I'll be free. I promise myself this every night before I go to bed.'

I didn't have the heart to contradict him. Perhaps he would

---

[1] Nobleman (Castilian in the original text).

do it, sooner or later. If only he could, I thought. Rodolfo bit his lower lip.

'Sometimes I hear a voice inside me, and the voice announces that I'm never going to see the sea.'

All at once Rodolfo was no longer the same Rodolfo. He threw his body back, his gaze lost somewhere. He made me think again of an old man with no will to struggle, resignedly accepting the caprices of destiny. I tried to cheer him up but I don't know if he even listened. He was a long way from the hostel dining room.

In the afternoon as we completed the itinerary, absorbing a thin, really annoying rain, neither he nor I resumed the conversation. At dusk we took our leave. From inside the car I told him that I would almost certainly return the following day because I wanted to see the interiors of some of the houses and visit the Dominican convent. Rodolfo assented with a nod. The sky had closed in still more, an immense stain, coloured like a partridge wing. Through the rear-view mirror I saw Rodolfo, immobile on the road, an absurd figure slowly merging with the grubby pallor of nightfall.

I spent the night in Santander and the next day, just after eleven, I arrived again in Santillana. I didn't find Rodolfo at the Campo de Revolgo where we'd agreed he'd wait for me, nor in the streets, nor anywhere. An old woman all in black who, under the lintel of a dark doorway near the Collegiate church, was offering a piece of spongecake and glass of cow's milk for a couple of coins, informed me that she knew of no child Rodolfo. I got the same response from a barefoot, bandy-legged lad with a cheerful, slightly ironic expression. Then came the negative answers from a young matron, a shepherd rugged up in a sheepskin jacket, a white-bearded peasant and a little girl with hairy legs and curved body.

In the end it occurred to me to relate the family history that Rodolfo confided to me, but then they looked at me in stupefaction, and I learned that the present Duke of G.'s house was uninhabited except for a poor old fellow who was half-blind because of trachoma, who answered to Rodolfo, and who for ages, for years and years, had been a sailor in the Duke of

G.'s mercantile fleet. When he got old and was gradually losing the sight of both eyes, and since he had no family, the Duke of G., a wonderful person in the opinion of my informants, entrusted the old man with looking after his palace in return for a roof and his keep.

The day was ashen again, but dry. The air clean, fresh. Perplexed, I found the old Rodolfo in the entrance to the Duke of G.'s palace. Though not very tall, he was thick-set, the skin of his face a map of innumerable wrinkled furrows, toasted by the sun on the high seas, dried out by the salinity of the water. His small eyes had a Chinese slant, were weepy, dim, expressionless. He propped his body against a knotty staff.

I observed him from the distance. Not only was he not the child Rodolfo but not a single detail of his physiognomy reminded me of him. The old Rodolfo was absorbed in rolling a cigarette. He put it between his lips and spat from the corners of his mouth. I admit I felt afraid. I turned my back on him, containing my urge to walk faster. I started the car and reluctantly left Santillana.

When I went back there that summer, everything was exactly the same. I searched the streets hopelessly for the presence of the child Rodolfo. Above a spread of low-hanging mist enveloping the timeless peace of the living-dead Santillana, I suddenly noticed four branches protruding from the crusted wall of a large house. They were a hand's breadth from my nose. The small leaves were crystal green, dewy-damp. Could it be that the child Rodolfo would emerge from the mist and with his mere apparition spare me from having to drag around with me, probably forever, the dead weight of the mystery? Now I know that what one wants to happen never does and I'm condemned to live in company with the impenetrable. Until I'm accustomed to it. Then it will no longer seem to me that I walk with heavier step than before.

In any case, it must be said that I like to think that on the first and only afternoon of our acquaintance, the child Rodolfo began his run, carried off by an idea, tired of waiting for his purse to brim with small change, and that ever since he has sailed the seas of the planet, never stopping because he still hasn't come up against the wall that separates him from nothingness.

The other one, the old Rodolfo, did, I learned, take the leap over the wall, driven by late autumn blizzards. A throng of faded leaves accompanied him, the colour of Santillana's gold-tinged stones bathed in the still-warm setting sun.

(*Translated from the Catalan by Julie Flanagan.*)

Ana María Moix

That red-headed boy I see every day

For Rosa Regás, who wanted to publish this book, but malheureusement, *or by the will of God, was unable to.*

'Ooh! This is Hell! We're entering the jaws of Hell!' shrieked Marga. At Marga's side, she was gripping onto the wooden seat of the little train that was going through the dark caves. 'Don't be stupid, open your eyes, silly, what are you afraid of?' laughed Marga. She opened her eyes but shut them again straightaway. On either side of the narrow track down which the little train was moving, red lights lit up the walls and shadows flickered amidst flames; cardboard legs and arms hanging from the roof of the cavern flapped about over their heads, and large signs with phosphorescent letters glowed and then faded announcing the entrance to the next cave: 'Into the jaws of Hell.' Marga's shrieks, together with the blaring of the sirens and the unending lamentations of tormented souls who were being consumed in the infernal pit, reverberated in her aching head. Before leaving the house, Mamá had made her take a pill with her breakfast, because of the pain, but her head went on hurting. So did her eyes, which were swollen and reddened. She'd cried the whole night long. Where was her Puss? She'd noticed the cat wasn't there when she'd got back home, the evening before. Had Mamá thrown him out, fed up because he broke vases and scratched curtains with his claws? Remembering Puss her eyes filled with tears: he would climb stealthily up onto the chest in the hall, approach, slowly, the vase in which Mamá, every morning, placed a spray of carnations in front of grandmother's portrait, sit on his hind legs near the spray, smell the flowers, touch them with his little paw and then bite them. It was when he tried to eat them and pull them out that the vase would fall onto the floor. Before the impending crash Puss would leap off the chest and rush and hide under the bed, under her bed. Because Puss knew she loved him and would defend him against Mamá who would come rushing furiously into the room with a slipper, shouting 'Where's that wretched cat? I'm going to call the RSPCA and tell them to come and take him away before I clobber him to death.' She didn't understand Mamá. Why couldn't Puss eat the flowers? What was the harm in it? Why did she buy flowers for grandmother, who was dead, and not for Puss? Grandmother couldn't eat them now, and besides, she'd prefer them to be for Puss, she'd never loved grandmother who, while she was alive, was always scolding her and calling her a sinner for being disobedient and using bad language. At night she'd hardly slept, thinking, with tears of despair, what could possibly have happened to Puss. Mamá must have taken advantage of the fact that she had gone out of the house to church for confession because the next day was the feast day of the school's patron saint and they all had to take communion, and called the RSPCA to come and take him away. Or else she'd put him in the car and then abandoned him in some lonely place, far from home, so that he wouldn't be able to get back. But Mamá, seeing her crying and going to bed without eating, swore she hadn't thrown Puss out. She swore it with tears in her eyes; Mamá was sorry too about Puss's disappearance because, as she admitted, even though she sometimes used to hit him for breaking vases and tearing curtains and upholstery, she'd got fond of him, and if she shouted at him it was only to try and teach him a lesson. Had he gone off by himself, fed up with Mamá hitting him? In that case, it was Mamá's fault too. Didn't she understand that Puss just had to scratch the sofa covers? How else could he keep his nails sharp? The science teacher told them animals always acted from necessity, driven by instinct. Mamá didn't understand. She, Mamá, went to the manicurist's when she needed to have her nails done, or she cut them herself with a pair of scissors and then filed them. Puss didn't criticize her for this, he was cleverer and he understood Mamá's needs. But Mamá . . . what did Mamá want, Puss to go to the hairdresser's to get his nails cut? At night she imagined her Puss, lost in some lonely place, wandering along the streets, alone, miaowing with sadness because he couldn't find the way back home. For Puss would certainly try to come back to her, to sleep with her, in her bed, as he did every night. Mamá didn't let him, nor did Martina, the servant. But Puss and I were cleverer than them and we knew how to trick them. After supper I'd go up to Puss and whisper in his ear: I'm off to bed, you stay here with Mamá, Papá and Martina, and, when the TV programme's finished, and they've gone, you come to your little girl's bed. I liked it: feeling the weight of his body on my legs, and the way he moved the bed when he licked or scratched himself. In the dark, Puss, suddenly, would start walking on my back, very slowly, and I'd feel, in my body, steps advancing till they got to the pillow. He'd play with my hair. I liked his little paws nuzzling my neck, my ears, my forehead. It was a very nice tickling. Then I'd take him by surprise and catch him, I'd hug him, his fur was soft, soft, ever so soft; I'd take a paw and, guiding him, get him to caress me: my face, my arms, my chest, my legs . . . I felt his little hairs, and the claws between my fingers, a shiver down my spine and a feeling of well-being. I seemed to be floating, like at mass, the days the nuns celebrated important feast-days and decorated the altar and the choir stalls with a lot of white flowers, and lit all the lights in the chapel, with candles burning and the organ sounding. A calm and warm sleep would come over me. I know it's wrong to say warm sleep, I know because the literature teacher gave us an essay to write and when he corrected mine he crossed out 'warm sleep'. He said sleep could be heavy, calm, broken, restorative, deep, and I can't remember what else, but never 'warm'. But I say warm because during mass, and when I got Puss to caress me, I felt sleepy, I seemed to be floating in a bluish empty space (the teacher also told me you can't call me an empty space bluish, not bluish nor orangey, nor white nor black, because you can't call an empty space anything) but I saw it bluish and a very gentle heat came over me, I felt the blood flowing warm through my veins, warm and blue blood. That's why I saw the empty space blue coloured and I call my sleep warm, because, when sleepy, blood, veins, sleep and empty space all got mixed up together. That's what the doctor told me the other day, he also advised me not to worry if the teacher said I wrote badly and used the wrong words. According to the doctor I wasn't writing about what was there but about what I saw and felt. So that if I saw the empty space bluish, it's quite right to put bluish empty space. But the literature teacher didn't understand, nor did the physics teacher when I wrote in an exercise: bodies don't swell with heat, they float. I gave him my own example: when I'm overcome with warm sleep, because the blood is flowing more warmly through my veins, I don't swell, I float. That's what happened when I felt Puss's paw. Then I'd take his head and kiss his eyes. I liked putting my lips to his eyes: I felt him blinking against my skin. I'd ask him to open them. They were big, yellow, brilliant in the darkness. But he'd shut them at the touch of my lips and I was never able to kiss them. Mamá and Martina scolded me when they saw me kissing Puss, they insisted cats spread diseases. It's a lie, they were fooling me, they were always fooling me. They scolded me too the day they saw the way I was kissing Javier, the boy next door. When I came back from school I used to find him nearly every day, sometimes at the corner of the street, sometimes on the landing. Javier would ask me for a kiss and if, when I grew up, I'd marry him. I didn't want to marry or to kiss anyone who hadn't got yellow eyes like Puss and nails that tickled when they caressed me. 'I've got yellow eyes, I swear I have,' said Javier. But when I asked him to take off the dark glasses he always had on, he wouldn't. One afternoon, as usual, I found him on the stairs. 'Marry me, I'll buy you cats and ice-creams, we'll go to the cinema in the evenings, we'll go abroad, you won't wear school uniform and you'll look much prettier.' Javier was a red-head, his hair wasn't exactly like Puss's, which was yellow and brown, like a tiger's, but it wasn't that different. The important thing, though, was that he must have yellow eyes. 'OK, agreed,' said Javier, 'I'll take off my dark glasses; you shut your eyes, and when you open them, you'll see what colour my eyes are.' I shut them and he kissed me. I felt the movement of his lips on mine: like the blinking of Puss's eyes, when I kissed his eyes and he shut them beneath my lips. Warm sleep enfolded me. Javier's fingers brushed my cheeks and my neck, his nails caressed like Puss's: I saw the bluish empty space and I started floating. But before I could open my eyes and see what his were like, I felt a hand grabbing me by the arm, pulling me and dragging me inside. I heard Martina's voice, shouting insults at Javier who was already racing down the stairs, Mamá slapped me hard and went on scolding all afternoon till Papá came home and was told all about it. I was crying with rage: they hadn't let me see Javier's eyes. Papá tried to console me (he thought I was crying because I'd been slapped) and sitting me down on his knees, he started explaining very strange things, that I didn't understand, like when Martina scolded me for kissing Puss telling me that cats spread diseases. Did boys spread diseases too? Even redheads? All of them or just Javier? Then why did Papá kiss Mamá? Not diseases but something like that, according to Papá, from whose sermon I only remember two lies: that boys were dangerous, that you could only kiss them when you were a woman and that I wasn't a woman. Lies: Javier wasn't dangerous, he'd never stolen anything from me, nor hit me, nor shouted, nor scratched, nor had he tried to kill me, on the contrary, he'd given me a kiss as sweet as Puss's. A lie too that I wasn't a woman. At least that's what Mamá had said a few months before, one morning when I woke up with a tummy ache and felt that my legs were wet. I screamed. When I got up I saw bloodstains on the sheets, on my nightdress and between my legs. I thought I'd burst open inside and I almost fainted with fright. Mamá, when she saw me, began crying, and so did I: I thought Mamá was crying because I was going to die. It's exciting, my love, she said, now you're a woman, you've become a woman. She called Martina and they whispered together. And the blood? It went on flowing. I'd be taken to hospital, the doctor would come, I'd be given injections, I'd have to stay in bed, maybe I'd be operated on. I cried and cried, I was so upset, my tummy was hurting and Mamá took no notice. She took off my nightdress, she made me stand up, she walked around me, looking at me and laughing with Martina, she talked about buying me bras, she advised me not to have a bath that was too hot or too cold, not to eat ice-creams or do gym and, above all not to tell anyone what had happened. And the hospital, when was the ambulance coming? Mamá laughed: no hospital, silly, get dressed and off to school. Martina came in with cotton-wool and gauze. Were they going to bandage me up? And when I wanted to . . .? Mamá laughed, and so did Martina. I got to school late. All the other girls had already gone into class and I couldn't slip in without being seen by the Sister who, as soon as I appeared in the classroom door, stood up. 'You're late again, may we know what has happened today?' Mamá had ordered me not to say anything about what had happened. I was trying to invent an excuse, but if I tell a lie I go red and it shows. Don't tell a lie or you'll get a sign on your forehead. She got the truth out of me. 'Sister, it's because last night I became a woman and . . .' Without letting me finish she began shouting: 'Quiet! Quiet, you wretched girl!' But Sister . . . it's true, I swear to God, I can show you, there's even blood coming out, it seems as though I've burst open inside and I'll come out of the gap but as a woman . . .!' The Sister hit me twice and grabbing me by the collar of my uniform dragged me out of the class. 'Sinner! Wretched girl! You've got the devil inside you!' She shut me in the chapel. I had to miss the break and got no points for a month. Mamá was right, I shouldn't tell the truth. Perhaps the Sister's words were true and I did have the devil inside me, perhaps it was he who was making the blood come out. Becoming a woman must be a really mortal sin. I could tell this from the Sister's reaction, from the tummy ache, from Mamá's tears (no matter how much she said they were of excitement), and from the punishments I was given without any explanation: they wouldn't buy me ice-creams, Sunday visits to the houses of Mamás friends were stopped because according to her they had sons (a silly excuse), and, on top of that, instead of toys Mamá began buying me bras, a piece of equipment that imprisons your chest, maybe, I thought, so that the devil I had inside me wouldn't get any bigger. Puss was the only one who didn't cast me off in my misery. At night, when I showed him the signs of my misfortune, he just looked at me, surprised, with his yellow eyes wide open, stretched out his head and sniffed me. That was all. Yes, Puss loved me, and I loved him, that's why I hugged him and tried to kiss his eyes, so that I could set him free from the spell that had taken away his human form, because I'd read tales where bewitched animals turned into princes when they were kissed on the eyes by their beloved. I wanted to be able to set Puss free from his fatal enchantment, but he shut his eyes when I tried to kiss him, and I couldn't accomplish my dearest wish: to give Puss a proof of my love. That's why I cried so much that night, the first one I spent without Puss by my side. Next day I didn't want to have breakfast and I refused to go to school. Mamá made me: it was the feast of the patron saint and I couldn't stay away. There was high mass. They'd decorated the altar and the choir stalls with white flowers, they'd lit all the lights in the chapel, and hundreds of candles, the organ was sounding, but, this time, I wasn't floating in the bluish space enveloped in a warm sleep. I was crying and crying inconsolably. All the girls looked at me, amazed, and the news went round from one to the other: she's lost her cat. A nun came up to me and whispered in my ear: 'Don't cry my child, one should never give up hope. Today is our patron saint's day, beg her to intercede with Our Lord and He will help you find your little cat. Pray, and when you approach the altar to receive the holy sacrament, surrender yourself to God in a spirit of true devotion, and this very day you will find your cat.' I prayed, and I kept on praying. I took the ring off my finger and placed it between the floor and my knee: as a penance. The Sister used to tell stories of saints who tortured themselves in order to gain the Lord's favour. With the brooch which held my mantilla, I pricked my fingers, between the nail and the skin. All the while I was praying: Our father, I want to find my Puss! Hail Mary, I want to find my Puss, I want to find my Puss! Lord Jesus Christ, God and very man . . .! I want to find my Puss! I want to find my Puss!' There was a lunch in the school, but I didn't eat anything: I'd made a vow not to eat anything till I found Puss. Afterwards, two Sisters took us to a Fun Fair up on a mountain-side. 'Do not lose faith, child, God is great, and through him you will find your cat.' 'I shall find him, I shall find him.' We climbed up to the observation point, and then to a little train that went round the gardens. It was when we were in the elevated railway that Marga began getting on my nerves: 'Hey—do you know that red-head, the one who's spying on us right now from the battlements of the Enchanted Castle? He's been following us ever since we left the school.' I saw a figure, hiding behind a battlement, and red hair waving in the wind, I saw him again, behind me, when I went into the hall of mirrors and found myself multiplied a hundred times, and in each of the hundred mirrors, a hundred looks of mine fixed upon a hundred pairs of dark glasses of a hundred red-heads. And in the Enchanted Castle: I was slipping as I crossed the Bridge of a Thousand Snares and there was the red-head's hand, I was leaning out of the window which gives onto Paradise, and that window gave onto another window out of which leant a red-head with dark glasses. Marga opened a door which had Danger written on it and a cardboard skull came rushing towards her. I opened it, and there, calm and smiling, was a red-head. 'Is he your boy-friend?' asked Marga, laughing. 'No, my boy-friend's got yellow eyes.' And I was searching for them, looking everywhere. And my heart almost missed a beat when I spotted them, shining, at the back of that cave, full of furnaces in which a thousand cardboard bodies were flailing around, full of red lights, of flames which reached up to the roof of the cave, of blaring sirens and of howls. There he was, majestic, unique, with his trident on high, his body as red as the flames over which he reigned. 'The King of Hell!' shrieked Marga. I recognized that mouth, the thin lips that turned up at the corners, the sharp pointed ears I'd so often caressed, and the eyes, the yellow eyes shining in the darkness. The Sister was right: the saint had heard my supplications. I had found my Puss, Puss was there, and he was the King of Hell. 'Once more,' I begged Marga when the train came out of the caves, 'please, just once more.' 'Impossible, the Sister must be looking for us, she's been waiting for us for more than half an hour. They're about to shut, and we've got to go home.' 'I'll go now, I promise,' but I didn't, I stayed hidden for I don't know how many hours, and then I made my way towards the jaws of Hell, not in the train, but walking so that nobody would see me, so that nobody would try and separate me from Puss, now that I had found him. The journey, through the cave, was dark, I heard footsteps at my back, perhaps it was Marga, or the Sister coming to look for me; but I was afraid of nothing: a pair of yellow eyes were looking at me from the back of the cave. There he was, and on seeing me he let fall his trident beside the cardboard figures and advanced towards me. He took me in his arms. He laid me on the ground. 'Puss, you think we're in my little bed, do you? We'll go back home right now, I've got to take off this disguise of yours.' I wanted to kiss his eyes, but he didn't let me, on the contrary, it was he who was kissing me, my mouth, my face, my neck, I was stripping him of his King of Hell disguise and he me of my school uniform. His hair appeared, so soft, redder than before perhaps because of the flames that surrounded us, and dark glasses covering his eyes. 'Oh, take off those glasses, Puss, let me see your eyes,' I begged him while he caressed me with his fingers and nails and I began feeling I was floating in a bluish empty space, overcome by a warm sleep from which I was about to awake because of the pain that pierced me. 'You're a bad cat, why are you hurting your little friend, when she's had such a time finding you!' Soon the pain disappeared and I was caressing that red hair. His eyes were blinking beneath my lips. I don't know how many hours I spent submerged in a warm sleep from which I did not emerge for nine months, despite the shouts and tears of Mamá, the beatings of Papá, the questions of the doctor who, like the rest of them, doesn't understand, and asks me daily why I call a little cat I have at my side day and night, Puss, instead of baby, a little cat with yellow eyes that he shuts when I bend over to kiss them.

(*Translated by Dinny Thorold.*)

Manuel Vázquez Montalbán

Helena, of Paris, France

I had never really expected that this would turn out to be the final landscape of my life. Like all men of my generation, I came into the world at a time of romantic thinking—the years when people believed that everything was possible: possible like the islands and the sailors on the sea; possible like ideals, and an attractive range of absolutes. At least, that was what the textbooks said, and the songs, and the radio programmes, in an age when television was still out of reach of the majority of Spaniards. It didn't cost me much to decide to forego surprises and travel. Life tends to generate a useful inertia that is orchestrated by a harsh mechanism which disenchants in one sense and enchants in another. I too had rebelled against this scenario, against this setting, against all settings in fact. As an adolescent, those grey roofs, those grey posts, those patches of green between the sandstone chimneys, the flapping sheets on the line, the plump arms of the women doing their washing, all filled me with nausea and a desire to run away. But nowadays I lean against the windowsill and somehow I find the view soothing. I enjoy it as evening comes on and the jumble of noises rises from the narrow street; the optimism of summer, half traffic, half voices and other noises vying with one another across open balconies where men in vests and soft, moist women take the evening air. I go through onto the balcony and I remember back to when I used to go round that corner in a daily search for knowledge and the unknown: first at school; then the three years I spent at university. But I knew that one day I would be coming back for ever. I already knew that around that corner a short journey was awaiting me, but that it was a journey which would have an end and a return. Since then this has been a consistent pattern of my life. I could sum it up by saying that I have managed to avoid ending up as a second-rate bureaucrat, and that while I nurture hopes of becoming a professional in the field of culture, I have achieved a position as a top-notch bureaucrat in a publishing house that deals in the publication of specialist dictionaries. I could also say that I don't have much left from my short voyage: a habit of buying books which I never finish and which sometimes I never even open; the occasional night out at cultural events which have become less rigorously avant-garde with the passing of the years; something of a taste for good films and quality theatre which I can't particularly explain; and of course, something which has been very important for me—my relationship with Helena, and the letters that we have written each other.

By the age of sixteen, Helena had already travelled to Fez and to Reykjavik. Like a character out of some novel by Vicki Baum or Lajos Zilahy, her father was a powerful businessman, a widower, who took his only daughter with him wherever he went. By the age of sixteen, Helena spoke English, French, Italian and German—all of them well—and she was applying herself to the study of Russian, as a language with a future, a thesis which set me on the track of understanding where Helena was coming from ideologically. Helena preferred her name to be written with an H, and when I told her that I had enjoyed *Lavorare Stanca*, she understood that, embodied in yours truly, she had hit upon a goldmine of possibilities for socio-cultural investigation.

At first we used to stroll round the university precinct together, and it didn't take many walks for us to realize that we were different from the rest, and that we were something of a race apart. Helena was white-skinned and slender, and the way she moved her hands was as if they were actually shaping her ideas. We used to enjoy reading together, and we enjoyed silences together. We were also able to share the fact of being apart for one summer. At the start of the following term we kissed for the first time. A few months later we realized that the way we were behaving qualified us perfectly as lovers. I have often reproached myself for not having had the courage or the decisiveness to suggest that we actually get engaged, but among my kind of people an engagement was a slow and chaste experience on a par with building up savings in a bank, an experience which would never have suited Helena, and which I, for reasons which were basically aesthetic, was not inclined even to broach. In short, any idea of an engagement was effectively impossible, unless I were to engage the kind of thoroughgoing exercise of will that was not really in my upbringing. Because in the slow education of a social climber, the cost of the vaulting pole and of experience engenders at first a terrible fear of specific things going wrong, and then, later, of things going wrong in general; a hellish mechanism which becomes almost metaphysical and all-enveloping. There is a deformation of will, directed like a draught-horse to a concrete task; the point is to limit your vision; in fact it almost calls for a multi-dimensional castration in order to avoid the possibility of going off the straight and narrow. Undoubtedly Helena was my voyage and my hope. Never had one person offered so much. She gave me books and words, her white body, and all the expanse of heartlands that a woman can give to a man. She also furnished me with the pleasure of doubt and crisis, experiences which could be turned to poetic use, and this was useful in the sense that I might say that I wrote poems, some of which were not bad at all, and which were even about to be published in *Papeles de Son Armadans*, thanks to a poet by name of Goytisolo, a friend of Helena's family to whom she introduced me one day.

Helena's future was already well mapped out. At the end of her second year, she went to Paris and enrolled at the Sorbonne. We continued writing to each other, and had the possibility of making love during our Easter holidays. But by the age of eighteen Helena already had Paris in her pocket. She had become friends with a leading lawyer who had made his reputation defending the leaders of the Algerian FLN, and through him she had found her way into cultural circles: Sadoul, the wife of Gérard Philippe, Yves Montand, Simone de

Beauvoir, Gisèle Halima . . . When these names cropped up in her conversation it was clear that she knew the people concerned and that some of them were also friends: Gisèle . . . Yves . . . Simone . . . Françoise (Sagan) . . . One day she mentioned someone called Henri, who turned out to be Henri Lefebvre. At about this time it was becoming obvious that my continuing at the university made no sense because it would open no doors for me. My brain had been trained in things that were real and concrete. It wasn't prepared for conceptual language and the subtle ins and outs of Kant; scientific abstractions generally proved too much for me and demanded an effort which I wasn't willing to make. But by now I knew that I had amassed sufficient knowledge not to end up as a second-rate bureaucrat. I was young, and when you're young it's easy to find justifications to help you through your traumas. I left university, but left it triumphantly and with contempt.

Helena was of the opinion that I deserved better than my first job: editing the A to M volume of an Italian dictionary. The editor who was doing the N to Z volume was a decent enough sort of fellow, a graduate, who ended up getting himself a halfway-decent teaching post in a secondary school. I too thought that I was cut out for better things. Helena never returned to live in Spain for any significant period of time. She wrote to tell me about her marriage to the lawyer, and she enclosed a pretty good poem which was all about our love affair. The fact of Helena's marriage afforded me a comfortable amount of suffering which I tried to extend for as long as possible, but Helena herself prevented me from extending it too much.

A year after her marriage she rang me, and we arranged to meet in a bar in one of our old haunts. By that time I had improved my professional status considerably. I was perfectly at home with the mechanics of the publishing world, and my superiors were quite happy for me to move on to more responsible work, including overseeing the editing process and exploring the possibilities of co-publishing projects. I talked about all this with Helena, albeit rather off-handedly and without going into too much detail, because I realized that it sounded pretty mediocre, as life experiences went. Helena, on the other hand, gave me a fascinating résumé of her life in Paris over the preceding year. The Evian talks were just getting under way, and her husband was very busy. The various left-wing groupings (Helena seemed to belong to most of them) were becoming a serious force. After two hours of talking, I seriously thought that it was all over between us, but Helena suddenly kissed me, and we retired to bed as usual, and I might even say that we still had the same old passion, the same commitment as before. I looked at Helena and rather ingenuously tried to identify the effect that married life had had on her. All I could see, and even this I wasn't sure of, was that she was less coy about getting undressed.

About a year later, Helena came back again. She was in town for a week, and she rang me three days before she left. We slept together again, and I went to see her off at the airport, convinced that we had set up a mechanism that would stand the test of time. There was no fixed timetable to it. Helena came back to visit maybe twice or three times a year. On each occasion we tried to pick up where we had left off, but we knew tacitly that what was important was that she should do the talking, and that she should tell me about Europe, like a news report from some forbidding world. And so it was, in the half-light of that room, where a group photograph of a year's output of teachers of commerce hung unchangingly on one wall and where white lilies slowly faded in water made white by aspirin, that Helena created, almost as if by magic, an Anglo-Franco-Italian cultural carousel into which occasionally she would also introduce elements of German. Like the time when she told me a delightful story involving Heinrich Böll and her husband. One day Böll had said:

'These days you Marxists seem to be reading less and less Marx.'

And Helena's husband had replied: 'And you left-wing Catholics seem to be becoming less and less left-wing and more and more Catholic. Or vice versa.'

Helena reckoned that her husband was becoming bourgeoisified.

'I find it quite deadly in France. All the communists seem to be so well-off. Over there everyone's got their hopes pinned on Spain, while here everything's still to be done.'

Subsequently Helena struck up some fascinating friendships, and she would parade them past in the half-light like performers in a circus: a North Vietnamese with a specialization in phenomenology; a Neapolitan singer who sang sparkling songs in dialect; John Osborne; Juan Marinello; Rafael Alberti; Louis Aragon; Elsa Triolet; Robbe-Grillet . . . And whenever Helena mentioned them, she was completely matter-of-fact, as if it was the most normal thing in the world. She was so immersed in the normality of it all that sometimes it used to annoy me—for example taking it for granted that when she said 'Michel' I would know that she was referring to Michel Butor. And as time went by we found ourselves talking less and less.

When my parents died, unexpectedly, Helena sent me a lovely note, which I still have. A month later she met me in our usual café, and she was obviously upset. On that occasion we didn't make love, even though in our heart of hearts we would probably both have wanted to. By this time I was almost thirty, and I'd been promoted to head of the production department. To give you an idea of the sort of money I was earning, I was now in a position to buy a decent car and pay it off over two years of instalments, and I could allow myself the luxury of going out for supper at seventy or eighty pesetas a time, and spending money on half-way decent lunches. I began to put on a bit of weight. But whenever I suspected that a visit from Helena was in the offing, I would go on a punishing diet so as not to show it. This didn't stop her looking at me every once in a while and passing comments:

'It's strange . . . You're changing physically. Alain is too . . .'

The Alain in question was Alain Resnais. Comments like this alarmed me a bit, and from that moment I decided to embark on a more or less permanent diet, which has given excellent results.

Helena's relationship with her husband had gone from bad to worse in the course of ten years of marriage. Two years ago she told me that she was trying to get a divorce. This alarmed me considerably, and I tried to dissuade her. Rather naïvely I imagined that the harmony that had been set up in the yearly triangle involving Helena, her husband, and me, was somehow fixed for all time to come. The idea of Helena getting a divorce suddenly threw up new unknowns, a new balance of things, and I found it alarming.

'I don't know whether to come back to Spain or not . . . Deep down I've always felt rather lonely in Paris. Do you think I'd be able to find a job here . . .?'

'Very unlikely.'

I'd said that rather too hurriedly. I had suddenly had an alarming picture of life becoming very different, with a Helena who was more or less on my doorstep on a daily basis.

'If you come back, I won't have anyone to write to me from Paris . . .'

She didn't laugh.

In the event, though, she didn't come back.

It's now two years since I last saw her. She has written once or twice, but most of the time she's sent postcards. The last card was from Genoa, just as she was about to leave on a cruise around the Greek islands with her father.

'George and I have decided to separate. I'm going on a cruise to relax a bit. It was Nathalie's suggestion . . .'

It took me a couple of days before I decided that Nathalie was probably Nathalie Delon. Then I received other postcards, from Corfu, Athens, Cairo . . . and six months later came a letter: 'I'm sure I must have told you about him. He's extremely intelligent—one of Lucien Goldmann's assistants . . .'

I bought myself a television, and this drastically reduced the number of times I went out. I was also of an age to discover the possibilities of paid sex. I pay very little by way of rent on this old flat, which was handed on to me by my parents, and this enables me to spend money here and there, and even to save a bit. I'm hoping to buy an apartment on the Costa Brava over the next four to five years, and I have a decent car which I can keep an eye on from my balcony. It's parked just on the corner where I used to wave goodbye to my mother and father as I set off for school. Twice a week one of my neighbours comes to give the flat a good clean, and I find that I feel increasingly at home within these four walls, with all the history and melodrama that they contain.

I've taken out subscriptions to a couple of French journals, which enables me to follow the fortunes of Helena's various friends. Sometimes I venture beyond my little corner, and I make the occasional trip to the smart part of town where she used to live. I walk slowly along the railings, and watch the acacia leaves falling from the tree in her garden. A few months ago I was on the point of renting an apartment very close to Helena's old place. But then one does one's sums so that, for example, I decided to spend some money on buying another television. The fact that I was paying cash gave me a twenty per cent discount.

Helena will never return now. If she does come back, she and I will never be together again in that room with its fading lilies. I'm sure of it. And it's almost as if, in my late thirties, I've been hit by the melancholic hysteria of the male menopause. I've begun to feel increasingly lonely. I did think for a bit about joining a tennis club. Nothing too fancy. Down to earth, and not in the upper part of the city.

The fact is, I'm beginning to feel more and more at home with the four-cornered view that I get from this window, and with the sense of freedom that I get from being able to sit out on my balcony—although sometimes the sound of the phone ringing still makes me jump, and the continuing vision of that street corner is capable of bringing on a sudden wave of sadness.

(*Translated by Ed Emery.*)

Javier Tomeo

Short-sighted

A spring morning in the most cloistered corner of the West Park. The girl proceeds slowly through the recently flowering roses (on a terraqueous scale, her buttocks reproduce the movement of the planets) and sits down on her usual bench. Five minutes later, I sit down beside her, but at the other end of the bench, and for quite a time I admire her in silence. I hold my unfolded paper close to my nose, but she knows very well I'm not reading. She's one of those exciting pre-war women, with a snub-nose which suggests that her virtue is far from impregnable. She shields herself behind the sort of glasses short-sighted people wear, and knits without enthusiasm, as if she didn't give a fig for what she was doing. She manipulates the needles awkwardly and with a suspicious infrequency, raising her eyes to gaze, enchanted, at the statue in front of her, in the middle of the rosegarden.

'Excuse me, Miss,' I say at last, 'but you're probably wondering why I sit next to you every morning. I don't want you to get the wrong idea. The thing is, I'm very fond of knitting, too, and my guess is that what you're making is a jersey with a rice stitch.'

'You've guessed correctly,' the girl murmurs, with a slight smile.

'I suppose that yarn will vertically cross the first row,' I venture.

'You suppose rightly,' she replies, opening all the pores of her skin to the beautiful baritone of my voice.

'It seems to me,' I continue, 'your jersey is going to be a bit tight for you, but it would go very well with some close-fitting jeans.'

'I never wear jeans,' she states, still not daring to give me too much encouragement.

'Why?' I ask, ardently staring at her knees; 'do you find them indecent? Do you prefer short, pleated skirts, like the one you're wearing now?'

She nods vaguely, a gesture that could mean anything.

'Getting back to jerseys,' I go on, 'I must confess I've a special weakness for those teenagers who wear openwork jumpers made with stretchy wool. I find them adorable.'

'Yeah,' she mumbles, still smiling.

'Ah well,' I sigh, shifting my right hand to my genitals. 'Each has his own tastes. You, too, no doubt.'

'Of course,' she murmurs, looking towards the statue.

'On the subject of knitting,' I expound, 'I prefer, for one, the Russian stitch. Do you know how to do a Russian stitch? It's not hard. All you have to do is work the needle over the open loop in the middle stitch, put it in the first hole on the right, work it two loops lower in the middle stitch, then do two rows in the opposite direction, and so on.'

'Your needle's movements seem pretty suspicious to me,' she states.

I don't want to frighten away the hussy in advance and so I resume a more sensible posture. I don't withdraw my hand from between my legs, but I try to hide it with the paper. She goes on knitting in silence and, with the precision of a metronome, every now and then she stares at the statue's lower abdomen. At the end of ten minutes, I summon up enough courage to make my true intentions quite clear to her. I lean against the back of the bench, spread out my legs, put the paper on one side and begin to breathe obscenely through my nose.

'Why don't you tell me once and for all what you're after?' she asks, turning her head and focusing on me the thick lens of her glasses.

'You know very well what I'm after,' I say. 'For four days I've been sitting next to you on this bench just to admire your beautiful profile.'

'Do you really think I've got a nice profile?' she asks, finally giving up her knitting.

'The profile of a goddess,' I reply. 'Some might rate you snub-nosed, but for me that snub-nosed quality, instead of spoiling you, makes you even more appetizing. You know what they say about snub-nosed women. Your dainty little nose has an element of supreme delicacy, a sweet challenge to the most amorous of teeth.'

'What about you?' she asks, blinking behind her lenses. 'Let's have a good look at you.'

She subjects me to an uncertain look, as if she really were unable to make me out clearly. I decide that the moment has come to let her know that she can't put one over on me.

'You, Miss, can see me perfectly well. Your myopia is feigned. I found that out the first day. You're wearing spectacles with plain glass.'

'How can you possibly imagine I'm not short-sighted?' she exclaims, surprised.

'I've three important reasons for supposing so,' I explain. 'My first reason: you knit clumsily. Your fingers don't move with that speed and skill, which all those who suffer from short-sight invariably possess, forced by their condition to make constant use of their hands and the sense of touch. My second reason: you parade—forgive me for being so explicit—a phenomenal pair of breasts, out of place in someone really short-sighted. And my third reason—the most important of all: you always sit opposite that statue of Apollo. Every morning you do the same thing. There are a hundred other benches in the park, but you prefer this one. And however much you try to disguise the direction of your gaze, every now and then you take your eyes off your needles and gently rest them on the god's lower abdomen. You should see how the wings of your nose tremble then!'

By the time I finish saying all this, she's blushing to the roots of her hair.

'So you can't fool me,' I go on. 'Like a lot of other women in this country, you're randy, but repressed.'

'What exactly do you mean by randy?' she enquires, still

trying to lead the conversation in a different direction.

'I mean what I mean,' I reply without removing my hand from between my legs, but a little worried about the outcome. 'If you'd like me to put it another way, I'd say you're the victim of a deplorable sexual repression, like so many other of your sisters. You don't want to pretend you're completely blind, because that would be too uncomfortable. But for many years—from your first period, perhaps—you've passed yourself off as short-sighted, so as to be able to look at what you want with impunity, and without being afraid you'll get called immoral. People feel sorry for you, thinking you can't see what's right in front of your nose, but the fact is, my dear lady, you enjoy yourself, covertly observing all that's sinful around you.'

She takes off her glasses at last and I'm confronted by the most beautiful pair of eyes I've ever seen.

'I've finally been exposed,' she whispers, but without lowering her gaze. 'It had to happen some day.'

'Quick, give me your nose,' I implore, immediately excited by her confession. 'Give me your tiny pea-nose and together we'll cook up the most delicious soup you'll ever have tasted.'

'You're quite a cheeky fellow,' she murmurs.

'Oh yes, my sweet Messalina,' I explode, lowering my pants in the twinkling of an eye. 'Forget about that statue and surrender yourself to this Priapus of flesh and bone who hasn't been able to sleep for the last five nights, thinking of you.'

I see her smile sweetly with her lips half open. Groans are beginning to erupt as I spring towards her.

'Afterwards, you'll think I'm just one of those,' she moans, overcome by my exuberance.

At this precise moment, from behind the hedge which has been protecting us from any tactless observer, appear two policemen. The wily creature, who has spotted them before I do, puts her glasses back on and begins to scream.

'Don't be deceived,' I warn the policemen. 'It was she who invited me, up to a point! It was she who was determined to lead me up the garden path!'

The policemen pay no attention to my explanations, however,

and lead me off to the nearest police station. So now I've got a fresh reason not to trust women.

(Translated by Anthony Edkins.)

Javier Marías

As the women sleep

A Night of Love

For Bianca Andreu,
on her day.

My sex life with my wife, Marta, is most unsatisfactory. My wife is not very lustful or very imaginative, she doesn't say nice things to me and yawns as soon as she sees that I'm in the mood for love. That's why I sometimes go to whores. But they're becoming more and more apprehensive and they're very expensive, and what's more, they're creatures of routine. Not very enthusiastic. I would prefer my wife, Marta, to be more lustful and imaginative and to be satisfied with her. I was happy one night when she was enough for me.

Among the things my father bequeathed to me when he died was a packet of letters that still give off a faint scent of eau de cologne. I don't think that the person who sent them perfumed them, but rather, that at some moment in his life my father kept them next to a bottle of cologne and it tipped over onto them. The stain can still be seen, and so the scent is doubtless that of the cologne he used and didn't use (since it had all been spilled), and not that of the woman who had been sending the letters to him. That odour, moreover, is the one characteristic of him that I was thoroughly familiar with and it never changed and I've never forgotten, always the same during my childhood and adolescence and a good part of my young manhood, which I'm still in or which I haven't yet left behind. And so, before age could dull my interest in such things—whatever is dashing or passionate—I decided to have a look through the packet of letters that he bequeathed me and that up until that point I'd lacked the curiosity to glance at.

These letters were written by a woman whose name was or

still is Mercedes. She used blue-tinted letter paper and black ink. Her handwriting was bold and maternal, set down in quick strokes, as though she no longer aspired to make an impression, no doubt because she knew she had already done so till eternity. For the letters were written as though by someone who had already died when they were penned, and they maintain the pretence that they are messages from beyond the grave. I can't help thinking that it is a game, one of the ones that children and lovers are so fond of, and that consist essentially in passing oneself off as someone other than one is, or in other words, in giving oneself fictitious surnames and creating fictitious existences for oneself, out of fear, surely (not the children but the lovers) that their overpowering feelings will be the end of them if they admit that it is they, with their real existences and names, who are undergoing the experiences. It is a way of softpedalling what is most passionate and intense, of acting as if it is happening to someone else, and it is also the best way to observe it, to be a spectator too and be aware of it. Besides living it, being aware of it.

The woman who signed herself Mercedes had opted for the fiction of sending her love to my father from beyond death, and she appeared to be so convinced of the place or of the eternal moment which she occupied as she wrote (or so certain of the acceptance of that convention on the part of the recipient) that it seemed of little or no importance to her that she posted her envelopes in the public mail or that they bore ordinary stamps and the postmark of the city of Gijón. They had a date on them, and the one thing they were missing was a return address, but this, in a semi-clandestine relationship (the letters all belong to the period when my father was a widower, though he never spoke to me of this belated passion), is more or less a necessity. The existence of this correspondence, which I have no idea whether my father answered in the usual way or not, would also not be in any way out of the ordinary, since there is nothing more commonplace than the sexual surrender of widowers to daring and ardent (or disillusioned) women. Moreover, the declarations, promises, demands, recollections, vituperations, protests, fits of fury and obscenities with which these letters are filled (the obscenities in particular) are conventional and stand out not so much for their style as for their audaciousness. None of this would have anything remarkable about it, I repeat, were it not for the fact that a few days after deciding to open the packet and have a look at the sheets of blue paper, with more equanimity than shocked offence, I myself received a letter from the woman called Mercedes, about whom I am unable to add that she is still alive, since she seemed, rather, to be dead from the very beginning.

Mercedes's letter addressed to me by name was most proper, she did not take liberties because of the fact that she had been on intimate terms with my progenitor nor did she yield to the vulgarity of translating her love for the father, now that the latter had died, into a morbid love for the son, who remained and still remains alive and was and is myself. Unperturbed at knowing that I was aware of their relationship, she confined herself to worry and complaint, demanding the presence of the lover who, contrary to what he had promised over and over again, still had not arrived at her side. Six months after his death, he had not joined her at the place they had agreed on, or perhaps it would be better to say *when*. To her way of thinking, that could be owing to only two possible causes: to a sudden and final falling out of love at the moment of demise that would have made the deceased break his word, or to the fact that, contrary to the prior arrangements that he had made, his body had been buried and not cremated, which—according to Mercedes, who remarked on it forthrightly—might, if it did not render it impossible, at least place difficulties in the way of the escatalogical encounter or re-encounter.

It was true that my father had asked to be cremated, although without insisting too adamantly (perhaps because he was alone at the end, with his will destroyed), and that he had nonetheless been buried alongside my mother, since there was still one remaining place in the family burial vault. Marta and I decided that this was more proper and sensible and more convenient. Mercedes's jest struck me as being in bad taste. I threw her new missive into the wastebasket and was even tempted to do the same with the packet of letters from long ago. The new envelope had current stamps and Gijón postmarks as well. It had no scent. I was not prepared to dig up my father's remains merely to set fire to them.

The next letter soon arrived, and in it Mercedes, as though she were aware of my reflection, pleaded with me to cremate my father, since she couldn't go on living (that was what she said, go on living) amid that uncertainty. She preferred to know that my father had decided in the end not to join her rather than go on waiting for him for all eternity, in vain perhaps. She even spoke to me about you. I cannot deny that that letter moved me for a brief moment (that is, *while* I was reading it and not afterwards), but the conspicuous Asturias postmark was something too prosaic for me to look on the whole thing as anything else but a macabre joke. The second letter also ended up in the wastebasket. My wife, Marta, saw me tear it to bits and asked:

'What's that that's irritated you so?' My gesture must have been a violent one.

'Nothing, nothing,' I said, and I carefully picked up the pieces so she wouldn't be able to put the letter back together again.

I was waiting for a third letter, and just because I was waiting for it, it took longer than expected to arrive or made the wait seem longer. It was not very different from the ones before and resembled those my father had received for a time: Mercedes addressed me in the familiar form and offered her body to me, if not her soul. 'You can do whatever you like with me,' she said to me, 'everything you imagine and everything you don't dare to imagine can be done with a body not your own, with the body of the other. If you accede to my plea to disinter and cremate your father, to allow him to join me, you will never again forget me in your whole life or even in your death, because I will gobble you down, and you will gobble me down.' I think that when I read this for the first time I blushed, and for a fraction of a second the idea of making the trip to Gijón crossed my mind, so as to put myself within her reach (the unusual attracts me, I'm filthy sexually). But then I immediately thought: 'How absurd. I don't even know her last name.' Nonetheless this third letter didn't go into the wastebasket. I still have it hidden away.

It was at that point that Marta's attitude started to change. Not that she turned into an ardent woman from one day to the next and stopped yawning, but as time went by I noticed a greater interest and curiosity concerning me or my no longer very young body, as though she had intuited an infidelity on my part and was on the alert, or else she was the one who had committed one and wanted to confirm if what she had just discovered was also possible with me.

'Come here,' she sometimes said to me, she who had never made overtures to me. Or else she talked a little, saying for example: 'Yes, yes, yes, now.'

That third letter promising so much had left me waiting for a fourth even more than the second irritating one that had left me waiting for the third. But that fourth one didn't arrive, and I realized that I was waiting for the mail every day with greater and greater impatience. I noted that I felt a jolt each time an envelope had no return address, whereupon my eyes swiftly shifted to the postmark, to see if it bore the imprint Gijón. But nobody ever writes from Gijón.

Months went by, and on All Souls' Day Marta and I went to take flowers to my parents' tomb which is also that of my grandparents and my sister.

'I don't know what's going to happen to us,' I said to Marta as we were breathing in the pure air of the cemetery, sitting on a bench near our family vault. I was smoking a cigarette and she was inspecting her fingernails by stretching her fingers out a certain distance away from her, the way someone calms down a crowd. 'I mean when we die. There's no more room left here.'

'The things you think about.'

I looked far off into the distance so as to take on a dreamy look in order to justify what I was about to say and said:

'I'd like to be buried. It suggests an idea of repose, while cremation doesn't. My father wanted us to cremate him, do you remember? and we didn't abide by his wish. We ought to have done so, it seems to me. It would trouble me if mine, the wish to be buried, weren't carried out. What do you think? We ought to disinter him. What's more, that way there'd be room in the family vault for me when I die. You could go to your family's.'

'Let's get out of here, you're making me sick.'

We began walking among the burial vaults, looking for the exit. The sun was shining. But after ten or twelve steps I stopped, looked at the glowing end of my lighted cigarette and said:

'Don't you think we ought to cremate him?'

'Do whatever you like, but let's get out of here.'

I threw the cigarette down and buried it in the earth with my shoe.

Marta wasn't interested in attending the ceremony, that lacked emotion and had me as the sole witness. My father's remains went from being vaguely recognizable in a coffin to being unrecognizable in an urn. I didn't think it was necessary to scatter them, and furthermore, such a thing is prohibited.

On my return home, at an already late hour, I felt depressed; I sat down in the easy chair without removing my overcoat or turning on the light and sat there waiting, mumbling, thinking, hearing Marta's shower running in the distance, perhaps recovering from the responsibility and the effort of having done something that had been left unresolved for some time, of having fulfilled a desire (someone else's desire). After a while my wife, Marta, came out of the bathroom with her hair still wet and wrapped in her bathrobe, a pale pink one. The light from the bathroom, in which there was steam, illuminated her. She sat down on the floor at my feet, and leaned her damp head on my knees. After a few seconds I said:

'Shouldn't you dry yourself off? You're getting my overcoat and my trousers wet.'

'I'm going to wet you all over,' she said, and she was not wearing anything underneath the bathrobe. The light from the bathroom, in the distance, illuminated us.

I was happy that night because my wife, Marta, was lustful and imaginative, she said nice things to me and didn't yawn, and I was satisfied with her. I'll never forget that. It has never happened again. It was a night of love. It has never happened again.

A few days later I received the fourth letter, awaited for so long a time. I still haven't dared open it, and at times I'm tempted simply to tear it up, never to read it. In part it's because I think I know and fear what that letter will say. Unlike the three that Mercedes sent me previously, it has an odour, a slight scent of cologne, a cologne I haven't forgotten or am very familiar with. I haven't had another night of love, and for that reason, because it hasn't happened again, I sometimes have the strange sensation, when I recall it, nostalgically and intensely, that that night I betrayed my father, or that my wife, Marta, betrayed me with him (perhaps because we gave ourselves fictitious names or created existences for ourselves that weren't ours), even though there is no doubt that that night, at home, in the darkness, on top of the bathrobe, only Marta and I were there, Marta and I as always.

I haven't had another night of love nor has she again been enough for me, and so I also continue going to whores, who are becoming more and more expensive and more apprehensive, and I don't know whether to have a try with transvestites. But all that is of little interest to me, it doesn't worry me and it's temporary, even though it has to go on for some time still. Sometimes I surprise myself thinking that it would be most desirable if Marta died first, because that way I could inter her in the place in the burial vault that is still vacant. That way I wouldn't have to give her explanations about my change of mind, because what I want now is to be cremated and not buried, not buried under any circumstances. I don't know, however, if I'd gain anything that way—I surprise myself thinking—since my father must be occupying his place alongside Mercedes, my place, for all eternity. Once cremated, therefore—I surprise myself thinking—I would have to do my father in, but I don't know how you kill somebody who's already dead. I sometimes wonder whether that letter that I haven't opened yet won't say something different from what I imagine and fear, whether it wouldn't give me the solution, whether it won't encourage me. Then I think: 'How absurd. We haven't even seen each other.' After that I look at the letter and sniff it and turn it over and over in my hands, and finally I always end up hiding it, still without having opened it.

(*Translated by Helen Lane.*)

Juan José Millás

The lecture

In the rush about the journey or perhaps out of anxiety, I remember I neglected to clean my teeth that morning and all day kept poking around inside my mouth with the tip of my tongue.

At the time I had just turned forty and had taken to drinking heavily, though without really registering either fact. Indeed I found my job so all-absorbing that the only signals I was sensitive to were those relating to my research work in the laboratory.

What happened was that the University of S. had invited me to give a lecture about the influence of cigarette smoking and diet on coronary disease. I was to deliver my paper in the main auditorium of the medical faculty before an audience of professors and postgraduates, all of whom had been following with interest the articles I had published over recent years in an important scientific journal.

I decided to make the journey in my own car, intending to revise the most important points of my lecture on the way. I've always enjoyed driving—as long as I'm travelling alone, that is. The car is a warm, enclosed space in which everything one could possibly need is within easy reach, Generally speaking, I find long journeys highly conducive to thinking; I usually make good use of the ideas I set out with, to say nothing of any other ideas that find their way into the car en route, sparked off by my contemplation of the passing countryside or by my chance reactions to the changing atmospheric conditions.

Accordingly, I spent the four hours it took me to reach S. in a fruitful revision of the concepts that formed the backbone of my lecture, and I realized with pleasure that I would be able to speak without notes or use them simply as a back-up to give me the confidence I lacked. The only thing bothering me was what seemed to be a coating of fur where my gums met my teeth, which ended up producing a slight soreness on the tip of my tongue on account of the obsessive probing I have described above.

I reached S. at two in the afternoon; it was a Wednesday (I remember what day of the week it was because I still never clean my teeth on Wednesdays—a kind of superstitious whim). My lecture was timetabled for the following day at ten in the morning. There was a message at the hotel reception desk from the University requesting me to get in touch with them on my arrival. However, I decided not to do so until later that night in order to savour to the full my few hours alone in a strange town, a town in which I would soon find myself trapped, as in a snare, by a sequence of events that some would call chance and others fate, and which was resolved with the precise efficiency of a hammer blow, disrupting, in a single moment, the whole course of my life.

I had a leisurely lunch in the hotel restaurant, enjoying the slow pace apparently imposed by the town's own internal rhythms. The town was still unknown to me, but its secrets would be revealed that afternoon, when I walked its streets without the fear of being recognized, as if I were a foreigner, as if, in short, I were someone else.

The waiter at my table gave me excellent service without being overly deferential or bothering me with banal questions. He recommended a local wine, to which I did full justice and with which he simply topped up my glass whenever the contents dropped below a certain level.

A foreign couple—American tourists, as far as I could tell— were sitting at a table near mine with their adolescent son, whose voracious appetite was the delight of his parents. They made a happy threesome, absorbed in their own contentment in a manner that was both active and in keeping with the zest for life that shone in their faces.

Somewhat befuddled by drink, I peered in at my own existence, like a Peeping Tom through a crack in the door, and I deduced from what I saw that in my life too there was a measure of happiness, albeit of a passive nature and tempered by an utter predictability that had doubtless further encouraged my dedication to my work in the laboratory. Admittedly my wife and I had been unable to have children and that failure, which we never spoke of, had been transmuted into something like an intangible lump that would occasionally get in the way of our caresses or hinder communication when we discussed certain topics. But, in a way, we were very happy, I could see that now; it was suddenly as apparent to me as the fact that I had begun to drink rather heavily or that my youth had been finally laid to rest.

I think I've always been rather slow on the uptake when it comes to recognizing the really important things affecting my life.

Anyway, I decided I would phone my wife and share with her my thoughts on the subject of our unsuspected bliss.

The waiter, meanwhile, recommended a special dessert and then served me coffee accompanied by a glass of the local brandy; this had the same stupefying effect on some part of my brain as an adolescent's first glass of cheap cognac.

I was distinctly drunk by the time I got up from the table and so decided to take a short nap before venturing out to see the town.

I slept for two hours that felt more like five centuries and during that time I remained locked in the same circular dream of being inside a fantastic waterwheel with buckets that seemed to represent all the different segments of my life.

I woke up feeling confused, as if I had just received a message I could not read. I was seized by a terrible sense of my own fragility and sat for some minutes on the edge of the bed, not moving, fearful lest the simple act of standing up and walking over to the bathroom might cause my skeleton to fracture, the way a glass object would break and shatter if struck at the base.

I realized then that I lacked the necessary courage to face the delights of visiting the town alone. I needed someone to name me, to certify that I was indeed a well-known research scientist who happened to be in S. to give a lecture at the University. I remembered that I was married, that I had no children and that I wasn't American—as the people on the neighbouring table in the restaurant had been; I ran through a brief curriculum vitae and thus acquired an equally brief identity. But it was a precarious identity, ready at any moment to burst the bounds of my body, like wine gushing out of a badly sewn wineskin. I then phoned the University and gave them my name, and, to my relief, a voice assured me that someone would pick me up in about an hour to take me for a walk round the town and then out to supper.

I showered, shaved and put on the kind of suit lecturers are supposed to wear, but I still didn't brush my teeth, despite the unpleasant taste in my mouth, for the simple reason that it seemed the only stable point of reference in the general disorder of the day.

Shortly afterwards I was informed that someone was waiting for me in reception.

That someone was a woman of mature years, on whose features, however, time had worked with great subtlety, giving her the look of a rather weary adolescent. Her dark wavy hair set off her face perfectly, the way a carved frame sets off a baroque painting.

Something's happening, I thought, as I shook her hand and took in the information conveyed by her lips. She introduced herself as technical assistant to the professor of cardiology and apologized for the latter's absence; he had been unavoidably detained on business. Then we set off for the Plaza Mayor, both of us cheered by the trivial conversation that flowed easily between us, as if we were each playing a long-rehearsed role with which we had not yet, however, managed entirely to identify.

The Plaza Mayor was rectangular in shape with numerous small cafés sheltering in its arcades, their tables occupied by young people whose laughter and excited eyes spoke of the coming of spring. We sat down at a table that afforded us a clear view of the square; she ordered a cognac, thus allowing me to order an alcoholic drink too, without fear of incurring her disapproval.

'It's good for the heart,' the woman joked.

We sat for a long time in silence, as if letting the gentle effects of our mid-afternoon drinks permeate through us. We each ordered another drink and gradually the space and time contained by the square began to change into a different kind of space and time, one isolated from the general order of events. I had the feeling that we were a tiny scrap of history which, due to some minor cataclysm, had become cut off from any normal sequence and been condemned to live in an eternal present. Doubtless noticing my air of bewilderment, she said.

'See that balcony on the top floor, the one with the doors half-open?'

'Yes,' I said, 'it's nice.'

'That's my flat,' she replied with some satisfaction.

By the third drink, which coincided with that moment in the evening when the light seems just about to disappear but doesn't, the birds arrived, obscuring the voices of the young people in the cafés with their screeching. They did not seem like birds to me, but small, flying artefacts wheeling blindly about, following trajectories determined by the hand of some invisible mechanic. Then desire surfaced, and that too seemed manipulated by a power beyond our own wills. Her gaze had become clouded, like the past life of a traveller, and words fell in fragments from her lips. I looked at her now with the insolent gaze of a client assessing the body of a prostitute whose services he is about to avail himself of and asked in a hoarse, broken voice:

'Do you live on your own?'

'Oh, worse than that,' she replied, 'Let's go.'

I paid for the drinks and we went up to her flat. From its balcony I could look down at the chairs in the café we had occupied only moments before, but our bodies were not there now, a fact that filled me with an inexplicable sense of relief.

It was an old house and had a multilated air about it, the cause of which I could not quite put my finger on. It wasn't just that there were pictures missing, their absence signalled by the marks they had left on the walls; it wasn't the lack of books, although the bookshelves did seem strangely empty; nor was it that the place seemed sparsely furnished or that some of the lightbulbs were bare. No, the mutilation was of a different order altogether and the apparent absences were just a pale reflection of a far greater absence, of which no visible trace remained, however. It was then that I understood her reply to my question about whether she lived alone.

Meanwhile, she had come back from the kitchen with a bottle of cognac and two unmatching glasses, which she placed on the table. Then I seized her by the wrist and clasped her to me with a kind of calculated violence to which she responded with a wild cry, very like that of the birds disrupting the peace of the square.

However, just as I was beginning to explore the edges of the more mysterious nuclei of her body, the woman pulled away.

'I'm going to get undressed,' she said.

She disappeared down the corridor and I stayed on the balcony watching the birds (whose flying activities had diminished now), still probing the inner recesses of my mouth with the tip of my tongue.

After some time had passed, I called out to her but received no reply. I walked down the corridor, whose walls seemed clammy like the walls of some internal organ, and reached her room, where I found her lying dead on the bed. She had not even had time to undress.

I've seen a lot of corpses in my time, but none as beautiful as hers. She wore the same look of weary adolescence she had worn in life, and death had added a touch of despair to it and only made her all the more desirable. However, fear of finding myself caught up in some dubious and complicated situation prevented me from studying this more closely. I ran out of the house, went back to the hotel and phoned the University. After telling them who I was, I explained that I would have to cancel my lecture for the next day, as a sudden family crisis obliged me to return at once to my home town.

The person who answered the phone had no idea what lecture I was talking about and put me through to another department, who in turn put me in touch with the office of the chair of cardiology, where they also knew nothing of my lecture. Perplexed, I hung up, packed my things and fled. I arrived home at dawn but only realized the next day that I had left my wallet in the woman's flat. I had put it down on the table moments before embracing her because it made a hard, uncomfortable lump in the thin jacket I had on.

I spent the next few days in a state of unbearable tension, knowing that when they found the body, they would also find my papers, and I would become embroiled in a scandal that would ruin my career and have serious repercussions on my family life.

I considered suicide, but lacked the courage to go through with it. Meanwhile, the days passed and no policemen appeared at the laboratory or at my house. After ten days, I calculated that the corpse's advanced state of decomposition would make discovery inevitable. A month passed, then two, and so the months went by one after the other and my life underwent none of the changes I had expected. I got back into my daily routine, but the constant fear of discovery aged me and plunged me into terrible alcohol-soaked dreams.

When a year had passed, I decided to go back to S. and find out what had happened. The Plaza Mayor was still bathed in the same light and the birds still traced the same trajectories around the statue standing in its centre. The balcony windows of the woman's flat stood ajar, exactly as I had left them twelve months before. I went up to the flat and knocked at the door. When I got no reply, I slid a credit card in between the doorframe and the lock and the latch gave beneath the pressure of the plastic with astonishing ease.

The flat was just as I had left it, that is, it had the same half-lived in, half-abandoned air; its walls still exuded dampness as if they were made of some organic, porous matter that sweated and breathed. My wallet was still on the table, lying at the same angle and in precisely the same position. I went down the corridor to the bedroom where I gazed again upon the woman's body, entirely untouched by decay. Her skin was the temperature of someone who had only recently died and her breasts had the firmness of someone newly expired. I wondered if perhaps that space was like a fold in time or a splinter, a fragment broken off from the laws of succession and condemned to last for all eternity.

I did not dare pick up my wallet for fear that any change—however slight—might set in motion the complex machinery of time that corrupts all things subject to its laws.

So I returned to my normal life, in which I've grown used to living with the threat that, just when I least expect it, something beyond my control (the disappearance of one of the birds from the square or a gust of wind blowing shut the balcony doors) could trigger a dormant mechanism and set in train the scandal caused by that death.

And, as I said before, that is also the reason I still never clean my teeth on Wednesdays.

Oh, well.

(*Translated by Margaret Jull Costa.*)

Carme Riera

Report[1]

Deyá,
22 September, 1980

Dear Helen,

 I need you to find out for me whether a woman named María Evelyn MacDonald, aged about forty, is living in Santa Barbara. For the moment, I can't give you any more details. It's absolutely essential for me to locate her and make contact with her, as you'll see from the story I'm sending you. I'll call you when I can from New York and will keep you informed. Please don't think I've gone crazy. Do everything possible to help me. Ask around, look in the telephone directory . . . whatever you can.

Love,
Stephanie.

 This is a small village on the north coast of Mallorca. The stone houses look out over the stream, offering up their tiny mauve gardens. Still-flowering bougainvillaea competes with the ivy in its endeavours to scale house and garden walls. Only from the highest windows can you see the sea penetrating the

---

[1] This story, like almost all of Carme Riera's work, was originally written in Majorcan, the variation on Catalan spoken in the Balearic island of Mallorca. Unfortunately the manuscript was lost and this English translation is, perforce, from a Castilian version the author prepared for the anthology *Doce relatos de mujer* (Alianza, 1982). (Trans.).

rounded deserted cove in the distance. The last summer visitors, the faithful and the stragglers, left a few weeks ago. They held out until the damp and first autumn rains threatened to vent themselves on rheumatic anatomies addicted to central heating. Apart from the sparse foreign colony established in the village years ago, there are very few of us outsiders still here. I confess right away that I'm leaving soon too. There's no reason for me to delay my departure any longer because yesterday, what I was waiting for, the only thing that kept me here, happened. And yet I'm sorry to go. But I have no other option. I must leave here as soon as I can.

It would never have occurred to me in the early days after my arrival that I'd spend the whole summer here toiling away simply in search of information to write a report. The fact is, I got carried away with the whole affair. Right from the start, I thought the hostility of the local people to the matter seemed abnormal. People living here are used to dealing with foreigners and are by nature helpful and hospitable. Why then did they persist in keeping silent? Even the money I offered them failed to refresh their memories . . . The younger ones made excuses saying they'd never heard anything about the case, while the older people who might have known at close quarters what happened, or who might even have experienced the events, refused to make any statement.

Nobody remembered Anaïs Nin either. 'So many artists come through here . . . you will understand . . . we are used to seeing so many people . . . new faces . . .' Thanks to Robert Graves's wife, I found out where she had lived. A cottage in the 'Clot'[1] with a little garden, just like all the rest. Its present owner, a black girl who spends her summers here, was very happy for me to visit her and delighted with the news because she didn't even know that Nin had stayed in Mallorca, let alone in her house. 'I could come to some arrangement with the people who own the cells where Chopin and George Sand stayed in Valldemossa and for a bit more money they could

---

[1] 'The Gully' (Majorcan).

round off the tourist trip with a visit to my house. You can't tell me Anaïs Nin isn't someone with international prestige . . .'

Needless to say, the house retained no trace of the writer's stay, but I took photos anyway to illustrate my report which still wasn't making any progress.

I was really very dispirited, realizing that it had begun badly, that I was getting nothing clear; the best thing I could do was to forget about my commitment with Partner and the special number his magazine was putting out in homage to Anaïs Nin, and devote myself to sunbathing. After all, it was my fault. You should never take literally the assertions of any writer who claims she heard the story she's about to tell from other lips . . . But it was difficult for me not to take the case of Nin seriously: 'I was spending the summer in Mallorca, in Deya[1] . . . A strange story was told of the place by the fisherman.' These two sentences at the beginning of her story 'Mallorca' struck me as being credible enough. Without doubt, the strange story would have unfolded around the forties when Nin was here. If they told her about it then, why didn't they want to mention it now? Did they find it so shameful that a local girl should have a relationship with a foreigner and make love with him on the beach? Was it more outrageous then than now? It was absurd to believe such a thing. But why did they refuse to talk about it? Gisele, my black friend, suggested that maybe they were all telling me the truth . . . they didn't know the story because it had never happened.

I wrote to Partner. Anaïs Nin had only used her imagination. It was a mistake to suppose otherwise. The story 'Mallorca' figures amongst the pages of her book *Delta of Venus*, a collection of stories written on commission. I was very sorry to have got it wrong. As an alternative, I proposed to write a long piece about Graves and his world . . . Partner telegraphed me from New York. He wanted something on Nin, and fast. I re-read her *Diaries*, looking for any item that might orient me . . . How did Nin manipulate reality? What was her concept of

---

[1] The accent is absent in Nin's English version, *Delta of Venus* (1978, A Star Book, W.H. Allen & Co. Ltd.).

truth? I remembered a letter from Henry Miller to her: 'All your lines are loaded with meaning, but no matter how much anyone explains their sense, the enigma will persist because you are the only one who can explain it. And in the enigma resides the key to your triumph: you will never reveal it . . .' I underlined several paragraphs of her voluminous confessions, ending up with one succinct affirmation: 'What kills life is the absence of mystery.' I began to think it all through. Partner had asked me for an article, something light, so I tried sending him a short essay which was too esoteric for the public for whom the magazine was destined. I sent it by urgent mail. He telegrammed me again: 'Take time necessary. We delay publication. Get what happened with story. You have key. There's a mystery.'

I renewed my enquiries, but changing tactics. I didn't mention Nin at all, nor did I ask if the fisherman's daughter and the young American were still alive, nor whether it were true that in their youth they had made love publicly, in the moonlight. I confined myself to finding out if there were in the village any couples of a foreign man and Mallorcan woman, or the reverse, if this were at all usual, and if it were looked upon favourably. They said no, that there were very few cases, that such relationships always ended dramatically . . . the customs are different, way of life, temperament . . . Not one of these conclusions seemed sufficiently valid to me, nor even explicit. I protested, asked for more details. The little woman who was letting a room to me confessed that every time such a union occurred, some calamity fell on the village . . .

'Such as?'

'Calamities . . . A house collapses, a wall falls down, a rainstorm washes away the vegetable gardens.'

'It could be coincidental.'

'Don't you believe it. It's a punishment.'

'Why?'

'Up there, they don't like people doing such things . . .'

'How long has this been going on?'

'Since they died.'

'Who?'

'The ones you're trying to find out about . . . But I'm not telling you any more.'

All my efforts were useless. I begged, made offers, promised to keep the secret. Futile. I couldn't get another word out of her. For some days after our conversation she was evasive, and managed not to see me or have the least contact with me. Gisele congratulated me when I told her. 'You've got a very strong lead; it's a good starting point.' It was her idea: I went down to Palma, and, in the small newspaper archive there, consulted the papers from the summer of '41. Anaïs had been in Deyá during those months. I found nothing of interest. Then '42 . . . In the copy of *Correo*[1] for 21 September 1942, there was a brief item: three bodies had been found floating in the waters of the cove at Deyá. Two of them were women, María Sarrió Companys, daughter of village fishing people, and Evelyn MacDonald, American subject, while the third was a man, George MacDonald, brother of Evelyn. It appeared that heavy seas had swept them from the rocks where they were walking. There were no witnesses to the unfortunate accident and therefore no help was available.

I returned to Deyá with a photocopy of the newspaper item. I discussed it with Gisele. There was no doubt that Anaïs Nin had used part of the story, speaking only of the love between María and Evelyn's brother, without mentioning their tragic deaths . . . Nin wrote before this happened . . . What really occurred? Why was there so much mystery about such a stupid and cruel accident? 'There has to be something more to it,' Gisele insisted, 'for sure.'

I had quite a job getting my landlady to read the document. She couldn't see well without her glasses and she'd lost them months before. Nor did she want me to read it to her aloud. Finally, after much persistence, I put it before her myopic eyes. Her chin trembled and she started to cry.

'It's them. Leave them alone. Yes, they're dead, but if you call them, they'll come back again and it will be horrible. They'll

---

[1] *Post* (Castilian).

come back and they won't let you sleep. None of us will ever sleep again.'

'Why? Tell me, please . . . don't cry . . .'

'They died because of their terrible sins. It was a punishment from above, there's no doubt of it. They bewitched her, miss, they bewitched María . . . I can't tell you any more. I can't. If I say anything, they'll come back. At night the sounds of the sea won't let us sleep, the waves will flood this house and with their noise will come the gasping . . . They used to make love on the beach, the three of them, naked, all together. Do you understand? They didn't care if anyone was watching, it was so obscene. Nothing like that had ever happened in the village before . . . It was their fault, those two foreigners. They'd come to Deyá, away from the war,[1] they said, at the end of thirty-nine. They rented a house outside the village. They used a typewriter, like you. We thought they were married. They used to embrace in public, with no respect for us. The priest gave them a talking to once, but that made it worse. From then on they used to swim naked in the cove, a disgraceful custom which unfortunately became fashionable along this coast more than forty years ago . . . One evening María was walking on the rocks at the cove—she was my friend, did you know that? The same age as me. Evelyn called out to her from the water. María took off her dress and jumped into the water in her chemise. She swam up to Evelyn. The chemise made it hard for her to move. Evelyn pulled her over to the boat landing and undressed her there. They swam back to the shore and lay on the sand resting in the moonlight with Evelyn's arm around María's waist. They went back there to meet each other every afternoon. María was fascinated by Evelyn's beauty, and the stories she beguiled her with. I was confidante and I knew all too well she'd been bewitched. One day George joined them. He swam out to them and then lay naked on the beach with them. María let them both make love to her . . . That night she got a tremendous beating from her father. She was in bed a week because of it. As soon as she could get up, she disappeared from the village with them.

---

[1] The Spanish Civil War.

We had no news of her for two years. The Palma police visited us once trying to get information that would help them find out where she was. It was about then that the writer you're working on appeared. I remember her vaguely. Someone told her the story; she was American like them. Later we found out she'd been merciful with María . . . she'd only written about the love affair with George. The next summer, towards the end of September, they came back. They brought a little girl a few months old with them. The father was George, but we didn't know which of the two women was her mother . . . María came to see me but I didn't want to receive her. Nobody in the village did. That evening they went down to the cove, taking the little one in a carry-cot. Everyone in the village was spying on them from behind the bushes. They were making bets about their shamelessness and said we had to teach them a lesson before we called the police. I still marvel at how naturally they took their clothes off. Then, instead of going into the water, they stayed next to the rocks at the right side of the cove. They lay down there and embraced. Their gasps came up to us mixed with the sounds of the waves. It was something disgusting to see the way their bodies moved when they were making love. Some of the men left their hiding places and went across to them with sticks to threaten them. They didn't turn a hair. They had to beat them apart. The three of them were hurt and they ran to the sea. It was their only possible escape. We assumed they'd try to save themselves by swimming to the far end of the cove and climbing up the cliff from there. The sea was coming in furiously, with the waves getting bigger and bigger. We could hardly make out their heads and arm movements. We thought we could hear their voices calling out to each other. The baby started to cry. I took her home with me. Really, it was just an excuse to get away from there. One by one, all the people went back up to their houses. The next day their bodies appeared floating at the mouth of the cove. Dead. The judge from Soller came to take charge of the corpses, but nobody could be surprised by their deaths . . . They took too many risks and everyone had seen them swimming when the sea was rough . . . I took the little girl to the police and it was then that they told me that George and

Evelyn were brother and sister. The American consul in Palma contacted their family. Later I found out that María Evelyn went to live with her grandparents in Santa Barbara. To be frank with you, I've done everything possible to forget about it . . . For years I've had terrible problems with insomnia and awful nightmares because of this story, just like everyone in the village, only nobody dares to confess it. Often at night when the sea is rough we've heard them calling out for help from the cove and on other nights when it's calm, their soft voices come up to us and you can hear the panting of their bodies at the moment of pleasure . . . But there's more yet, a lot more. For years after this terrible thing happened, none of the fishermen from here could put down nets anywhere near the cove without putting themselves in grave danger: a tremendous weight dragged them down to the bottom . . .

'It's the first time I've told anyone about it. Maybe you'll think I'm exaggerating, or not right in the head . . . The pity is that these things happened, just as I've told you. If they haven't come back to worry us lately, it's because nobody's mentioned their names, but I fear that without meaning to, you've called them again . . . Ever since you've been trying to find out about it, I've had trouble sleeping and it's the same with some of my neighbours who saw these terrible things . . .

'Do you want proof that I'm not lying? Then go down to the cove on the night of the 21st. It will be thirty-eight years since their deaths. Just like every other year, only the boats of the youngest people and the foreigners will go out. They'll come back without catching a thing. The sea is rough and there's usually a storm. Stay by the water's edge and look carefully: at midnight you'll see them come out of the water and lie naked on the beach to make love until morning . . .'

I was totally overwhelmed by the story. I hurried to tell Gisele.

'Your landlady was talking nonsense, sweetheart. They tell me she's crazy. Apparently she was the schoolteacher when she was young but they took her off it because she had bad attacks of depression . . .'

Gisele left at the beginning of September and I stayed on,

waiting. Yesterday I went to the cove. It was full moon. The sea was sparkling. Suddenly I saw them. They were swimming in towards the beach, young, amazingly beautiful as if death and time hadn't been able to touch them. And there near the water's edge, they began their amorous games which lasted until daybreak . . .

When I went back to the house, I couldn't tell my landlady what I'd seen. She wasn't there. She'd left me a farewell note saying she was going, as she did every year, to spend a few months in a sanatorium. She left me instructions for closing up the house and wished me a happy return home. I tried to sleep but couldn't for the murmuring of the sea that came insistently to my ears.

Barcelona, October 1980.

(*Translated from the Castilian by Julie Flanagan.*)

José Maria Merino

Cousin Rosa

Forcing the key into the lock, my cousin used both hands to turn it. She pushed at the door, which grated open. The darkness rushed out at us, was contained on the threshold, and suddenly became flecked with streaks of brilliant sunlight.

'Come on in,' she said.

Inside, the mill was also built of unplastered stone. In the centre of the dark room lay the huge mass of the grindstone. The sound of the stream rose from deep within, endowing it with the mysterious air of a live object.

The only light in the room came from a tiny window with dusty panes. Some stairs led up to the loft. They were made from stone flags driven into the wall at one end and fixed at the other to a long wooden beam that rose diagonally from the floor supported on three posts.

With no landing of any kind, the stairs ended abruptly in front of a door, which my cousin now opened. At the sight of the bare timbers of the sloping tiled roof which ran the length of the loft, with the crossbeams holding up the wooden floor, I imagined I was being ushered into a cabin far removed in time and space from the reality of that moment: my uncle and aunt's village, this June afternoon, my cousin showing me what was to be my workplace. An open window set in the far wall offered glimpses of the river, its tree-lined bank, the hills beyond it and their violent contrasts of light and shade.

In the middle of this room stood a dark, almost black, table, and next to it a wicker chair.

'No one will disturb you here,' my cousin said.

From the moment I set foot in the village (gingerly, still stunned by the protracted bumpy ride on the open bus lined with wooden benches on which passengers, packages and chickens were all crammed together in the afternoon sun), I had understood that my cousin would rule with a rod of iron. After the customary kiss on both cheeks, the very first thing she said to me was:

'I hope you haven't forgotten your books.'

I didn't say a word. By way of reply, I half lifted the bundle dangling from my left shoulder. She took me to her house, where I was able to greet my uncle and aunt briefly and leave all my luggage apart from the books, before she hauled me off after her without any opportunity to rest. We walked along the main road until we left the last houses of the village behind us. Then my cousin led me down a narrow track lined by dense clusters of foliage, pierced here and there by sudden sunbeams teeming with dust and insects, until we reached the watermill. The atmosphere created in that late afternoon by the building, the river, and the landscape, engraved itself deeply on my mind despite my torpor.

'You'll be able to study here to your heart's content,' she added. 'And I'll test you every morning, after breakfast.'

My cousin succeeded in instilling fear into me in a way that not even Don Fulgencio himself had managed to do, despite all his fury when on Mondays he used Latin as a bludgeon to crush the hostility he imagined he saw in his students, and which seemed so to embitter his days.

The summer days were radiant even though the thick foliage filtered the sunlight and swathed the mill in a cool green shade. The room I studied in was filled not only with the constant noise of water (in itself a double sound, a high-pitched rushing of the river outside, combined with a deeper but softer murmur of the water under my feet, beneath the mill itself) but also with the song of thrushes, the lowing of cattle, the twitter of swifts and swallows, dogs barking, and every now and then a voice, which always fragmented and dispersed on the breeze before I could catch the words being said.

The summer days were radiant, and all the sounds evoked the

completeness of something full and irreplaceable. And yet I grew to loathe them every bit as much as the dark days spent shut in the seminary, or even more—there at least the tedious routine and tasks were shared with others, and misfortune was spread among us all, whereas here, in this solitude, I was all alone to suffer the strictures of my teacher.

I tried to spin things out over my morning bowl of milky coffee, but my cousin would have none of it.

'Come on, wake up, don't play the dummy.'

And she was a zealous examiner of everything I knew, checking each question with a scrupulous attention that even my tiny writing could not deflect.

For the first few days, I was caught up in a strange kind of lethargy that I sought to blame on the stupor of the journey, as well as an ill-defined but determined desire not to have to do anything. This made it hard, even physically, for me to concentrate on the pages of my books, which swam before my eyes. All this prevented me from responding to my cousin's questions with at least a modicum of dignity. She said nothing on the first day, or the second. On the third, she slammed the book shut and looked me sternly in the eye, her own face flashing with aversion and distaste.

She had small eyes that were hazel-coloured with streaks of gold and red. One of them was darker than the other. Her insistent stare, combined with this disparity, threw me even further into confusion.

'Listen, don't think you can make a fool out of me,' she said. 'If you carry on like this, you'll pack your things and go home. The first thing I'm going to do is to write to your father, this very afternoon.'

I imagine I must have turned pale. I could still almost feel the thrashing my father had given my round my head, my neck, and the beneath of my back.

'No, cousin,' I shouted in alarm. 'I'll study, I promise you I'll study. I don't know what's been wrong with me these past few days.'

My mother took fright at the beating. My father turned bright scarlet, and was gasping for breath.

'I'll kill you, you booby,' he spluttered.

That same night he decided to send me to his brother's house so that my cousin Rosa, who was his god-daughter and a student teacher, could take me in hand. While I sobbed in bed and my brothers and sisters lay in terrified silence, I could hear him and my mother discussing all the details of a lengthy letter in which they were outlining my situation in the most dramatic terms: a school year full of absences, waywardness, and a steady worsening that had culminated in the catastrophe of failing several exams and a warning about my future from the headmaster.

I forced myself to study, elbows jammed on the table, painfully struggling against the repugnance I could feel in my whole body. I occasionally left off reading to go down to the millpond to relieve myself. It was only at those moments, when the stream of my piss was splashing the smooth surface of the water, setting up ripples and for a few seconds clouding the crystal clear view of the gravelly bottom of the pond, that I recovered a sense of the sweet gratuitousness of summer, which dragonflies and swallows crisscrossed so contentedly. As I finished, the memory of the book waiting for me up on the loft table fell across my mind like the blade of the guillotine must fall across the neck of its victims, forcing me into an immediate renunciation that was both absolute and irredeemable.

There never was such a lovely, full summer as that one, and I have never missed it so completely. I gradually became accustomed to the arduous days of study and examination, sunk in a state of stupefaction like that which galley slaves must have felt as they plied their oars day after day. Whenever I lifted my gaze and saw the hillside blazing with sunshine, the leaves on the trees shimmering in the gentle breeze, I realized I was condemned forever to contemplate paradise from outside the gates.

And yet as the days went by, my dogged determination made the routine of study a little easier, so that it became possible for me to pass my cousin's implacable examination each morning and yet still have some time free in the afternoons to gaze out at the landscape. That was how I saw her.

The first time it was only an instant: a female shape which I guessed to be that of my cousin flashed across the path in a patch clear of brambles and trees. A short while later, I heard a splash, as though someone had dived into the water.

The next afternoon I was on the alert, and although she again ran quickly by, this time I could clearly see it was my cousin. The splash which followed confirmed my suspicion that she must come to the river for a swim.

I began to feel a great curiosity to watch her bathing without being seen. I don't think there was any lasciviousness on my part in this (at that time, the delights of the flesh were still very vague and imprecise for me); it was more to wreak a kind of revenge. It seemed to me that by watching my cousin swimming without being aware of it, I would be somehow avenging myself for the strict authority she wielded over me at all times, and especially during her morning examinations.

That afternoon I was engrossed in imagining the details of my act of revolt; the following one I could scarcely glance at a book, such was my expectation of her appearance. When I saw her flit by, I ran down stealthily, found the path and followed it until I reached the reeds at the river's edge. I finally discovered the spot where my cousin had stripped off: her clothes lay carefully folded on the stump of a tree at whose base grew the fat golden-coloured dishes of some large fungi.

When I heard a loud splash I moved cautiously forward among the branches, expecting to catch sight of her in the part the noise had come from. But I saw nothing except the deserted stretch of water, disturbed only by the slight ripples of the current.

This unexpected emptiness baffled me, until another splash, this time down by the mill, made me realize that my cousin must have swum over in that direction. I was afraid she might discover me in my hiding-place, so I crept back along the path until I came to a spot where I could see the river clearly again.

From here there was no sign of my cousin either. In the background the silent, ivy-covered mill, which I had never seen from this angle before, led me to think of myself, shut in behind the open window which now peered down on the dark, motionless mass of the building like an empty eyesocket.

The river swept on along one side of the mill, while the water of the millrace, darkened by the building's shadow, plunged underneath it as if swallowed by an enormous mouth. The sun was already so low that it had sunk behind the trees at the water's edge, and there was a bluish, almost violet glow in the air. I remember being overcome by an odd sense of fear, so strange was the atmosphere the whole place had taken on at that moment. Then I saw the trout.

It was right next to where the main current and the millrace divided, and it was huge. I had seen large trout in my own village: there was one they hauled out on a gaffe that weighed close on thirteen kilos. In the water it had not looked half the size of this one. For a split second I told myself (though in my heart of hearts I knew the truth) that it was simply a long, dark stone that I had not noticed before. But its unmistakable shape, which allowed the play of light underneath, and its immobility in which it was nonetheless possible to sense an incessant quivering, were conclusive proof that this was indeed a trout. The shallowness of the water made it look even more impressive.

I stared at it in rapt attention for many minutes, while the sky grew darker and darker. In the end, the trout suddenly swung round, and with a flick of its tailfin disappeared upstream like a streak of lightning.

That enormous trout became for me a distorted image of all my winter longings. During all the boredom of the seminary, whose nets I was caught in for the whole school year, I was filled with a nostalgia in which my home river and its trout played a large part. That year, my second at the seminary, the hypnotic routines which dragged on amidst the smell of stews, chunks of stale bread, and greasy marble tabletops, in chilly rooms and high dark corridors, through interminably dreary days that seemed exactly like purgatory, convinced me of the value of all I had lost. One of the greatest treasures stored in my memory was the days when I had gone fishing. Ever since I was a small boy, I had devoted myself to learning and trying out all the different ways of catching trout. Even before I could swim I could tickle them under stones, pursuing them relentlessly even if a water snake appeared. Later on, I learned to fish with a rod, and to prepare my own flies for my hooks, which despite my clumsy fingers proved successful in catching these beautiful, shimmering creatures.

This gigantic trout was therefore like the phantom of all those I had been unable to catch, but had dreamt of with such longing during those endless days in the seminary: outside it was winter, a weak sun lit the dusty courtyard, the stumpy, bare trees, the brick wall enclosure, but in my mind I painfully dreamt of that same day and hour back in my own village, close to the river. Now, at the height of this summer I was also being robbed of, the trout appeared like a mysterious sign: surely nobody could ever have seen the likes of it.

That night I went to sleep in a happy frame of mind, my imagination filled with the image of its huge dark flank, the sure flick of its tail, its swift but stately movement. It almost made up for all the afternoons spent in forced study, and the mornings of gruelling questions.

As soon as I saw the trout, I was determined to catch it. The two months in which I had been obliged to subdue my real appetites had succeeded in creating in me the previously unsuspected ability of keeping something alive in my imagination while still following the thread of abstruse academic topics. Faced with my cousin's tireless daily evaluation of my progress, I was able to maintain the same frenetic pace of the first days at the mill, but also to create a space in my mind which I could fill with my daydreams.

I now slipped my new idea into this context. I began, so surreptitiously that it was not even suspected, let alone discovered, to conjure away bits of line, hooks, and feathers from my uncle, and with the new patience I had learnt to acquire, I made up flies that seemed most like the larvae laid in those days.

I left my tackle tied firmly to the river bank in different spots I could see from my window. My cousin still came to bathe in the river, on the far side of the bend, and the trout swam downstream until it came to its usual resting-place.

Finally, one afternoon it took one of my lures. A loud splash heralded the capture. I had tied my hooks to strong bits of twine, which were fastened at the other end to tough cord. The trout took the fly right by its hiding place.

I rushed downstairs and without a second thought leapt into the water, which in that stretch did not come up any higher than my thighs. The trout's body slithered in my hands, and I was afraid I might lose it, until I managed to plunge my fingers into its gills. The fish was far stronger than I had expected, and succeeded in knocking me over. I have no idea how long we struggled, but I do remember that we rolled over and over in the water for quite a distance. I think it was only my intense excitement that saved me from having to let go of the fish, half-drowned as I was by all the thrashing about in the water. Eventually I dragged myself to the bank and with a great effort threw the trout out of the water. Both of us lay panting on the path.

Stretched there beside me, the trout seemed bigger than ever. It was beating its tail furiously, and gasping for air. All down its huge body, the markings shone like precious stones. I lay looking at it in wonder.

Suddenly a discovery brought me down to earth. The trout's eyes reminded me exactly of my cousin's. It seemed to me that like hers, the fish's eyes were of different colours and even had the same expression. I felt frightened. It was that blue, mysterious hour of the evening. The watermill looked like some huge animal lurking in ambush. The gasping trout was staring at me with my cousin Rosa's eyes.

I pulled out the hook and pushed it back into the water. For a while the trout hardly moved, but then it swam slowly off until it disappeared in the middle of the stream, which was getting darker and darker as the light faded.

When I got back to my uncle's, I wasn't the only one who had met with an accident: my cousin had got caught on some branches, and sported a bloody tear on her upper lip. My aunt scolded both of us. To ward off the pneumonia she forecast for me, she made me drink a glass of homemade brandy (which, after burning my throat, left me drowsily tipsy). She also tended my cousin's wound, taking her to task for her crazy habit of going for a bathe every day. The peroxide bubbled gently on my cousin's lip. She stared at me, but I wouldn't return her gaze.

That was the last time she bathed in the pool near the mill. Nor did I ever see the enormous trout again.

(*Translated by Nick Caistor.*)

Alvaro Pombo

Mouse Island

An island in an island. Reaching an island, however small, made him feel better. Victorious. Sure of himself. A broad definition of islands. Not just any piece of earth surrounded on all sides by water—islands didn't have to be stable. So islands were divided into the stationary and the mobile. At low tide, there was a flowering of sandy islands in the big bay. Sometimes there were quite a few of these freshly appeared islands where the boat could be beached. Some people said that the bay ought to be dredged from one end to the other, that sand was slowly smothering it. The islands could last a whole morning. Keeping straight ahead, you suddenly arrived. To the sandy island from the Maritime Club would be roughly half a mile. Once on the island and sitting on that underwater sand—damp and dismal, although it was sunny—you waited for the tide to rise. A slow, fascinating feeling—like coming, only better. So when, little by little, the tide started coming in, you could be seen squatting in the middle of a shiny grey, motionless sheet—the whole bay—which was gleaming dangerously around you. And, in that situation, imagining you were part of some important shipwreck, which, seen through binoculars from the quay or the Maritime Club, you could well be. Then you could make weird, contorted faces and open your mouth wide, as if shouting in terror, in the hope that the horrified pilots, seeing you from the port, would immediately order the easily recognizable launch to come for you. The island, however small, invested itself with an uneasy theatricality, like an aura. Once back in their depth, the fish would lightly graze the same coarse, rough sand on which we were now sitting. Sand that was coarser than the Playa de la Concha, which Granny Carolina used to descend upon to put a stop to the goings-on of brassy French girls. Grazing it, the fish would slightly stir up the sand, the silent minute granules of rock and shell. The little red bits of sand included crabs and crustaceans powdered by the clash of the sea against the headlands. No one imagined, of course, that the sand's underwater movement was anything like the bits of sand moving at the bottom of a fishbowl. The image of the sea's vastness changed everything. The depths of the sea, however dark (as they probably would be round Mouro Island—the very word *mouro* brought to mind a deep, dense, chilly sea, its mass full of big black fish, gigantic sea-bream and mussels devouring each other), however slow and violent and uninhabitable the depths of the sea were, they always seemed to us far and wide, lit up, a darkened suffocating replica of the dreaded, dark blue surface which stretched, undulating, towards the horizon. You had to cross this deep, sensitive, power-driven surface in the dinghy, rowing. Doing it that way, you got to understand the sea, not any other way. The bay was the sea, the beaches were the sea, even the tamarinds in the Piquio Gardens were the sea, but—above all—out at sea was the sea and, even more above all, the depths of the sea were the sea, like the surface mightily pliable and revealed on windy days by intertwining white crests. The sea could be seen from everywhere throughout autumn and all winter and during Holy Week, with its extremely long services and the Sermon of the Seven Last Words in the Plaza Porticada. Just by leaning out of the window, you could see the sea, gigantic and nearby. The sea of the appearing and disappearing islands was aloof and temperamental. A sea to be looked at and left in peace, down bay, almost up to the Remonta district, the fisherman's quarter and the Remonta, where Uncle Alvaro and my father had lived. Throughout the autumn and winter of hats and berets, of raincoats and umbrellas, of the Alameda cinema and a bottle-green colour south wind, he thought of the sea as an infinitely desirable but forbidden place. In the mind's eye, they were the months of boarding ship and weighing anchor, no longer thinking about anyone else, not even the bloody Father Superior, or about getting good marks. Because weighing anchor was a perfect moment. The distant, blurred outline of the transatlantic liners and even of the coastal shipping, the cargo boats going to Gijón. Whose name we knew, whose sailors, with blue jerseys and cigarettes hanging from one side of their mouths, we knew, it least some of them. That's why, on Sundays and even in the afternoons after class during the winter, we'd go to examine the piles of dark green coal on the cargo wharves beyond old Peña's shop (may he rest in peace!) and the railway station and the non-bonded warehouses and the wooden coal wagons (God bless them!). The sea smelled wintry then, with a reflection of the sitting-room's enclosed balcony—its golden brass lamp, mirrors and dirty, cream-coloured lampshade. A good Thursday walk in winter was going to look at the boat run aground in Pompeyo's little shipyard. There it was, green and white, with its bottom full of black water, because of the heavy rain, and its skinny and somewhat frail ribs, like those of alley cats. Winter was also the time of the cats. The cat from the neighbouring block and the fried potatoes cat, who fought to the death in the Plaza Pombo. We went fishing for sea-bream spawn and *porredanas*. On afternoons which were sunny—or cloudy, but without rain—we fished from the jetty that closed off the smaller port. At its tip, there was a diminutive red lighthouse, with a fixed light, where, hidden at nightfall, lovers used to kiss. Manuela and the man who limped, for example, both of whom could be seen on the very same tram, travelling separately, not even greeting each other, so that La Negra wouldn't notice them. Or the red-haired Rosalía, Godofredo's niece, who fell in love with a married draughtsman, a fair-haired fellow with long legs who lived directly opposite. Rosalía, who came from Alhucemas on her Goda side and who finally threw herself from a window, a tiny lavatory window, although no one could understand how she got through it. From Fräulein Maria Hirschle's small flat, which still exists. That remote agony which, through the window and the arch suggested by the two lace curtains, goes on being repeated. That milky skin, speckled with freckles, and her big eyes like distressed eggs, the impossible lover with his slender legs and wasp waist. They were afternoons right by the cranes or—better still—alongside the moored ships, whose cooks fed the fishes, filling up—without meaning to—the whole stretch under the stern with potato peel and left-overs from the crew's quarters. You could see hungry, silvery-backed fish gleaming green, pink and gold as they turned over. But the biggest catch was an octopus. At that time I was reading *The Treasure Hunter* and *Twenty Thousand Leagues under the Sea*. All the dead octopuses you saw in Esperanza plaza were an image of those terrible giant squid with jaws. The octopus was on its own, separated from other fishes, a cephalopod, all arms, an incalculable creature, with its halo of navigating carnivorous blossom, who could drag you to the back of a cave with algae for ever. Days of low tide, in summer, you'd go after shrimps in the pools with a net. They weren't like the ones in paper cones, pink and salted, they were raw. There were big greenish ones, nervy and pop-eyed, investigating the flowery side of the rocks with their invisible erect antennae. You could go barefoot into the same pool because they had no escape. And there were thin, small ones, the little shrimps, which were better left to live a little longer. But the sea's greenest and darkest production was the octopus. Not only because of Jules Verne, but because of the dead octopus itself, lying in the fishmonger's scaly, wooden boxes, with its head inside out, more threatening than ever, almost more spectacular dead than alive. There, inert, its real marine danger was revealed. Its erect, reddish-black tentacles recalled ferocious suckers fastened onto waist and legs. Even though you never got to see the really ancient and enormous octopuses, who didn't let themselves get caught and who, stretched out, expanding and contracting, swam in the waters surrounding Mouro Island. Even the middle-sized ones seemed dangerous enough. One middle-sized octopus was strong enough to drag a dog to the bottom, even a big water spaniel. And the pull of an octopus, who had caught you by the foot, was enough to duck your head and hold it under till you drowned. Because the immobility of an octopus in a fishmonger's was and is deceptive. The octopus quietly waits with all its tentacles spread out over a clean, slippery rock. They prefer bare rocks and, whenever they can, avoid ones with algae, with which they hate to be confused. The octopus is the brave, flesh-eating mollusc that attacks man because he can. He attacks those who stare stupidly at the sea. People from Palencia, Madrid and Avila—landlocked summer holidaymakers—were the most exposed. Holidaymakers always went about in canvas shoes that had been whitened. (Whitening is the name given indiscriminately to the sub-nitrate of bismuth and other sub-nitrates.) And it's precisely that thick, lumpy whitening, smelling of carpet and waxed corridors, that upset the octopus and unhinged him to the point of aggression: octopuses detest that smell of freshly-applied cleanliness. Just as they hated kids from Valladolid, older than us, who'd learned to swim in a real pool and who did the crawl. The true octopus only respects the breast stroke, the way sailors swim, those who live from the sea; nothing to do with sport, none of that shit. You had to respect the octopus, almost like the ray or skate, or the jellyfish. But the jellyfish is disgusting, a sea nettle that eats transparent treated filth from the sewers. That's why the coelenterate is an intestinal animal, asexual like little girls. Except that the jellyfish was sexual and had a prick, which touched you and peed on you. What's special about the ray or skate is that it's electric. The colour of sand, hidden flat on the sand, with an electrified spike that paralyses a man. So at low tide you have to go with care, prodding with the oar if you see the slightest protuberance—it may be a ray or a skate. But the island that brought together all the mystery of islands, and was easy to get to and from any time, was Mouse Island, with its tumbledown, cubist club—in those days: the days when the house on the way to the lighthouse belonged to Laxen-Busto. What happened with Mouse Island was that, although you'd got to know it well, you were quite scared of it. It was known that there were a lot of octopuses there. With a very deep channel, at least half a mile. And with the engulfing memory of 'The Ten Little Nigger Boys'. Very easily, something could always happen there—with luck, a crime! In the days before Uncle Pedro let me have the dinghy, we went in a big boat, slowly, which very soon lost its charm. Except for Paco Vázquez, with his springy fair hair, who, marvellously, arrived swimming. And so it came round to low tide again. You could almost get there on foot. From early on, it was a day with very blue breaks in the clouds, and the clouds themselves ragged and moving very fast. He had gone very early, on his own, with the shrimp net, to investigate the new pools, some dark green, very deep, among the sticky, bare rocks. It must have been September. It wasn't very hot, but it wasn't cold either. He was wearing swimming shorts and a shirt. Although it was obviously a perfect day for octopuses, he wasn't thinking about octopuses, but about succulent shrimps, prawns almost, which there had to be in the deep bits between the island and the beach. Shrimps fed on the freshest, least black algae. In fact, he caught some very good ones, but less than he'd expected. Actually, it was a somewhat dismal spot, the same one as usual, in fact, but approached for the first time on foot. There, in a round pool among the smooth rocks, you could see sand and a starfish on the sand. There were even *porredanas* in the transparent water, or one at least. To catch the starfish, he submerged the handle of the shrimp net halfway or more, soaking his shirt sleeve up to the shoulder and stirring up the surrounding sand, which clouded the pool; but in spite of this, the starfish could still be seen. At this point, wham! out comes the octopus. He came from the side as I'd expected. Stretching his three-legged, four-legged, arm out for the starfish. You could see that was why he had kept himself hidden in the pool, he was stalking the starfish. It was genuinely frightening, even though he was only medium-sized, probably young, that octopus. He didn't have to think twice. Nothing could be seen apart from the blurred, whiteish-pink octopus, very excited, dilated and inflated in the turbulent waters. The octopus was going to attack. He caught him with the shrimp net, which all at once snapped; the amazing octopus, switching between sheer rage and suffocation, wanting to get out while we ran, like bats out of hell, to where there were people. The end was a bit sad. A brawny fellow whom I didn't know seized it by its tender head; it was beaten half to death. He turned it inside out like a defenceless sock. Some more blows against a dry rock till he'd killed it. Then they gave me the octopus, ugly and vanquished. I'd hardly had time to see it in the pool, like a great living flower, eating the starfish. I'd have preferred it to have grasped me by the arm, even to have drowned me, than to kill it. I think I've recounted the essentials. That was how this story was.

(*Translated by Anthony Edkins.*)

Esther Tusquets

Summer orchestra

Summer was already well advanced—more than halfway through August—when it was decided to begin renovating the smaller dining room of the hotel and move the children, together with their governesses and their nursemaids and their mademoiselles, into the grown-ups' dining room. Throughout the whole of July and the first two weeks of August the children had formed a wild, unruly and increasingly uncontrollable gang that invaded the beaches, raccd through the village on bikes with their bells ringing madly, prowled with restless curiosity around the stalls at the fair, or slipped—suddenly surreptitious, silent, almost invisible—into secret places amongst the reeds. Year after year they built the huts there that housed their rarest treasures and where they initiated each other into marvellous, secret and endlessly renewed transgressions (smoking their first cigarettes, often communal, crumpled and slightly damp; getting enmeshed in poker games played with a ruthlessness that would have astonished the grown-ups—games so intense and hard-fought that the participants often preferred to play on rather than go down to the beach—and venturing into other stranger and more ambiguous games, which Sara associated obscurely with the world of grown-ups and the forbidden, and to which, during that summer, she had reacted with both fascination and shame, eager to be a spectator but very reluctant to take part. She—possibly alone amongst all the girls—had been astute or cautious enough when playing forfeits and lucky enough at cards to get through those days without once having to let anyone kiss her on the mouth or touch her breasts or take her knickers down), transgressions which were doubly intoxicating because they were the culmination of that parenthesis of temporary freedom provided by the summer and would be unthinkable once they were all back in the winter environment of schools and city apartments.

But within a matter of two or three days the summer community had broken up and with it the band of children, some being transported inland to spend what was left of their holidays in the mountains or in the country, most of them going home to prepare for the September resits. And Sara had stayed on as the one female straggler amongst the decimated gang of boys (Mama and Mademoiselle had promised consolingly that, at the end of August, her four or five best friends would be allowed to come up for her birthday) but the atmosphere had changed, it had grown suddenly tense and unpleasant, the general mood of irritability and discontent aggravated perhaps by the frequent rain and the shared feeling that all that remained now of summer were a few unseasonable, grubby remnants. One thing was certain, the boys' pastimes had grown rougher and Sara had simply had enough of them, of their fights, their games, their practical jokes, their rude words and their crude humour, had had enough of them spying on her through the window when she was changing her clothes, of them upending her boat, of having three or four of them corner her amongst the reeds. That was why she was so pleased about the change of dining room: there, at least during mealtimes, the boys would be forced to behave like civilized beings. And they must have had the same idea, for they protested and grumbled long and loud, complaining that, now there were so few of them and the rain deprived them not only of many mornings at the beach but also of almost every afternoon previously spent amongst the reeds, it really was the end to be expected now to sit up straight at table without fidgeting, barely saying a word, eating everything that was put in front of them, being required to peel oranges with a knife and fork and, to crown it all, wear a jacket and tie to go into supper.

But Sara was radiant and so excited on the first night that she changed her dress three times before going down—opting in the end for a high-necked, full-skirted organdie dress that left her arms bare and which her mother did not much approve of, saying that it made her look older than her years and was inappropriate for a girl who had not yet turned twelve—and then caught up her long, straight, fair hair with a silk ribbon. What most excited Sara that first night was the prospect of getting a good look at the adult world, until then only glimpsed or guessed at, since during the long winters the children's lives were confined to school, walks with Mademoiselle, and the playroom. There was hardly any contact between children and parents during the summer either—not this year nor in any previous year. (Sara had overheard Mademoiselle making a comment to one of the chambermaids about the delights and charms of the family holiday, at which they had both laughed, only to fall silent the moment they realized she was listening, and the whole episode had filled Sara with a terrible rage.) For the fact was that while the grown-ups slept on, the children would get up, have breakfast, do their homework or play table tennis and be coming back from the beach just as their parents would be finishing breakfast and lazily preparing themselves for a swim; and when the grown-ups were going into the big dining room for lunch, the children would already be off somewhere, pedalling down the road on their bikes or queueing at the rifle range at the fair. It was only occasionally, when Sara—quite deliberately—walked past the door of one of the lounges or the library, that she would catch sight of her mother sitting, blonde and evanescent, amongst the curling cigarette smoke. She would feel touched and proud to see her here, so delicate and fragile, so elegant and beautiful, like a fairy or a princess hovering ethereally above the real world (the most magical of fairies, the most regal of princesses, Sara had thought as a child, and in a way still thought), and for a moment her mother would stop playing cards or chatting to her friends to wave a greeting, call her over to give her a kiss, or pick out a liqueur chocolate from the box someone had just given her. At other times her father would come over to the children's table and ask Mademoiselle if they were behaving themselves, if they did their homework every day, if they were enjoying the summer. And, of course, they did coincide at church on Sundays because there was only one mass held in the village and the grown-ups had to get up early—relatively speaking—but even then they would arrive late and sit in the pews at the back, near the door. Although they did wait for the children on the way out to give them a kiss and some money to spend on an ice-cream or at the rifle range.

So Sara dressed with great care the first night the children moved into the big dining room—where they occupied only four tables—and she entered the room flanked by her brother and Mademoiselle, both of whom looked bad-tempered and morose. Her own face was flushed and her heart beat fast, and she was so excited and nervous that it was an effort to finish the food they put on her plate, and she felt she could see almost nothing, that she was unable to fix her gaze on anything, such was her eagerness to see and record every detail: the women in their long dresses, with their shoulders bare and their hair up and the earrings that sparkled on either side of their neck; the men, elegant and smiling, so different from the way they looked in the morning on the beach or on the terrace, and talking animatedly—what about?—amidst the laughter and the tinkling of crystal glasses. The unobtrusive waiters slipped furtively between the tables, treading lightly and barely uttering a word, so stiff and formal and impersonal that it was hard to recognize in them the rowdy, jokey, even coarse individuals who, up until yesterday, had served them in the children's dining room. And no one, neither the waiters nor the other diners, took the slightest notice of the children, so that any attempts by governesses and mademoiselles to stop the children fidgeting, make sure they left nothing on their plates and used their knives and forks properly were futile. As was the music played by the orchestra (hearing it as she crossed the foyer or from far off on the terrace, Sara had imagined it to be larger, but now she saw that it consisted of only a pianist, a cellist and a violinist, and the pianist, it seemed to her, had terribly sad eyes) for no one appeared to be listening to it, or even to hear it. People would merely frown or raise their voices when the music increased in volume, as if they were obliged to superimpose their words over some extraneous noise. There wasn't a gesture, a smile, even a pretence at applause. That surprised Sara, because in the city her parents and their friends attended concerts and went to the opera (on those nights her mother would come into their room to say goodnight, when the children were already in bed, because she knew how Sara loved to see her—the way she was dressed now in the dining room—in her beautiful, long, low-cut dresses, fur coats, feathered hats, jingling bracelets, with the little gold mesh bag where she kept an embroidered handkerchief and her opera glasses, and all about her the sweet, heavy perfume that impregnated everything her mother touched and that Sara would never ever forget). And in the library there were several shelves full of records which on some nights, when her parents were not at home, Mademoiselle would play so that Sara could hear them from her bedroom and drift off to sleep to the music. But here no one paid the least attention and the musicians played for no one and for no reason, so that when Sara went over to her parents' table to kiss them goodnight she couldn't help asking them why that was, at which they and their friends all burst out laughing, remarking that 'that' had little to do with real music, however hard the 'poor chaps' were trying. And that remark about 'poor chaps' wounded Sara and, without knowing why, she associated it with the jokes the boys told, with the stupid acts of cruelty they perpetrated amongst the reeds. But she immediately discounted the thought, since there was no possible connection. It was as irrelevant—and she had no idea why this came back to her now either—as Mademoiselle's tart sarcastic comment about the delights of family holidays.

Nevertheless, the following night, because she still thought the music very pretty and because it infuriated her that the grown-ups, who did not even bother to listen, should then condescendingly pass judgement on something to which they had paid not the slightest attention, she said to Mademoiselle— 'The music's lovely, isn't it? Don't you think they play well?'— and Mademoiselle said yes, they played surprisingly well, especially the pianist, but in the dining room of a luxury holiday hotel in summer it made no difference if you played well or badly. It really was a waste of good musicians. Then, screwing up all her courage, with her cheeks flushed and her heart pounding but without the least hesitation, Sara stood up and crossed the empty space separating her from the orchestra and told the pianist how much she enjoyed the music, that they played very well. She asked why they didn't play something by Chopin, and the man looked at her, surprised, and smiled at her from beneath his moustache (although she still thought he looked terribly sad) and replied that people there didn't normally expect them to play Chopin, and Sara was on the verge of saying that it didn't matter anyway since they wouldn't be listening and wouldn't notice and then she felt—perhaps for the first time in her life—embarrassed by her parents, ashamed of them and of that glittering grown-up world all of which seemed suddenly rather less marvellous to her. And before returning to her table, without quite knowing why, she apologized to the pianist.

From then on Sara put on a pretty dress every night (alternating the three smart dresses she had brought with her but had not worn all summer, because up till then she had gone around in either jeans or a swimsuit) and she did her hair carefully, brushing it until it shone, tying it back with a silk ribbon. But she still felt awkward and self-conscious when she entered the dining room (the boys made angry, spiteful, possibly jealous comments but Sara no longer heard them, they had simply ceased to exist) and she would mechanically eat whatever was set before her because it was easier to eat than to argue. She still observed the women's lovely dresses, their new jewels and hairstyles, their easy laughter and chatter amongst the clink of glasses; she still noticed how elegant the men looked and how gracefully they leaned towards their wives, smiled at them, lit their cigarettes and handed them their shawls, whilst a few waiters as insubstantial as ghosts bustled about them. The music played and outside the full moon shimmered on the dark sea, almost the way it did in technicolour films or advertisements. But her eyes were drawn more and more towards the orchestra and the pianist, who seemed to her to grow ever sadder, ever more detached but who, when he looked up from the keyboard and met Sara's gaze, would sometimes smile and make a vague gesture of complicity.

Suddenly Sara felt interested in everything to do with the pianist and discovered that the pale, thin woman (though she was perhaps faded rather than pale, like the blurred copy of a more attractive original) whom she must often have seen sitting on the sands at the beach or strolling along the farthest-flung and least frequented paths of the garden, always accompanied by a little girl who would hold her hand or be running about nearby, this woman was the pianist's wife and the little girl was their daughter. Sara had never seen a lovelier child, and she wondered if at some time in the past the mother had also been like that and wondered what could have happened since then to bring her so low. And, having definitely broken off relations with the gang of boys, and Mademoiselle having raised no objections, Sara began to spend increasing amounts of time in the company of the woman and the little girl, both of whom inspired in her a kind of transferred or displaced affection, for Sara loved the pianist—she had discovered this on one of those nights when he had looked up from the piano at her and their eyes had met; it was a discovery that brought with it no surprise, no confusion or fear, it merely confirmed an obvious reality that filled her whole being—and because the little girl and the woman were part of him, Sara bought the child ice-creams, candied almonds, bright balloons and coloured prints and took her on the gondolas, the big wheel, the merry-go-round, to the circus. The little girl seemed quite mad with joy, and when Sara glanced at the child's mother, perplexed, the mother would always say the same thing: 'it's just that she's never seen, never had, never tried that before,' and here her look would harden, 'we've never been able to give her such things'; and then Sara felt deeply troubled, as if she were somehow in danger—she would have liked to ask her forgiveness, as she had of the pianist one night, long ago now it seemed, though she did not know for whom or for what—perhaps because she could not understand it or perhaps because something within her was doggedly coming to fruition—and because when it did finally emerge and spill out of her she would be forced to understand everything and then her innocence would be lost for ever. The world would be turned upside down and she would be shipwrecked in the midst of the ensuing chaos with no idea how best to adapt in order to survive.

At nightfall—by the end of August it was already getting darker earlier—whilst the woman was giving the little girl her supper and putting her to bed in the servants' quarters, Sara almost always met the pianist in the garden and they would walk up and down the road together, holding hands, and the man would speak of everything he could have been, of all that he had dreamed in his youth—his lost youth, even though he couldn't have been much more than thirty—of what music had meant to him, of how much he and his wife had loved each other and of how circumstances had gradually caused everything to wither and crumble, forcing him to abandon everything along the way. It was a bleak, terrifying speech and it seemed to Sara that the man was not talking to her—how could he unburden such stories on a child of eleven?—but perhaps to himself, to fate, to no one, and on the road, in the darkness of night, they couldn't see each other's faces, but at certain points the man would hesitate, a shiver would run through him, his voice would tremble and then Sara would squeeze his hand and feel in her chest a weight like a stone, whether pity or love she no longer knew, and she would have liked to find the courage to tell him that there had doubtless been some misunderstanding, that fate had conspired against them, that at any moment everything would change, life and the world could not possibly go on being the way he described them. And on a couple of occasions the man stopped and held her tightly, tightly to him and, although she had no way of knowing for sure, it seemed to Sara that his cheeks were wet with tears.

Perhaps the woman felt subtly jealous of their walks alone together in the dark or perhaps she simply needed someone to whom she could pour out her own anguish, someone she could justify herself to (although no one had accused her of anything) because she sometimes alluded bitterly to 'the things my husband has probably told you' and, however hard Sara tried to stop her or tried not to listen, she would go on. 'Did he tell you that now there are fewer guests in the hotel, the management won't even pay us the pittance they originally promised us, something he simply doesn't want to know about?' 'Did you hear what the manager did to me the other day, right in front of him, and did he tell you that he didn't say a word in my defence?' 'Did you know that I've borrowed money from everyone, that we don't even own the clothes on our backs, that we have nowhere to go when the summer season ends in a few days' time and that he just stands on the sidelines as if none of this had anything to do with him at all?' And one day she grabbed her by the shoulders and looked at her with those hard eyes that left Sara defenceless and paralysed: 'Yesterday I felt so awful I couldn't even eat, but do you think he cared or bothered to ask me what was wrong? No, he just picked up my plate and, without a word, finished off both our suppers. I bet he didn't tell you that.' And Sara tried to explain to her that the man never talked to her about real events, about the sordid problems of everyday life, about what was going on just then between him and his wife; he talked only, in melancholy, desolate tones, of the death of love, of the death of art, of the death of hope.

The day of Sara's birthday came round, the last day of the holidays, just before the hotel was to close and they were all due to go back to the city and, just as Mama and Mademoiselle had promised, her best friends travelled up especially and even the boys behaved better, wearing their newly pressed suits and their Sunday smiles, and she got lots of presents that she placed on a table for everyone to see, including a new dress and, from Papa, a gold bracelet with little green stones that had been her grandmother's and which signalled that Sara was on the threshold of becoming a woman. There were sack races, lucky dips, fireworks, mountains of sandwiches, a vast cake and a fruit punch with lots of champagne in it which, because it was the first time they'd ever been allowed to drink it, got them all a little merry and was just one more sign that they were leaving childhood behind them. And the whole afternoon Sara was so excited, so happy, so busy opening her presents and organizing games and attending to her friends that it was only when night fell, when the party was over and some of the guests were already leaving to go back to the city, that she realized that the musician's little daughter had not been amongst them, and, however much she tried to deny what to her seemed at once both obvious and inconceivable, she knew instantly what had happened. She knew even before she grabbed Mademoiselle by the arm and asked, shaking her furiously: 'Why didn't the little girl come to my party? Tell me!' and there was no need to specify which little girl she was talking about, and Mademoiselle blushed, she did her best to act naturally but instead blushed to the roots of her hair and, not daring to look at Sara, said: 'I don't know, Sara, really I don't, I think it must have been the porter who wouldn't let her in,' adding, in an attempt to placate her, 'but she is an awful lot younger than all your other friends . . .' She knew before she confronted the porter and screamed her bewilderment and spat out her rage at him, and the man simply shrugged and explained that he'd simply done as he was told, that her mother had issued instructions about who should be allowed into the party; and she knew before she went over to her mother, swallowing back her sobs, her heart clenched, and her mother looked up from her book with surprised, unflinching eyes and said in a slow voice that she had had no idea they were such good friends and that anyway it was high time Sara learned the kind of people she ought to be associating with, and then, seeing Sara's eyes fill with tears, seeing that she was shaking, said: 'Don't cry, now, don't be silly. Maybe I was wrong, but it's not so very important. Go and see her now, take her a slice of cake and some sweets and it'll all be forgotten.' But in the musician's room, where she had never set foot before, the woman gave her a hard look, a look, thought Sara, that was now fixed, a look the woman had been rehearsing and learning throughout the summer, but her voice quavered when she said: 'The worst thing, you see, was that she didn't understand, she saw you all having tea and playing games and she didn't understand why she couldn't go in; she cried a lot, you know, before she finally went to sleep.' But the woman didn't cry. And Sara dried her own tears and did not ask forgiveness—now that she knew for whom and for what, she also knew that there are some things for which one does not ask forgiveness—and she took them no cakes or sweets, made no attempt to give them presents or to make anything better.

She went up to her room, tore off the ribbon, the dress, grandmother's little bracelet and threw it all down in a heap on the bed, then she pulled on her jeans and left her tousled hair hanging loose over her shoulders. And when she went into the dining room, no one, not Mademoiselle or the boys, her parents or the head waiter, dared say one word to her. And Sara sat down in silence, without even touching the food they put on her plate, sitting very erect and very pale, staring at the orchestra and repeating to herself that she would never ever forget what had happened, that she would never wear a long, low-cut dress and a fur coat and jewels or allow men in dinner jackets to fill her glass and talk to her of love, that she would never—she thought with surprise—be like the rest of them, that she would never learn what kind of people she ought to be associating with, because her place would always be at the side of men with sad eyes who had had too many dreams and had lost all hope, at the side of hard-eyed, faded women, old before their time, who could barely provide for their own children, not after this terrible, complicated summer in which Sara had discovered first love and then hate (so similar, so intimately linked), not after this summer in which, as the grown-ups kept telling her in their very different ways, she had become a woman. She repeated all this to herself again and again while she looked and looked at him and he looked at no one but her, not even needing to look down at the piano on which, all through supper, he played nothing but Chopin.

(*Translated by Margaret Jull Costa.*)

Enrique Vila-Matas

A house forever

An Old Married Couple

You made me drink too much, or rather, your avowal that you liked to hear other people's stories prompted me to drink (as I once said to an elegant German of around seventy, with whom I went out every so often to a café in Lugano), and it's quite true that I'm a little tipsy now and a little keyed up, or to be more precise, I feel a bit as though I'm in a dream world and I'm of a mind to tell you that story I hinted to you about before when I told you that lately I've had a certain inclination to recount certain chapters of my life, chapters that I sometimes transform so as not to be repetitive and not bore myself, señor Giacometti, allow me to call you that, here everybody seems to be named Giacometti even though nobody wears a monocle like yours, don't tell me your real name, it wouldn't be of much use to me, I'm only interested in telling you what happened to me with a compatriot of yours, a story it might possibly give you pleasure to hear, señor Giacometti, allow me to call you that.

I wanted to get to know your country, or more specifically Bavaria, someone had told me that on the walls of many houses in that region shadows moved on the tapestries representing hunting scenes, and I had also been informed that strips of white bark trembled on the trunks of the birches when winter came. I loved snow and still do and that season of the year and the hunting scenes and the shadows and I wanted to see all that in Bavaria, so as soon as a chance came along for me to take a well-deserved vacation, I didn't think twice. During my first days in Munich I had a fine time all by myself; sauntering about and smoking and taking in a great many things, singing Tyrolese songs in the solitude of my hotel room. But one afternoon, as I was calmly strolling down the Kantstrasse, I saw a woman disguised as a snake watching me, winking her eye at me and smiling, and I, naturally, thought I had before me the prospect of a brief love-intrigue that would be a cinch. I approached unhurriedly, is something wrong? I asked, yes it is she said, and then she added, or rather mumbled, a few words I didn't understand, it's possible she said that life was a white tunic that looked like a blank page from a distance and a nightgown from close up, she didn't lack a sense of humour, she may have said that or something of the sort, whereupon she dropped a silk handkerchief on the Kantrasse and I, who couldn't get over my astonishment, took that to be confirmation that I had before me the prospect of a brief love-intrigue that would be a cinch, walked over closer to her and gallantly picked up the handkerchief, but looking at her, señor Giacometti, looking at her from so close up left me in a sort of trance, because the fact is that the mysterious face of that thirty-year-old snake had a pair of green eyes with an intense gaze that ensnared a person, so ensnaring, señor Giacometti, that I was left mute with terror, the love-intrigue still struck me as a cinch but no longer as brief as I had at first supposed.

After a week we got married even though I knew scarcely anything about her or about her life although I suspected, quite rightly, that she was a de luxe prostitute, which excited me, she said her name was Ida but on all her identity papers the name Helga appeared; she had told me the story of her fabulous past but quite obviously it was made up out of the whole cloth, and the fact is that Ida did not lack imagination when it came time to invent a new identity for herself, naturally I couldn't keep up with her, I too had invented everything about myself from the very first moment and had told her, for instance, that I was a doctor from the Piedmont and, although it was quite clear that I didn't know the first thing about medicine, I never took this back nor any of the other lies because she was plainly delighted with my fabrications, just as I was with hers, and the fact is that that tacit agreement interested both of us a great deal because it allowed us to flee from ourselves and afforded us that serenity that emanates from a union between two fictive beings, a fictitious serenity that hitherto we had never known, and the fact is that nothing, I thought, is as reassuring as a mask.

That was what I was thinking during the wedding ceremony in that church in Munich that no longer exists, which, believe me, señor Giacometti, no longer exists, just as doubtless there no longer exists that old rented Volvo in which, after the ceremony and in a drenching downpour, we began to glide like ghosts down the avenues of Munich first, then afterwards down the motorways leading to Italy. Of that day, like so many people who recall every last thing about their wedding day, I remember even the most trivial details, I can even close my eyes and see the Volvo moving along in the rain at dusk through the suburbs of Genoa, behind buses and trucks as mud spatters the sidewalks and the people walking along them take refuge in the doorways as we pass by, when that very peculiar-looking Volvo goes past.

I never saw a car like that one, it seemed to possess the ability to move along without making the slightest sound, as though the fact that it was transporting two passengers who appeared to have loomed up out of the fog of their respective invented lives and turned it into a special automobile, a phantom in all its manifestations save the visual one, for a person could easily imagine the car travelling swiftly down some dark country road, in the middle of the night and without lights, and slithering along in a terrible silence.

Around midnight and on the outskirts of Livorno, the car stopped in front of the Bristol, a hotel that didn't much look as though it were open to the public, and it stopped in a very strange way; normally when cars come to a stop the sound of the motor fades away and shortly thereafter someone gets out of them, but in this case nothing of the sort happened, the old Volvo simply came to a halt, as though there were nobody inside and there had been nobody during the entire trip, and it was then that there passed by our silent parked car, in the heavy downpour, the noisy, scandalous Volkswagen that I for my part was quite convinced had been following us for a long time now, perhaps from Munich.

I insist, Ida, that someone is following us. You're crazy, really crazy. I beg you, Ida, come back for a few seconds to accursed reality and tell me who can have an interest in following us. Perhaps reality itself, dear, didn't you say the other day that reality is always scandalous and mocks fiction without a let up? But, Ida, at the moment that isn't relevant.

We exchanged these words, señor Giacometti, and as we did so we saw the Volkswagen come back our way. To our left was the Mediterranean, the sea was very rough, the waves broke violently against the shore and the wind drove the rain and the sea water against the car. The Volkswagen passed by alongside us, it was obvious that it was searching for us, when it had gone by us it turned around, skidded on the asphalt and, in its attempt to keep from falling into the sea, wisely reduced its speed and placed itself directly behind ours, perfectly parked. But even so, Ida, who gave signs of being very distraught, refused to bow to the evidence that someone was following us, and that provoked an argument that went on until I could bear it no longer and lost patience and decided to resolve the whole thing in my own way: I got out of the Volvo ready to confront the driver of the car, but when, soaked to the skin, I reached the Volkswagen there was nobody inside, absolutely nobody, I already suspected that that too might be a phantom car when I saw that lights on the ground floor of the Bristol had gone on and I presumed that the pursuer had just entered the hotel.

Let's get out of here, I said to Ida. But, as though badly perturbed, she told me she sensed that that hotel had a magnetic power that attracted her more forcefully than life at my side. Listen, Ida, I said to her, I think you've talked enough nonsense, somebody is following us, perhaps to kill us even; luckily he's gone into the hotel thinking that we've already taken refuge in it, let's get out of here before it's too late. I can't, she said, I can't. And she sobbed, señor Giacometti, she sobbed and seemed lost in the night of rain and claps of thunder. Her lover or her pimp might be waiting for her in the hotel, and I didn't have much of an idea how to act, I felt immensely

confused, and became even more so when she said that a glove
for the right hand along with one for the left hand constituted a
whole, that is to say, a pair of gloves, whereas if we had two
gloves for the right hand we would have to throw them away,
and that the same thing was true of our relationship, which had
to be thrown overboard, since the two of us lived in the world of
fiction, with no contact with reality. Two bassi profundi, she
said, producing the same note, that's what you and I are; on the
other hand, there in that hotel is someone waiting for me who is
my ideal complement, which is the reality that has been
following me since Munich and who knows whether I'll return
to his arms because I am unable to live without his company;
without his necessary complement, I tried to rid myself of that
reality but did not succeed, I'm sorry, goodbye; a hook and eye
are a unity, but nothing can be done with two hooks, the same
thing happens with two fantasy-ridden beings like us, our union
isn't going anywhere, goodbye; it was all superb while it lasted.

For a moment I lost the roles and the masks, and my
composure as well, because I pushed my seat back and
pretended I was falling into a faint. I lied to you, I said, I too can
be a realist and a good complement for you, I'm not a doctor or
a Piedmontese or anything I pretended to be, I wanted to try
being someone else but I no longer have any thought of trying it
again, in reality I'm a ventriloquist, do you hear?, a ventriloquist, and I'm your husband as well and I order you to stay
with me. Forget me, Ida said, my fate is not yours. And I, señor
Giacometti, understood then and there that whatever I might
do would turn out to be useless, that I was going to lose her and
that when all was said and done she had never been mine; when
all was said and done she was the wife of another and formed
with that other an old married couple, whose tense relationship
went back to remote eras, as far-distant in time as the first night
in which reality and fiction coupled: a pair long married,
fighting it out in a nightmare with the same obstinate anguish as
the whore and the pimp.

But perhaps it's true, perhaps we're two bassi profundi
producing the same note, I said sarcastically and with my
feelings a bit hurt, perhaps it's true. I opened the door on her

side of the car, asked her to leave me and go inside the Bristol, the rain came into the car and lashed my face and I felt as though I had just awakened. I saw Ida walk away into the dark; I counted her footsteps in the mud as far as my eyes were able to make them out, and then, despite knowing that I was travelling with her luggage, I began to leave all that behind telling myself it had been a dream.

2

Well, let me tell you (Giacometti said, lighting a Havana in that café in Lugano), that just as it is surprising to discover the existence of a route that leads, in the space of a single day, from the closest union to the cruellest infidelity, it is no less surprising to discover how in many apparently happy marriages there is projected, invisibly and nearly constantly, the shadow of a third party that lives with them, silently and secretly, down through the years. For many years! That was my case, I was married to poor Bárbara for half a century, forming by the time we reached the end of our days a deeply affectionate old married couple, until, all of a sudden one night, in the middle of the year spent in Bandung, our union threatened to collapse on account of something she said, and as a result, from that moment on, nothing could go back to being as it had been before. It was different, I believe, from what happened to you in Livorno, because at least in your case in just a few hours you were aware of what was going on, whereas it took me fifty years and I was obliged to travel as far as Java in order to find out that for half a century I had lived trustfully and tranquilly, ignoring the presence of a shadow, the shadow of a dead man. Don't try to tell me that that's not reason enough to burst out weeping and ruin all the rugs of this old café with my tears.

But I'm not going to weep, it's most boring to do so, I will tell you of my drama, everything began when last year, as the date of our golden wedding anniversary approached, Bárbara and I decided to celebrate it a long way away from Franz and Greta, who are our two children and who, of course, are both unmarried and live together because they always wanted to marry each other, life has its oddities; in short, in their own way they too are like an old married couple; anyway, as I was saying, we decided to celebrate the occasion as far away as possible, on the island of Java, we said to each other, and we went there and in the beginning everything was very entertaining, since despite living together for so many years, we were not the kind of couple who bore each other to death or endlessly insult each other, we were not that type, we had established a tacit non-aggression pact and got along together very nicely, commenting gaily, every morning when we woke up, on the events that we had experienced together the day before and that reflected human stupidity, the imbecility of other people (never our own, which, because of that tacit accord, was safe from our viperous voices).

I am one of those who believe that people get married so as to be able to exchange comments between themselves on the world. And Java turned out to be a perfect place for us since we soon discovered that in the Javanese the conditions were ideal for us to laugh cruelly at them, every morning when we awakened, because the Javanese, among other things, had something in their faces that was not forthcoming, they still must have it, something that didn't make its way forward, but backward, it was as though their faces had been put in reverse, and that is the way it still must be, their faces looked as polished as the pebbles from a stream that have been smoothed by continual rubbing, their foreheads were rounded and seemed to be inviting us to circle about to the back of them, in fact the Javanese are people who sit down facing their houses, with their backs to the street, as though they had an eye behind them, in any case they have a presence in the back of them. And to top everything else off, we went one night to see their shadow theatre and discovered that Javanese actors, unlike almost all other actors in the world, wear costumes whose principal adornment is on the back.

The night on which we visited the shadow theatre and attended a Javanese version of the myth of the young lovers who commit suicide out of love for each other, we noted that the light onstage didn't move and that the characters remained almost constantly rooted to the base of a trunk of bamboo cut parallel to the stage. The characters moved their arms rather than their body, and they were flabby arms that floated about in the air with nothing aggressive about them, the way yours float, señor ventriloquist, allow me to call you that, the way yours float on that trunk that scarcely moves when you tell stories.

On our return to the hotel that night, unable to wait until the next morning, I began to laugh at the bamboo trunks, but Bárbara, instead of laughing with me, looked at me with eyes filled with infinite sadness and called me stupid and rebuked me bitterly for not having noticed the exquisiteness of the voices of those Javanese actors. Their voices, those of the actors who recite the story, she said, are sweet, melodious, low and reflective and as though filled with commiseration, courteous voices, sensitive, flowery, dreamy, almost absent voices, church voices, they remind me of Wim.

I smiled somewhat disconcertedly, and asked who Wim was. My first love, she answered, and my consternation grew. I asked her to tell me the story behind her reference to a first love. When I was still living with my parents in Rosenheim, Bárbara said, he fell in love with me the moment he saw me, and the same thing happened to me, it was love at first sight, but we were very young and our parents were opposed to our marrying, and the only thing left for us to do was to run away together; one night we left Rosenheim, and once we reached the outskirts of the city Wim proposed that we commit suicide so as to be able to live together for all eternity; but I wanted to be realistic, as you know I always have been, and I refused and decided to go back to Rosenheim, and in the days that followed Wim began to waste away with grief, and one night in a violent storm, he fled from the city and made his way to a monastery at the top of the mountain, twenty kilometres from Rosenheim, his grandfather had been the caretaker of that romantic spot and had shown him a dangerous place between the rocks where lightning bolts would often strike on stormy nights, and there Wim patiently waited in the rain hoping that a lightning bolt would split him in two, and he died some days later, a victim of pneumonia, and I'm of the opinion he died of love for me.

I felt humiliated, señor ventriloquist, by the summoning up

of the remembrance of that figure from the dead, and the terrible sensation came over me that I had not only lived for half a century with that Wim without my being aware of it, but that, in addition, at that very moment, I noted, I had him beside me, and that I too, like the Javanese, had an eye at my back and could feel and see perfectly the presence of the man who'd died of pneumonia.

I've invented the whole thing, Bárbara said to me then with a laugh, that is to say, I read it all in a book, how naïve you are, you'll never change. That was what she said to me, but her voice sounded veiled and sad, and I still had my doubts and was unable to sleep that night, whereas Bárbara immediately fell asleep, exhausted, leaving me lost in thought and feeling that my own identity was vanishing in an impalpable grey world inhabited by a dead man who was there, at our side, as dead as our marriage already was, back in Java, where actors wear their principal adornment on their back.

And now, señor ventriloquist, allow me to invite you to visit my hotel room, I would like you to believe my story and know that, every so often, the dead man appears at my back, yes señor, the dead man, and, in order that you may see that I really was in Java, allow me to present you with a few things typical of the island, I keep them in my hotel room, come with me, I want to offer you souvenirs of Java.

I have felt affection for you and trust in you, but don't get the idea that I don't realize that you and I also form an old married couple, because we've been a long time together here, you and I, in this old café in Lugano, exchanging stories, we are now an old married couple and I would like you to take something of Java with you: a parasol, for example, which has a secret spring that turns it into a very sharp, slender parasol, a sort of bayonet that, who knows, may be useful to you some day, and I would also like us to go to bed together and exchange comments on the world between ourselves, and in that way you could confirm, señor ventriloquist, how even in my hotel room my back freezes if I'm naked and behind me, like an old adornment, there appears the dead man.

(*Translated by Helen Lane.*)

Quim Monzó

'Oof,' he said.

They drank coffee and ate pieces of almond cake. *'Oof,'* he said, eventually (because he had his mouth full before, not just of cake, but of lethargy, and he wouldn't have been able to open it). She didn't even look at him (it was *so* hot and the window, as usual . . . shut . . .). 'The window, as usual . . . shut . . .,' she said. He didn't answer (he thought it was only logical that it should be hot in the height of summer). 'Open it if you want,' he said, because he felt he ought to say something. But she didn't get up from her chair and she made no comment. The weather seemed to be silently crushing them. She picked up the teapot and slowly poured herself a cup of coffee (it was a year now since they'd broken the coffee pot, and they'd decided not to buy another one: as they didn't like tea, they could use the teapot for coffee). A fly was buzzing round the cake. She lifted her hand to frighten it, but decided the fly wasn't enough of a nuisance as to warrant the effort, so she let it be. The hand hung dreamily in the air for a moment. Then she lowered it slowly and left it on the table. 'I think,' he said, sniffing gently at the air, 'that this heat attracts the flies.' Outside the window, the sun was strangling the syphilitic ivy that clung, more dead than alive, to the only clean patch of the dirty white wall. In no time at all the sunspot would get round to the window pane and would come into the room. 'Yes,' she agreed, turning her gaze on the cup and tapping it monotonously with the teaspoon (the ringing was constant and warm, minimal). 'Do you mind not making that noise?' he snapped. She let the teaspoon drop onto the table with a gentle, soft, orange-coloured sound. 'Before,' he went on talking, 'summer afternoons weren't so hot.' 'Everything's topsy-turvy,' they agreed. They sat in silence while the howl of the sun at its peak hung over everyone's head: those of the slow men in the street, of the children at the beach, blinded by the harshness. They shuffled the cards and cut the pack. She had a full house.

Before they realized, the sky was dark and the light black. They switched the light on and gathered up the cards. They turned the television on with the remote control. On the table there were still some sausage meats and pieces of cold toast, which they ate. Once all the programmes, anthems and flags were exhausted, the screen was flooded with rain and they fell asleep in the armchairs. Then, sometime around midnight, through the window came the pink she-doves and the black sugar-cane cockerels and the golden deer and the seagulls of lapis-lazuli and the ivory finches and the multi-coloured ivies and laughing heliotrope giraffes. They stayed until dawn, and when the sun came up, they left slowly; so that when he and she woke up (the sun was alrady stabbing the white wall in front of the window), the animals and plants were gone. They drank coffee and ate pieces of almond cake. '*Oof*,' he said eventually (because he had his mouth full before and he wouldn't have been able to open it).

(*Translated by Andrew Langdon-Davies.*)

Cristina Fernández Cubas

Omar, my love

I had planned it all, Omar. The colour of your robes, your smile, the cut of your hair. I bought a Kaftan to match your eyes. That was why, when we lost ourselves in the corridors of the tomb of Keops (ten pounds were enough to bribe the watchman), you saw yourself reflected in me, in my parted lips, in my look. I knew how to imitate all and every one of your gestures long before you moved a muscle. I understood your Arabic too, so clear, so concise, so free from unnecessary flourish. And, wearing that smile I had set on your lips, you welcomed my replies making the right and expected comments. I showed you that you were mine, the three nights we spent together in the gallery of the treasure, surrounded by masks, bracelets, papyrus, almost suffocated by the thin air in the tomb. You gasped, *ya* Omar, with occasional spasms that at times seemed to me strange and unreal. And you loved me and covered my body with ancient kisses and laughed. We laughed like mad, Oh *Hub*, offering Keops the best moments of our sacrilegious love, climbing down naked through the eye of the sphynx, sinking our exhausted bodies in that sea of sand. I remember, *ya* Omar, that the first rays of the sun shone on your curly hair when, dressed in Bedouin clothes (another ten pounds were enough), we decided to go into the desert. I covered my hair with a turban and pretended, in front of the dunes, to be a man. Though I didn't have to cross the river or show my frailty to make you aware of my deception. We kept laughing, drunk with love, sun and sand and finally lost ourselves, as we had foreseen, and surrendered to a sweet sleep.

We woke up, remember, days later surrounded by monks. St Macarios, *ya* Omar, a city lost in the desert, with streets, dwellings, walls. The friars prepared fortifying potions and got ready two pilgrim's cells. Next to each other, with narrow beds and books in Coptic writing. We learnt to intone songs of unfamiliar rites, till the fields, recognize the properties of herbs. They gave us two habits and I concealed my hair under a biretta. You didn't find it hard to excuse my ways. He is a stranger, you said, he's not used to our strong sun. And you still laughed, with that smile I desired, when you kissed me secretly in the corridors of the monastery and you caressed my knees under the table in the refectory, when you drank me in, always, every night, moments before I bound my breasts with linen and you returned silently to the solitude of your cell.

You grew a long beard, *ya habibi*, which emphasized the whiteness of my hairless skin and sometimes betrayed your looks and my joy. We could not stay much longer. The faces of the novices now flushed purple in my presence. They forbade me to work in the fields, in the orchards, in the gardens. And we had to take flight, *ya* Omar, wrapped again in our Bedouin clothes, mounted on a horse as black as your hair, drinking the waters of the Nile, feeding on prodigious herbs and roots. You became Omar again, the one with the smile, and I, for the rest of the world, turned myself into Ibrahim. But at night, in the intimacy of our desert tent, I would become Kalima again. You liked to call me that way and you were right. Because I, Kalima, had given you the word.

We covered mile after mile of desert. We reached remote oases and discovered forgotten temples. When we arrived in a city, I would unfasten my turban and you would plait my long hair, repeating my name—Kalima, Kalima, Kalima—until you remained exhausted. And then, as always, you would smile. But one day, oh *habibi*, a day I shall never be able to forget, your smile didn't fit the agreed plan. I couldn't make sense of it then. Your lips, Omar, opened too widely that day. Or perhaps not enough, my love. I only know that it was the beginning of our misfortunes. You begin to talk and talk, to play about with words that I didn't always manage to understand, you often smiled—too much or, perhaps, not enough—and your remarks suddenly seemed too frugal, or endless. What was happening, *ya habibi*? I wanted to retrace our steps, but you refused to ride the same horse or call me Ibrahim again. And you laughed. You laughed when you should have cried and cried when I expected a smile from you. I felt dazed, my love. That was why I didn't ask too many questions when I found myself locked in the tomb of Amenophis III, the most foul, the most impregnable in the whole Valley of the Kings, nor did I wish to know, once I was freed, who had bribed the watchman this time or why the keys of the heavy gate were now held between your fingers. I didn't show any curiosity either about the reason for your strange meetings. You made me scale the most inaccessible cliff, wait for you in a boat by an awesome waterfall, navigate a canoe without poles or sails. You wanted to free yourself from me, *ya* Omar, from the woman you owed so much.

I concealed fear and deception and, one night, leaving aside the ache in my heart, I ordered that you should vanish. But your only reply was to settle yourself more comfortably on your carpet and smile again at me. That smile in which I didn't recognize myself. A smile that was *yours*, *ya* Omar. And later, defying my fury, you started to doze, as was now your habit, unexpectedly.

So there was no other course left for me. I pretended to love you and admire you for what you now were. I laughed at your new ideas and tried to emulate your new gestures. I repressed within myself the repulsion your body suddenly provoked in me. I feigned, I feigned so well that your eyes were unable to conceal a glint of vanity, unfamiliar in you. You had fallen into my trap, *ya habibi*, and the rest was going to be as easy as separating the grain from that corncob with which you were now allaying your hunger. I used my wiles to convince you to take me to the city of Cairo (the place where you were born, do you still remember?), I talked to you about its crowded streets, its souks, its avenues. I promised you essence of musk, jasmine perfume, slippers embroidered with gold. And you succumbed, my love. We walked along Jal-el-Jalili arm in arm, like the lovers we had been. You hardly looked at me, *oh Hub*, absorbed as you were with your image reflected on the mirrors of Fishawuy, smiling at a youth with locks of gold, accepting the caresses of a fortune teller. And I, feeling ignored, recalled to myself some of the stories that you had insisted on repeating to me with a hateful voice, those last weeks. By the waterfall, on the cliff, in the drifting boat. Had you not told me—yourself, my love—how easy it is to die in Egypt? How the corpses are buried immediately? Of the terror of all Moslems towards putrefaction and decomposed matter?

We had arrived in Ramses Avenue, its chaotic traffic jams, its overpasses. I gathered up all my strength, overcame my pain and hurled you onto the pavement. You, poor vain creature, wouldn't stop smiling! You won't make it with me! you shouted, I am no longer yours! But your die was cast, my friend. His name was Omar, I said with a firm voice to whoever wished to listen to me. And you, on hearing your name, could do nothing but close your eyes for ever.

Then I returned to St Macarios and offered alms in your memory.

(*Translated by Miriam Frank.*)

Luis Mateo Díez

Albanito, my friend

1

Now that I am old and my fate has run its course, and the almshouse years prolong each crippled hour of abandoned corridors and courtyard in winter, I have been feeling the urge to tell old stories, as if memory were a sack that has to split its seams to free me from so much weight. This one today belongs to the life of a lad who answered to the name of Albanito Moreno.

He was part of that train of emigrants who leave the scorched hinterland, make their way to the coast, and then, unresolved whether to cross the pond, end up dossing out at the port.

With him I was linked by a long friendship, and the tragedy of his death—he was found scuttled with stab wounds at the end of the docks—is the main reason that I should speak of him now.

I met him at the Lugones tavern one November night in the year 1928.

Almost everyone in the port used to go there. It was a warm, spacious place with a bar made of chestnut, benches, long tables and the best wood stove in the neighbourhood.

I used to drop in there every night and dump myself like a sack of ballast by the corner of the stove, amending the day's labours with a bottle of red wine and some hot spuds.

Next to where the stovepipe came out, smoke stains oozing from the joins, the lad was huddled like a lost and hunted sparrow in search of its mother's warmth.

I observed his appearance, wizened and haggard under the cap and corduroy jacket. He looked the very image of Christ on the road to Calvary as he was hemmed in by the mob.

The idea struck me at once that he was an orphan trying to emigrate. He looked small and weak for his years, though he was already past the age of growing. His shoulders sagged like broken yardarms and he had the pointed, contrite face of an orphanage child. It was not hard to guess his background as a waif brought up on the Milk of Human Kindness at some charitable institution. Nor was it hard to predict, to judge by his appearance, that the world was for him a forbidden place and that limbo alone would quench his yearnings.

Spurred by the wish to throw the castaway a line in his distress, I drew my bench up to his side, filling his glass and saying,

'Prop yourself up here, matey, and accept a drink from a friend.'

And then, as I watched the shyness and suspicion in his woeful eyes which opened as if from a bleary dream,

'I've got it in my head that you must be emigrating to the Americas or some country or other on the far side.'

Albanito picked up the glass with a trembling hand and whispered timidly,

'Er, no sir; I've given up on that idea. I just came to the port to look for work and try to make ends meet.'

He drank with a slight wince and puckered his lips as if from the sharpness of the wine, which showed he was not used to it.

'Well, you have to belay cables and keep your sails to the wind, you know,' I said, 'because around here it doesn't pay to get downhearted.'

He managed to force a smile and it was clear that he valued the tonic.

'I'm a bit green, you see, because I only arrived two days ago and I don't know these parts.'

So we managed to tack together a conversation and he told me the sort of thing you find in those tales of woe that abound in misfortunes like cobs in a cornfield. I had not been wrong to surmise that his origins were amongst the chaff heaps of the bleak interior. He came from a village in the uplands of León, was an orphan and had only his corduroy clothes, the cap and a few solitary coppers to his name.

I am not fond of giving advice but I summoned up the effort to offer him some, not just as vain words but with the friendly intention stirred in me by that creature so full of fears and weakness. I pressed him with more wine to liven him up and he thanked me for each mouthful one by one while I briefed him on the possible jobs to be found in the port.

At this point the pity I felt went deep, for the cut of Albanito's jib did not presage much tolerance for unloading cargo, which was almost the only employment open to new arrivals.

It was the wine that finally provided a remedy for the gloom in which he was adrift.

In two hours we had sealed a quiet friendship. Later we left the thick air of the Lugones to walk off our muzziness, doing a turn of the estuary and then sitting for a while on the hull of an upturned barge.

Watching me roll a cigarette, Albanito was beginning to sound positively confident as he told me his plans.

'What I need to do,' he was saying, pronouncing the words carefully so as to convince himself, 'is to earn, to start with, just enough for the digs; and later, when I've found my feet a bit, look for a better opening. Because you understand me, Braulio, you know, I can do no more, and I don't want to trust to luck.'

And I tried again to stoke his spirits which had already started to falter,

'Don't you despair, Albanito, my friend, because however much things go astray here you'll never be short of a scrap of food, even if it has to be ships' biscuits.'

2

My memory is set on the wake of wretchedness that pursued Albanito through life. He was like one of those flatboats that crawl right up to the quay, splashing through the poor clogged waters and leaving a trial of miserable flotsam where they are destined to sink one day.

From the start his luck was black, beset by woe and twisted with adversity. He lasted a month and a half as a hand on the docks. With mediocre nourishment his health was failing him, while bouts of fainting confirmed the weak condition that had led me to dread seeing him in such a job.

He was summarily given the sack and told to look for another way of making a living. After that he tried to find work on board ship as a reefer but the first trial unleashed on him a mortal terror of the sea, provoking vomits and the sort of fear that sends rash novices to the dry dock.

Three weeks without work exhausted his savings and at that point I found him living on credit in a shared room at the San Telmo pension.

Then a job came up for him at the fish market. It was poorly paid but sufficed for him to get by. I told him he should swipe the odd fish but Albanito, as well as being daft, had the moral integrity of a saint and said it was a rule of his never to betray anyone who had placed their confidence in him.

While he was staying at the pension, where the bedbugs set your blood on fire and the fleas did St Vitus's Dance, he caught a rash which put the wind up his work mates at the fish market. He was laid off and they said, or so a trader I knew down there told me, that when he got better they would see if they could take him on again.

The rash subsided within a fortnight but he came down soon after with a venereal affliction. I was astonished by that bizarre turn of events and even helped him to expel the crabs that were scouring his privates and groin. I could not get my head round the absurd irony of that infestation, knowing as I did that Albanito had never known a woman and was in no condition even to think about them.

He ended up in the Provincial Hospital where they diagnosed his condition as suspiciously grave and isolated him in a room in the right wing of the building where there was a sign that read 'contagions'.

At about that time I signed up for six months bound for Gran Sol, and the memory of Albanito faded from my mind, allowing me a great rest after so many trials and tribulations.

I do not know what kind of star can have guided the relentless destiny of that wavering and weakly youngster, who was satisfied with the very minimum a man could need but who only found true rest that night on the dock.

I had been in port for three days after the six months at sea when I found him again in an even worse state. He had gone back to the job unloading cargo and was struggling on, convinced that it was his only hope of survival, but work and illness had sapped him to such a point that he was scarcely recognizable.

He gave the impression of having aged prematurely, as people do when they are overwhelmed by unforeseen tragedies; he looked more sickly and distressed than ever, with a weak thread of a voice that could only be heard by asking everyone else to be quiet.

I used to come across him almost every night at the Lugones, dozing in a corner, absent from the hubbub the seamen raise in the fellowship of those beached hours, when flowing wine is the only remedy for the bitterness of toil and salt-spray.

It was almost impossible to make him follow a conversation; I felt wounded and tainted by his misery as if the contagious, implacable leprosy of his ruin were infecting me too.

Albanito was by now refusing to touch wine and I was at my wits' end. A sense of hopeless doom filled me when I went to meet him, often with a strange weariness, something that would gnaw at my conscience afterwards.

I remember that period as a dark gale at sea, when a trusty crew mate is washed overboard by the waves and you are left, clinging to the rigging, unable to arrange any means of rescue.

3

The north wind must have been blowing or the hermitage bell was pealing fears of a northeaster, or perhaps I dreamt that of the lighthouse the Sotondrio lantern had gone crazy, that February night, the last one Albanito was alive.

As on so many others, we were at the Lugones. I had a few coppers to spare so I ordered a bottle and two plates of sprats. I had resolved to raise the boy's spirits, if only by getting him drunk, but I realized straight away that it would be impossible even to bring about the ephemeral cheer of a moment.

He was more withdrawn than ever and shuddered with intermittent fits of trembling. His eyes were fixed on the floor and his breathing cracked with a dry cough.

It was a Saturday and as usual the tavern was packed with revelling seamen and busty street women coming in to do business: plunging neck lines, painted with rouge, engulfed in cheap perfume, acting saucy and offering a bed for low water at their pensions on Nazareno street.

Seeing the futility of my intention I felt an urge to ditch that desperate friendship, abandon Albanito and put myself under the wing of one of those strumpets who would make me forget everything for a while. But as these thoughts were going through my mind the boy's voice reached my ears, the sick words uttered with painful effort.

'Forgive me, Braulio, if I don't accept your invitation, but my whole body hurts and the wisest thing would be for me to get to bed for as long as I can. Please don't take it as a snub, you know you're like a father to me.'

I told him not to worry about it, that we should go out for some fresh air and head for home later, and for a moment I had twisted my intentions and it was as if that lantern had shone into my head, illuminating what should be done in a case like this.

The darkness lodged the black thought in me and the cold, incessant sting of drizzle sharpened the tension in my body, fixing the crossed emotions that flowed amongst the drops, like sad, irremediable tears.

Scarcely a light showed from the lower parts of the port as the hermitage bell tolled through the silence of the fishermen's quarter.

Albanito walked at my side, dragging his feet over the flagstones and racked with shivering, not noticing that our steps were leading to the outer recesses of the dock, where the darkness was thicker.

I was kneading the handle of the knife in my pocket, softly and gently, just as I caress the sides of my wine glass before draining the last drop of the last glass of each day.

We had been walking through that gloom for a good stretch when I let him draw ahead a little. I took out the knife and opened it half way, muffling the sound of the hinge. Albanito turned to face me and I could barely make out his silhouette against the blackness, just the faintest glimmer in his eyes from some distant glow, with all the sadness of his poor life.

I threw myself on him and gave him six jabs above the stomach, to the hilt, one after another until the blade started to drip.

There was not the slightest groan.

The boy's hands clutched at his chest where the knife remained buried and seemed to press my hand, trying to push it further in.

Then I held him in my arms for a long time, caressing his forehead, bearing the choked gasps which gradually grew quieter until they disappeared, while on my face the raindrops mixed forever with two tears shed for the tenderness of a feeling that cannot be explained.

When I lowered him to the floor he was already dead. I cleaned the knife and put it back in my pocket.

Kneeling for a moment, I saw his open, staring eyes that wore the sadness of his absolute resignation and at that point my tears brimmed over, furious and abundant.

An infinite tremor nestled in my fingertips as I touched his eyelids and slowly closed them.

That night I returned to the Lugones tavern and there I sat, alone and dazed at the very table where Albanito's glass remained still full, knocking back the almost untouched bottle.

And even now, with this solitary obsession for digging up so many memories in my old age, that of Albanito rocks me like a gentle ripple that still refuses to accuse.

I am fully certain that he was grateful to me for those definitive thrusts, and that his was no loveless, callous death like others that feature in the gazettes, but rather it was born of the desperate tenderness of a friendship that I still keep in my heart.

(Translated by David M. Lambert.)

Valentí Puig

First days

The first days of work at the blacksmith's, he hadn't got his blue overall dirty yet and he envied the polished gleam of grease on the overalls of the other apprentices, who would whistle, sing and laugh until Master Lluc struck a ringing blow on the anvil. Biel still got the tools and names mixed up and the sparks from the oxyacetylene welder distracted him. The thought that he was going to learn the blacksmith's trade—recognizable in any town by the metallic din—and that soon he'd be able to buy a racing bicycle with gears, made up for the cruel pranks the others played on him and for always being the last at everything. He wished he could put on the welder's visor, beat out fancy pieces on the anvil, whistle as loud as the others or go and fix the lock at the Widow Timpano's.

Every time she came into the blacksmith's, the crash of metal would be cloaked in human silence.

'Master Lluc, I've got a broken lock. Could you send me someone?'

No one left off working, but the whole smithy throbbed expectantly.

'You go, Bernat,' Master Lluc would say, and he always warned, 'But not a word of this, here or outside.'

Biel would have liked to go and mend the Widow Timpano's mysterious lock. She had a tender look in her eyes, like an eddy in a spring stream, and a remote, weightless profile. The lucky apprentice would return in silence and with a look of triumph on his face.

In the evenings, his mother muttering to herself as she

dropped the clay plates onto the wooden kitchen table, Biel sat entranced before the great saucepan of steaming soup, intrigued by the mystery of the Widow Timpano's lock. In the mornings, the din at work took his mind off his bold decisions from the evening before. He had already made friends with Colau, another apprentice who also wanted to be a cyclist, and who fell smugly silent whenever Biel tried to start a conversation about the widow and her lock.

As if it had been planned in advance, the day that marked half a year of Biel's apprenticeship, Master Lluc sent him to mend the Widow Timpano's lock. She had come in the middle of the morning with a peasant's shawl thrown over her shoulders. Her eyes glazed, as though lost along the way, under the row of elms by the lane to Son Banya where she sought out Master Lluc, who was fixing a harrow. The hammers were ringing and the metal was taking shape, as when the first inhabitants made their arrowheads. Whenever the widow appeared, all the music of the metal went on without the din of talking, whistling and singing. This time, without looking up from his work, Master Lluc sent Biel.

The verse is yet to be written that describes the beating of a young man's heart who searches and doesn't know that he's found his first woman's body. All the way to the Widow Timpano's house it overwhelmed him: he was a shy lad of fifteen, inclined to be a bit distant and awkward. As he reached the end of the dusty path, pedalling mechanically, Casa Timpano struck him as an impenetrable home, a premonition of grief, a warning to turn back. Just remembering that he was there to fix a lock, and that as soon as he had finished he would be able to go, lessened the feeling of foreboding of the unknown house.

He found the door open and called out a Hail Mary. 'Come up,' called the widow down the stairs, and Biel heard the quick footsteps that made the beams over the entrance creak. At the end of the room, a stained-glass window opened onto the yard. As he went up the stairs, the ticking of a grandfather clock cut time into thick, even slices. 'Ma'am?' 'Come in. Come in.' He crossed a room with the walls crowded with portraits and holy pictures. He stopped in the doorway to the bedroom: the Widow Timpano was combing her hair before a rococo mirror as she waited. The four-poster bed dominated the room like a ship about to set sail.

'You're new... What's your name?'

'Biel. The lock, ma'am...'

'Not so fast, little Biel. You were quick getting here. I'm not ready yet. Look, come closer...'

Biel went closer and she held up a grey hair, very long and thin, showing it to him as if it were the proof of an argument he didn't yet know.

'How old are you?'

'Fifteen.'

'Where are you from?'

'My father was Felip from the inn and my mother's from Binimeca.'

'Do you like it at the blacksmith's?' she asked, but without waiting for an answer she rolled her blouse up to her breasts and pulled it off over her head, raising a curtain for Biel in a theatre full of giving, secrecy and trembling. She was barefoot and she stretched out naked on the bed, her hair loose again. With her right hand, she summoned Biel to her side.

'Take your clothes off.'

Biel undressed clumsily, while from the corner of his eye he stole a glance at the widow's milky white body, at the fullness and the standards of woman's flesh. As he lay down, he was all tension and readiness, and as the widow silently and surely initiated him, he felt for an instant the trembling of a distant tide, the steel of an invincible sword, the return to the perfect stillness. Then, his eyes closed, he heard the widow washing in a basin. When he opened his eyes he was almost surprised to find himself still in the same room.

Back at the blacksmith's Master Lluc said to him, 'Biel, not a word of this to anyone.' The eyes of the others, fixed on his back, accepted him reluctantly. All that was needed now was for a new apprentice to arrive.

Every night, Biel would carry on a frenzied monologue with

his body as he let the images of that morning with the Widow Timpano flow beneath his closed eyelids and he plotted other bold exchanges in his flesh. He became even less talkative, adding silence to his remoteness as the price of a secret. Every time the widow went back to have a lock fixed, Biel felt as if his heart were about to burst from his fingertips, and without turning round, he tightened his grip on the tool he had in his hands. The widow's visits were unpredictable, like a voluble moon, unheeding of the established cycles. Master Lluc, with instinctive justice, kept sending her apprentices. And at night Biel would exhaust himself alone in bed as he heard his mother grumbling over her rosary.

One night he dreamt that the widow was sitting up in the village square and she laughed and cried as he rode round and round the fountain on a new bike. Next day, Master Lluc sent him to Casa Timpano to fix a lock. The widow had turned up dressed from head to toe as though she had been to town. When he got to the house, he found her sitting and rocking herself in a canvas rocking chair. 'You're Biel, aren't you? Would you like to marry me?' She rocked faster and Biel said yes. 'Then you'll come upstairs when I call you,' she said, and she got up quickly. He heard her hurrying from room to room, pulling out drawers and opening the creaking doors of mirrored wardrobes. She was singing softly to herself. This time, eager as he was, Biel saw the large house and the bougainvillaea in the yard as they really were, rather than as plasma beating in time with his runaway heart.

In the distance he could hear the monotonous chanting of the children at the convent reciting their two times table and, almost more remote, the voice of the Widow Timpano as she sang to herself. She stopped moving around the bedrooms and called to him. She was lying on the bed waiting for him, all in white in her wedding dress, with a veil over her face and a bunch of white cloth flowers. Her eyes were closed, Snow White guarded by her widowhood and her feverishness. Biel lay down carefully beside her. They both breathed heavily, ardently, for a long moment. She took his hand. Everything was aflame, and the bridal dress, stiff with starch, smelled of closed drawers, crackling with memories, and it slid slowly up her legs to reveal the widow's body. To Biel, the scene was incomprehensible.

From that day on, the widow would go into the blacksmith's and say, 'Master Lluc, I've got a broken lock. Could you send me little Biel?'

Each time Biel went to put another lock right at Casa Timpano, mixed with the physical urgency there was a palpable transparency, an exaltation of their moments and the widow searching for something more, either the impossible permanence of pleasure or else the furtive joy of pain. Life didn't go on. Biel took his apprenticeship to heart and she recovered the clairvoyance of the wedding tie: to serve one another and the despair of death. It was also the flesh, and Biel was clever with his vigour and already knew all the clauses and lessons. Neither judged the other. Everything was frenzied haste. Backwards and forwards they followed the torrent of desire, neither of them aware of the other, without words. Just sighs, and gasps, and catching of breath. Biel learned the elemental scents, the secret lips, eyes of troubled water, stunned exhaustions, the torn silks of carnal fatigue.

One day the widow made him a present of her husband's wedding ring. She had got up from the bed in silence and rummaged in the drawer of the writing desk, from which she took an old gold wedding ring. It hung loose on Biel's fingers, like a dead weight with no possible relief. She clung to him, rubbing her face in the sweat on his chest. Then she started to scratch him with her nails. She clawed his chest, the chest of a man growing strong, determined to dazzle with his heart. She left five bloody scratch marks that followed the ellipse of his ribs. Then she threw him out.

A week later she was waiting for him again in her bridal dress. They came together roughly, like a swelling sea. Biel felt like a furnace fanned by all the winds, like a puddle of rain sucked down a storm drain. That day, when he was doing up his sandals to go, the widow started tugging at his hair until she pulled a handful right out. He thought it over rudimentarily as he poured water over his head in the sink at the smithy. Now he needed the strict ferula of the good blacksmith when he tames the unyielding bar and dips it in the sink to cool the red hot metal his work has already beaten.

Next time he went, he made her get up from the bed, and as she stood completely naked he took off his belt and beat her round the ankles with the buckle until they bled. She shuddered without protest. When Biel had finished, she said to him, 'There's no stopping you, is there?'

She was lying on the bed again, her ankles swollen and red. 'You're very clever. The others are so clumsy, so coarse.' She was looking up at the top of the bed as if waiting for manna. The morning was dry and penetrating and the pealing of the church bell could be heard clearly. As he fastened his sandals, Biel was fascinated for a moment by the pattern on the large carpet on the bedroom floor: it was a peacock with its tail puffed up forming different labyrinths of colour that had to be untangled before they reached the edge of the rug, and they did so by reproducing themselves and becoming smaller peacocks that spread their tails to create even smaller peacocks across the carpet to infinity.

The day they took the Widow Timpano away, the blacksmith's was just closing. The evening was ominous with rain and everything seemed to hang heavy in the air. In the blacksmith's backyard, their sleeves rolled up to their elbows, they were all washing their hands. One of the apprentices came out and said, 'Quick, they're taking the Widow Timpano away.' They went out into the street. A faded white ambulance was coming down the lane from Son Banya. They watched impatiently, reluctant to speak. A neighbour with a basket on her haunches said that the nuns had found her completely crazed, and another neighbour, who still held an embroidering frame in her hand, said no, they'd reported her because she took men home with her and sang indecent songs. The ambulance went past the blacksmith's towards Palma. All they could see inside was a white shape and the expressionless face of a male nurse beside the driver. They all bade a silent farewell and Master Lluc, before shutting the large door, watched them go.

On his way home, Biel, pedalling hard, decided to sell the wedding ring and buy himself that new bicycle.

(*Translated by Andrew Langdon-Davies.*)

Soledad Puértolas

The origins of desire

To my mother

My mother's relatives were in the habit of getting together every
summer at my grandmother's. She had an apartment which was
not very large, into which we, the two families, installed
ourselves. That is, in addition to the usual occupants: my
grandmother, her bachelor son, the cook and the maid. We
took over up to the last corner of her living space. I cannot
remember my grandmother ever getting angry, and yet she was
very formal. I can see her combing her hair in front of the
mirror, her hairpins on the dressing table, her grey tresses
across her shoulders, before arranging it into a complicated
chignon and fixing her black and white neckband in place.
Always in black, upright, impeccable. No jewellery, no paint on
her face. We would go out walking, held by her hand, and on
occasions she would buy us pastries, but she didn't like
anything fancy. She wasn't fanciful. She was content with her
black dresses, her neckband, her hair well brushed and combed.
She was not wealthy, she left us nothing. Yet she kept many
things in her cupboard and would sometimes show them to us.
Things of no value, mementos. She had a sister who was a
missionary and used to send her typical Chinese trinkets. There
was satin and ivory in the cupboard and, on top of everything,
there were many boxes and chests. In that divided and orderly
cupboard, the world was kept. China was the world.

Our grandmother spent part of every winter with us, so that
we were used to her, but it still surprises me that she should have

seemed so used to us. Neither of the two intruding families was very large but, in total, they brought six children into a house which for years had been inhabited only by adults.

That was our summer house and, like all houses, it had its dark areas that I never came to know altogether. There was the storage room, which was reached across the kitchen and where the suitcases and blankets were kept, and the odd warm clothes that didn't fit into the cupboards and a silver cutlery set that was never used. When the light was on in the storage room, it wasn't very scary. Something more than scariness as well as other vague things was aroused in the maid's room. She was in love with my uncle. I think I only went into that room twice in my life because, among other things, the maid always kept it locked—I suppose that was a sensible enough precaution considering our summer invasion. Of the two occasions that I went in there I have kept neither a bright nor pleasant memory. It was an austere room, very naked and very sad. It seemed unnecessary to keep it under lock and key. I think there was a suitcase under the bed, but I had no desire to open it.

The part of the house that was really dark, mysterious and profoundly appealing to us all was the other side of the door. The other side of the landing. There, next to us, lived the Arroyo family. My information about them was vague. They were always being talked about in my grandmother's house, even when we didn't speak. It was like a permanent whisper. The maid spent many hours spying through the peephole. The Arroyos always returned home late at night, drunk. Their life was a scandal. At night, a loud commotion would be heard from the street which would take some time to calm down and, finally, a clatter on the stairs and someone saying, 'the Arroyos are back', 'the Arroyos again'.

I never got to know them, though. Once when I was going along the street with my mother we passed one of them. She mentioned it afterwards and I turned my head, but only saw the back of a tall man dressed in black who was walking away. Another time we met my uncle near the house and were on our way with him to the gate when he stopped to talk with some friends. Again later, I found out that an Arroyo had been in front of me. The Arroyo family went unnoticed during the day. There was nothing that singled them out and I felt vaguely disappointed.

I don't know whether the only boy among my cousins envied them secretly, but among the girls there wasn't any doubt. We would all have given anything to get to know them and make them notice us. The maid as well, who was so devout and in love with my uncle. As far as my uncle was concerned, he was somewhat like them too and the whole family felt proud of him. He was an eternal student. And the central figure in the household. We all lived around him. He would often let us play on the beautiful parquet balcony of his room. He used to lock himself in there to study all night. The light used to filter out under his door. After supper we would all talk in lowered voices. He used to appear halfway through the morning in his silk dressing-gown and boxcalf slippers which he would later leave under the armchairs. He would install himself in front of the balcony and slowly consume a cigar and small cups of coffee. He seemed, at that moment, very satisfied with his life and, say what he might, he would win us over. Though he didn't stay in his room every night. He often went out, and his returns coincided with those of the Arroyos both in our imagination and probably in reality. And nobody criticized my uncle's outings. The next morning he used to appear later than usual. At times he didn't get up even to eat. But nobody spoke about him. All the criticism was reserved for the Arroyos.

In the end, however, everything melted into memory. One day, at noon, my grandmother's existence came to a quick and silent end. My uncle's death, also quick, was of a tragic nature. The maid withdrew into an enclosed convent in a sincere and dramatic gesture. My grandmother's apartment was closed up. The summers changed.

Only many years later did I ask my mother about the Arroyos. For the first time we spoke about them. The afternoon was drawing to a close and my room was almost in the dark while my mother, at the other end of the telephone, was telling me about the real life of the Arroyos.

That was how I came to know that, by the door next to ours, in the middle of the landing, their grandparents had lived. *They* occupied the apartment to the right. Behind the door which faced ours. They were five brothers and sisters. The two girls, of whom I had never heard, had died very young from painful illnesses. One of them in a convent. Their mother used to spend her afternoons in the grandparents' apartment, keeping them company and saying rosaries with the grandmother. Their father, a state engineer, seemed an extremely kind and good-natured person who aroused, among those who knew him, a kind of reverence. At home they all knew that the three brothers would go out in the late afternoon and return in the early hours of the morning, completely drunk. But no one told their parents, who surely knew it too. Nobody spoke about it. The night watchman used to help them up the stairs and their housekeeper, who had seen them come into the world, used to open the door carefully on hearing the commotion on the stairs. Between the two of them, they used to put them to bed. That is what their life had been like, day after day. Everybody was sure that the Arroyos would come to a bad end, and that is what happened. They had already died by now, sick and mad.

'Sick and mad'. Those were my mother's last vague words which spread stealthily in the semi-darkness of my room. Those tall men in dark clothes whom I had never managed to see, and their nightly sprees, personified the mystery of life for me. And how many times had I looked for them vainly across the door's spyhole, felt life vibrating inside me. But the landing was always empty for me. After so many years had gone by, I had to ask myself if the landing had not always been empty for them too. And I knew that what had drawn me from inside my grandmother's apartment towards them was, partly, that fear.

(*Translated by Miriam Frank.*)

Enrique Murillo

Happy birthday

Since the death of her mother when she had to live alone in the house with him, things had gone from bad to worse, but had never been as complicated as they had recently become. She could put up with her father's reversion to his usual heavy jokes—ignoring the mourning, and only a few months since the funeral—but that he walked around the house in underpants was too much to take. She could not tolerate this, yet at the same time didn't know how to stop him. As it was impossible to go and live elsewhere, she would have to suffer in silence, and resist.

The first time seemed like an accident. After all, it was completely dark, and no breeze had cooled that summer holiday's suffocating heat. Perhaps it wasn't strange that he too lay awake. But that he had opened the door, looking like that, just as she passed by on her way to the bathroom seemed too much of a coincidence.

'Fetch me a cool drink from the fridge, Remedios,' he asked, feigning surprise but without the slightest attempt to cover his hairy, retired docker's body. He was smiling too, as if appearing like that was perfectly normal, as if that kind of intimacy was quite all right between father and daughter.

After returning to her room to put something over her nightie, Remedios prepared a tray with water and ice cubes, without being able to banish from her imagination a body that had been so tough that even in old age it kept its metallic strength, with its rounded biceps, with the bulk of that enormous trunk mounted on proportionately skinny legs.

She passed over his move to start up a conversation, and placed his tray on his bedside table, and left, shutting his mouth with her severe 'good night'. But her firm tone of voice—trying to put things back in place—did not work because the same situation repeated itself at all hours of the day. Remedios was on holiday, and as usual had to spend it at home. Although he pretended to dismiss his daughter's financial help each month, he in fact continued to accept the half of a meagre salary that Remedios had started handing over ever since she started working in a box office. What was left over obviously couldn't cover her day dreams or plans for pleasure trips. Remedios knew perfectly well that her father's pension alone couldn't have given him the chance to drink a beer or bet a few pennies on his game every afternoon. She was just as sure that his beer and his game were the only things that prevented him from letting himself die, especially since he was widowed, because, quite certainly, it's what he would have done had he not had some hobby.

In each of his cheeky appearances in his underwear he made it seem as if it was natural, and at the same time, as if he expected something that Remedios preferred ignoring. What's more, he looked at her as if she was in the wrong. However, there was no room for surprise, because it was the same old thing as before; rather more exaggerated and out of place, but the same old thing. He had spent his life making what he alone called passes, at whatever women crossed his path. His wife's presence never held him back, but at the most, toned down crude flirtatious passes to simply amorous ones.

He had always found some women who accepted his passes and played the game, including some neighbours who more than once had had rows with their husbands for having entertained such witty but diabolic sentences, and such daring and disgusting glances. Vain, shameless women prepared to pay any price to be flattered by his advances.

Not even she was free of what he called his jokes. Especially since her adolescence, Remedios had to put up with his rushing up to her, saying he could eat her up with kisses, whether in the dining room, hall or on the street, and in front of everybody.

And not saying it. A couple of times he had knocked her to the ground, later saying, seeing her so offended while he helped her to her feet, 'Silly, more than silly, girl. Can't I tease you a little bit?' The worst was that her mother defended him, even laughed at his jokes, and to top it, ended up getting angry with her for refusing to accept his apologies. Then she would come out with that bit about being narrow-minded, that she'd never get married: 'And anyhow you know very well that he's a joker. Don't you know him?'

No, she had never got to know him, although she was sure that those assaults were far more than simple jokes, but she never imagined that things would get so out of hand so soon after burying his wife. Yes, she was a fool, but not for the reasons they decided but because she did not guess in time the way things were beginning to look. For having believed that his recent fits were fleeting, a strange but justifiable way of overcoming the pains that father had suffered.

Because he had really loved her mother in spite of everything. And not only loved. If it was true that he hardly considered the afflictions he made his wife pass through—however much he may have tried to hide what he did when she saw that her husband put his hand up the first tart that consented—it was also true that he even went too far with his wife. Although they were married, that was the impression given when, for example, he slipped his hand up her skirt when she came to table with the soup tureen. And how they laughed that day the soup was spilled over the tablecloth!

Remedios had never forgiven her mother for allowing him to get away with it, that she laughed at his most obscene jokes. But she knew that not even she could be forgiven because even if she had refused to applaud his effrontery, she had kept quiet, and keeping quiet is approval.

Now it was too late because nobody can change a fixed habit. To complain that he carried on with the same cheek in his old age was as lacking in respect as the vice that led to her complaints. There was no room for protesting nor moaning. However, it was urgent to stop him going any further because the situation was getting out of hand, and turning into something as unpredictable as it was sinister.

She felt unsure about herself, and even considered taking a knife to her bedroom to hide under her pillow. As soon as she was home from the swimming pool, or from a stroll, she was scared of seeing him appear like a ghost from out of the darkest corner wearing his clean, tight-fitting underpants, and smiling his usual dirty smile. What did he want? She did not have the strength to find out, and avoided reasonings that only heightened her fear.

One night she woke up with a jump. A strange noise came from a corner in her room. It was a soft crackling sound, like papers. She didn't know if it had woken her, or she was woken by a nightmare about shining yellow caterpillars with green, spiky bands and foul scratchy hairs. Only after carefully listening for a long time could she convince herself that the noise was part of her dream, and so dare to get up. She went to the window, rolled up the blinds and stood staring at the reddish mist that lay motionless and thick over the distant city centre. Little by little she managed to calm herself completely, and was about to get back into bed when the same crick-crick sounded again. She had not dreamt it. And she didn't want to believe it, but there was clearly somebody else in her room. Had he dared go so far! And what was he trying to do? She turned her head round slowly in case he was staring at her and, out of the corner of her eye, saw the only part of the wall that she could see from her strained position. She noted the frantic beating in her temples, the pain of nervously biting her tongue. The noise continued in intermittent bursts, but in the dark she could only see Rock Hudson's smile, and Gilda's magnificent shoulders on either side of her dressing table. Concentrating harder she believed that she had at last located the place where the noise came from on the other side of the cupboard where she had piled her magazines.

Her eyes had become accustomed to the half light. She took one step, then two, desperation having made her act, and cursing herself for having paid attention to her intuition, for not having anything to defend herself with, and let out a scream that came up from her belly when at last she saw the black creeping shape of a cockroach under the pile of magazines.

When she came to she was in her father's arms, and immediately began to punch him, pushing him away. The old man didn't appear to understand why she shouted and thrashed her arms about, repelling his concern. Until, staring into Remedios's eyes, he turned around, left his daughter in a chair, took one step and even though he was barefoot, squashed the cockroach under his heel. A lumpy brown paste burst out of the crushed insect's thorax and caused Remedios a last cry of disgust. But this time she did not resist her father's affectionate caresses. She cried awhile on his shoulder, let him stroke her hair, and slowly calmed herself down until she let him put her back to bed like when she was little.

During the following week the change in her father was dramatic. He took her to the fun fair, like old times, and simply walked with her, and talked. He became so garrulous that he even turned serious, recalling incidents from his youth that she knew by heart. But she found him so friendly and tender that she forgot the rancour that he had recently inspired.

However, it could not last. He returned to his games and beers, and she preferred to stay at home. Until the day when, after accepting a girlfriend's invitation, she went out and ended up thoroughly bored and fed up with people. To top it off, when she got home her father again turned up in that way of his. He had taken his siesta and had just got up, but had not had the decency to put on a shirt or trousers. He stretched in front of her like a gorilla, arching his sweaty chest and flexing his shiny arm muscles, and then went to the bathroom without even locking the door.

Remedios received his father's later entrance in her bedroom with a sulky pout. He had showered and shaved himself, and was friendly and good-looking so that despite him being in underpants she let herself be won over by his flattery. In such tender moments, and appearing to forget his nakedness, the old man seemed like a suitor trying to conquer a girl with his witty tongue, and he was so charming that he always lifted her out of her bad mood. That's how he was that evening, which continued after dinner up to ten or eleven. The trouble was that seeing that he had won her over he suddenly shifted to his dirty jokes and cheeky passes. Without realizing that she was not amused, drunk with his success, he got conceited and reached the limit, celebrating one of his jokes by slapping her thigh and leaving his hand there while he literally doubled up laughing, repeating the joke's last line.

When she got up from her bed, the old man froze with surprise, then lost his temper:

'Can I know what's going on now? You're as crazy as a loon, child.'

He had gone mad. He shouted all sorts of things at her, and there was a moment when Remedios thought he would hit her. But his fury quickly passed. He begged forgiveness, 'although I would like to know how I offended you, girl' and smiled again without checking if she too had made it up. He launched once more into his tiresome stories, told her more jokes, some of them so innocent and funny that even she laughed, and finally he left, kissing her on the cheek, calling her the prettiest, and finishing off the job in his usual way by his let's see if you find a boyfriend, that what she needed was to get married once and for all, that thirty something was the decisive age, because if she waited any longer she would turn into an old maid.

When he reached the door he turned round for a split second. He was smiling like a naughty, guilty devil:

'Who is the prettiest girl in the neighbourhood?'

And seeing that she answered with a grimace, added:

'You'll see tomorrow . . .'

Remedios didn't hear, or didn't want to hear, the rest of the sentence—something like 'the surprise you'll get.' It was hard trying to fall asleep. There was something strange in her father's tone of voice. 'You'll see tomorrow . . .' What did she have to see? Hadn't she been putting up with enough during that awful summer?

She rolled up the blinds to let the little light of that starless night in, and lay down on her bed concentrating hard on the noises that came from the other side of the dining room. She wanted to make sure her father had fallen asleep. But even when he was probably snoring she stayed awake, anxious. 'You'll see tomorrow . . .' Horrified.

If she finally fell asleep it was thanks to the bath. Or that is what she thought when her eyes closed not exactly calmly, but emptily, utterly empty. And clean, because she took a lot of trouble under the jet of warm water, she deliberately scrubbed herself until there were no more traces, until all evidence had gone. Clean and empty, invaded by a special, definitive drowsiness.

When her brother arrived the next morning with her birthday present he was puzzled that nobody answered the doorbell. He had his own key, and tired of standing on the landing, let himself in to wait more comfortably. His wife and daughter would soon arrive to prepare the meal because each year Remedios, poor Remedios, had to be the queen of the party, and nobody would let her lift a finger. He sat down in the dining room, and left the packet with its huge bow on the table. It was not the TV he knew she wanted, but he couldn't afford better. It was odd that when he suggested to his father that they go halves he had said no in a cutting way. After a while he went to the kitchen. He remembered the corner in the cupboard where the old man used to keep the whisky his son handed over secretly, to avoid severe Remedios. He first served himself a glass with ice, and after moving the jars with rice and flour noticed that there was less whisky left than usual. The explanation both of this circumstance and the father's refusal to share in the present that Remedios wanted, and dared not hope for, had an unmistakable, square and enormous shape. The old man had obviously bought the television set down in the harbour, where it had been smuggled in and sold for a song because the cardboard case for the 19-inch model had not been wrapped as a present. The rascal!

As the whisky did not turn up anywhere he went to the old man's bedroom, sure of finding it hidden there. But he did not have time to look, nor to open cupboards despite the fact that he had never needed it more than then. Sick, on the point of puking, he shut his eyes to stop seeing what he would go on seeing forever.

On the point of pushing open the door of his sister's room, he withdrew his hand, terrified, because a red stain had remained, damp, polished, on the varnish. He hadn't realized that he had touched that butchery.

Remedios seemed to be placidly sleeping, with a jar of barbiturates knocked over on the bedside table, and empty.

(Translated by Jason Wilson.)

Ignacio Martínez de Pisón

Buffalo

On the first day of last spring I could, at last, return to my office job. After a fierce struggle between life and death like the one I had just undergone, the picking up of old habits, however tedious they might seem, is always a kind of re-birth. I instinctively associated that re-birth with the figure of Elisa whom I had got to know precisely at that time. She had been dropped by her lover one or two weeks before—the only love of her life she claimed—and little by little was recovering from a depression whose self destructive urge she exaggerated while I, stupidly wounded in my pride, stubbornly played the matter down every time it came up.

The coincidence in our positions—both emerging from two different but equally sinister caverns—helped us comfort, if not understand each other. In the other's misery we found a tiny consolation from our own misfortune, and in every sign of its improvement a lively stimulant for our commitment to each other. That's how the other's company became indispensable, and how, united by shared miseries, we embarked on a brief marital relationship that would end the same way it began: silently, without our realizing it.

However, Elisa brought a sense of renewal to my life which soon spread to everything around me. The change she forced on my domestic set-up was radical: what had been the bedroom became the dining room; two empty rooms became the library and drawing room; pictures were finally hung on walls; piles of newspapers and magazines chucked out as rubbish, together with other useless household bits and pieces.

But her obstinate wish to change 'my place in life' was just a warning of her intention to change 'my life'. In a polite but relentless way she criticized my stubborn, bachelor's obsessions. She struggled to make me aware of the childishness of certain attitudes and inclinations that I had always thought were harmless, and even corrected some of those personal sayings whose absurdity I finally accepted like 'exquisite piece of cake' for 'pretty girls', or 'I don't give a damn' for 'I don't give a fig', among others.

Although I should acknowledge that I did become fond of her and wanted to be with her, I was, for the reasons given above, always sure that our relationship would not last long. What Elisa intended was to introduce me to her world without being willing to confess that her world had abandoned her at the same time as Oriol, her former lover.

Contrary to what happened when we first met when she referred to him almost obsessively, once we had begun the stage of living together she no longer spoke of him. If she alluded to events shared with previous friends, she spoke in forced and useless ellipses, concealing Oriol's presence in an ambiguous 'we', or simply suppressing all references to him completely. Instead of feeling grateful at the time for Elisa's tact—a show of her affection for me? a show of respect for me?—I felt on the contrary spited, like someone who impotently endures a humiliation. However, never once did I interrupt her. I let her go on talking about those old friends and that earlier world that she thought she held on to, embedded in the impossible geography of her nostalgia.

Our relationship took an unexpected turn around May when the staff at my office became overloaded by the amount of income declarations that they had to prepare, or check through. As my prolonged absence due to illness was still recent, and which my boss cynically referred to as my 'quiet winter vacation', I could find no excuse to refuse accepting all the extra hours alloted to me so that we could avoid hiring temporary employees. During a normal year I enjoyed working hours that were restricted to afternoons but over that period I had to resign myself to work without pre-established times, some nights even leaving the office later than two in the morning. We usually finished around midnight, which meant that I could get home about a quarter to one, or one. By that time Elisa, who taught at a village school 40 kilometres outside Barcelona, was fast asleep in bed because she had to get up at half past six to catch the 7.40 train. The incompatibility in our time-tables was absolute. Our everyday life together had shrunk to those four or five hours of sleep when we shared the same bed.

One morning when I woke up at about ten I found a note on the breakfast tray which read, in Elisa's small, round handwriting:

José: 'Did you catch the buffalo unaware?'

Elisa: 'What buffalo are you talking about?'

José: 'Those in the ash. Careful with your cigarette ash.'

I thought it was some game to puzzle me, and didn't give it too much attention. I ate early, went to the office, and returned home at two. I read a bit before going deciding to go to sleep. While I climbed into bed, Elisa made a movement that made me think she wasn't asleep.

'What did that note mean this morning?' I asked her.

'Concentrate on your work and you'll pass,' was her answer.

'What do I have to study?' I asked again, understanding.

'The fried-egg machine.'

Laughing to myself I got up, wrote that sleep-talking conversation down, and left the note on the breakfast tray.

In the morning there was another note next to mine:

José: 'One hundred, two hundred, a thousand . . . Against all odds.'

Elisa: 'The Pools?'

José: 'Voltaire, at last.'

Elisa: 'What's up with Voltaire?'

José: 'No, not Voltaire, ha ha ha. It's the king of clubs fighting Satan, ha ha ha.'

Something similar happened the next day. I'd jotted down the only sentence that I had managed to snatch from her sleep—'I don't know the path to the strawberries'—She too had caught the following absurd dialogue with my subconscious:

Elisa: 'What does my sleeping-beauty want to tell me?'

José, panting: 'They mustn't get in! The cloud has already fallen.'

Elisa: 'How did it fall? Tell me.'

José, without hearing me, 'Insects are still dying on the windscreen . . . that's how they get into our eyes when it's cold. Now! Haven't you seen how the clouds are racing? And they weren't the same trumpets we saw yesterday.'

These chats were noted down day after day. And through them—or their transcription—we were obviously trying to negate the irritating reality of our two bodies that scarcely shared brief intervals of absence. Because intervals of absence were, in the end, the few hours that we slept together, forced into a mutual ignorance. For several weeks, those notes were the only verbal contact we had on work days.

The opposite happened on Sundays. We seized the opportunity of not separating, and spent the afternoon laughing at our innate predisposition to talk in our sleep, and at the malice which at times we enjoyed using while the other was defenceless.

'By asking you questions I can arouse the stupidity you carry around inside,' Elisa would often pitilessly tell me.

Leafing through the small wad of notes that we kept in one of the desk drawers, I observed that some repetitive images occurred in her sleep: 'Don't throw sand in my eyes,' 'What has blocked out the seaside sun?' 'I lie down by your side to wait for the waves.' I was not motivated by any kind of suspicion when I asked her if she often dreamt of finding herself on a beach. To my surprise she lowered her eyes like someone caught out.

'I don't know,' she answered, 'I don't usually remember anything when I wake up.'

I pretended not to notice her odd reaction and with relish returned to reading those texts, those snippets from an intimate, remote world.

That week the breakfast tray continued to be our sole means of communication. I dreamt of transparent guitars, huge birds and members of my family I thought I'd forgotten. Elisa dreamt of her mother, the colour of wine and salt water in her mouth. On Sunday I made no comment about that. I still doubted my intuitions.

Monday night confirmed, however, my premonitions. While going to bed I asked:

'What's new?'

As if waiting for the chance to talk, she said:

'Let's go and swim, Oriol. The water is nice and warm, and the long hair of a star is floating.'

Sadly I thought that she continued to be obsessed with him. She hadn't managed to get over him. I jotted that sentence down on a piece of paper and kept it between the pages of a book.

In the morning only words from my dream accompanied my breakfast:

José: 'I was born with vertigo in my finger nails, like Plato.'

I did not leave anything written down for the next two days, knowing that when I woke up I would find a piece of paper with her handwriting and my words. I was moved by the devoted way Elisa insisted on maintaining such a weak link, as well as by her stubborn belief in a game I had stopped playing. My dreams about oil lamps and sharks seemed strangely sad now that she had chosen to keep hers secret.

With the transcription of my ravings about a supposed telegram from the fireman, her Friday morning note included the following question: 'What's happening? Have I stopped talking in my sleep?'

I placed a sheet of paper next to hers, with the text of all her latest dream declarations. I underlined Oriol's name the two times it appeared, as well as other references I thought were significant: 'The *beach* got drunk by my thighs', 'Choose, *Oriol*, the *sea* light and its smile', 'Let's *sink* now that the afternoon forgives us.' . . .

I came home before midnight and the house was empty. On the breakfast tray lay a short message whose content I guessed before reading it:

I'M SORRY JOSÉ.

I'VE TRIED TO LOVE YOU, BUT

I CAN'T FORGET HIM.

I let out a silent sigh.

(Translated by Jason Wilson.)

Javier García Sánchez

The fourth floor

It was the man's hand that first caught his attention. For a few seconds it hovered above the row of lift buttons that led to the ten floors and two top flats of the grey building where he had been working for over six years.

It looked as though the hand was about to press the button where the number four stood out. It was then he realized that, unlike all the others, this one was almost untouched. Most of the buttons had been tarnished by repeated contact with fingertips that were often damp and sticky, and had obviously been pressed many times. Although it was a relatively new building, which meant it was mostly occupied by businesses or offices, it was clear that a lot of people used the lift. Still the fourth floor button showed little sign of use.

He also suddenly called to mind all the people he had met in the lift during the years he had been using it at least six or eight times a day—people of all ages and appearance, whose destinations in the building were usually different and fleeting. Silent people with whom he had no communication beyond the habitual greetings, brief comments about the weather, the time of day, how bumpy the lift was, and of course mention of which floor they were headed for—people who avoided each other's gaze while peering round nervously like animals threatened by some greater danger. Not a single one of these transient, chance fellow travellers had ever said to him: 'Fourth floor please.' He dismissed the thought as mere coincidence.

Several weeks went by, and he soon forgot the incident, which had merely served to distract his attention for a few moments. One day however, just as he was about to leave, he had to wait for a colleague to finish work. He decided to wait for him downstairs, out in the street. It was pouring with rain, so he chose to shelter in the front doorway. As he stood there alone, a poignant silence seemed to take hold of everything. He walked almost mechanically over to the wall where the three rows of letter boxes were fixed. There was no indication from either the front or back fourth floor flats that they received any mail at all. Their locks looked as shiny and new as the lift button; the metal plate where the name of the firm or the owner of the flat or business should have figured was also untouched. He was slightly surprised to see there weren't even any publicity handouts in the boxes, which seemed very odd in an eminently commercial neighbourhood like this, where this kind of material was very common. That meant someone must be collecting it.

He was too embarrassed to share what he felt was his rather childish speculation with his colleague, but from that day on, his curiosity grew and grew. He even considered talking to one of the other residents, the owner of a flat on the mezzanine floor who, because he was one of those who had been in the building longest, carried out administrative duties that elsewhere would have been the job of a caretaker. After searching for some time for an opportunity, he managed to engineer a chance meeting with the man, a furtive sort whom he knew would not make things easy for him. Since he realized this might be his only chance in a long while, he questioned the man directly, with the excuse that he had been asked for information by someone interested in renting either of the fourth floor flats. All the man could tell him, in his grudging manner, was that despite the two doors on the fourth floor, there was in fact only one flat there. He said he didn't know anything more. However, just as he was about to give up, the fellow remembered another striking detail which apparently confirmed his initial belief that no one lived there. The man had once heard the cleaning woman say she had never seen anyone go in or out of the flat, or heard any noise that would mean movement inside.

All he could do was to try to contain his growing curiosity

about the fourth floor while at the same time glancing through the tiny lift window whenever he went past on the way up to his office or down to the street. The floor was usually completely dark, which gave it a both peaceful and gloomy air that was very much at odds with the comings and goings, the laughter, the knots of people chatting on the other floors of the building.

One day, around mid-morning, he was on his way back up to the office after having a coffee down at the bar on the corner. He walked in, his gaze straying vaguely over to the letter boxes. He felt out of sorts, and decided he'd have a good rest that evening. I won't go out or see a movie, he thought. The lift creaked and groaned as usual as the rubber seals that closed it airtight clanked together. When he pressed the tenth floor button, he realized he was perspiring. Perhaps he had a temperature. He decided that if he went on feeling this bad he would ask for time off to go and see his doctor before lunch.

As he passed the fourth floor something caught his eye. Not only did it seem there was more light than usual on the landing, but he thought he could hear the sound of voices. Without a moment's hesitation, he jabbed at the automatic stop button, something he had never done in all his years in the building. He was surprised at his own determination, and even more so at the haste with which, even though the lift had almost reached the sixth floor, he pressed the button for the fourth. The seconds spent in the descent filled him with an intense, inexplicable elation.

When he reached the fourth floor he opened the lift door as carefully as he could. He could still hear the confused sound of a throng of voices. A vertical shaft showed the door to the front flat was ajar. That was where the sounds were coming from. He could even make out some that definitely were a woman's voice. He thought of getting back into the lift, but the sight of the open door was too much for him.

He peered down the stairwell to make sure there were no inquisitive neighbours about, then strode across to the door. As he gently pushed it open, the voices became louder and more insistent. He stood on the threshold looking around him, bewildered by the sudden change of light, because in the large room where he found himself, which must have once been used as a reception room, he could make out shapes in pale white and neutral colours, their effect intensified by the high ceilings.

He took a few steps into the room to get a better view. Nothing, no sign of anyone. Yet the voices, closer all the time, were clearly happy about something. It must be a party of some kind, he thought. He was determined to reach the end of the corridor to see what was going on. If anyone asked, he could always say he had got out at the wrong floor.

Everything happened in a couple of seconds. The room was suddenly bathed in light. It was as if someone hidden just for that purpose had drawn back the heavy curtains that were now swaying to and fro, the starched tassels on the bottom folds clinking together. He heard a noise from the door at his back. He turned round to try to leave, but found the door had slammed shut. Yet there were no draughts of air. A premonition told him that it would be useless to try to force the door open. On the contrary: despite the sense of panic that was spreading up from the pit of his stomach, he stayed rooted to the spot.

One by one, figures began to appear at the end of the corridor. They were the oddest group imaginable. Old women, youngsters, infants, people who to judge from their dress and even their gestures were from very different levels of society . It was only when this happy, animated crowd had completely engulfed him that he noticed just how pale they were, how the adults' faces had a bluish tinge. They were laughing in unison, as though from somewhere deep inside them. Then they began to reach out their hands towards him in an irresistible desire to touch his clothes, his face. It took him only an instant to realize it was his own heart that was beating so wildly. The hands that touched him were as cold as icicles. And there was more than revulsion when despite his violent struggles he could feel them kissing, kissing, kissing him.

(*Translated by Nick Caistor.*)

Paloma Díaz-Mas

The resurrection of the young squire

To Adrian, the least I could do.

O nce the Lamb had broken the seven seals, and when the four horses (the reddish sorrel of war, the shadowy black of hunger, the diseased and dappled nag of the plague, the fierce emaciated colt of death) had struck out in all directions—opening up furrows of fire and tears—upon the face of the earth, and when the sun had veiled itself with veils of pestilential fog and had stained with blood the livid craters of the moon, and when the stars had fallen incandescent like dandelion seeds on fire—a magic rain which lasted some eternal seconds—the graves began to open.

Immovable slabs rose up as though made of feathers, to fall with a resounding crash on the dusty flagstones of deserted cathedrals. From the putrid damp of tombs, from the cavernous depths of recesses, glorious bodies began to emerge, wrapped in their rags of flesh and of cloth rotted through years, through centuries, through millennia of mould and worm. A smell like rotten flowers, like stagnant, greenish water, invaded the world: it was the perfume of the dead who were emerging from the graves, of disarticulated skeletons who were laboriously putting themselves together again in order to stand up, of flesh turned to dust becoming rose and lily coloured once more, of broken limbs regaining the gentle warmth of life, of hair that had crumbled into ashes turning back into plaits or waving in fresh curls once more. From the oldest tombs there arose, from between the crevices in rusty leaden urns, columns like mist which was soon revealed to be the priceless dust of the deadest of the dead: atoms of ashes which spun around in imperceptible whirlwinds, and then took form as a bishop or a maiden. Crumpled silks, brittle taffetas, moth-eaten wool, tarnished damasks, discoloured ciclatouns, cambrics mouldered with damp, unravelled lace trimmings, blackened frogging, rusted buttons of nacre and seed pearl—all recovered their former splendour; and there the gold began to shine, yonder the mother-of-pearl to glow, or the satin to gleam. Then was born again the ancient scarlet of cloaks and the carmine of lips, the red of cheeks next to the purple of cardinals, fair hair and bright yellow tunics, violet robes and indigo doublets, sea-green gazes and white ruffs. A pulse of life animated the cheeks of the young, and haloes—no one could say whether of earthly dignity, of lasting fame or of eternal glory—encircled the heads of the old. And from more than one tomb the dead came forth with roses in their hands: roses so fresh and full-blown that it was impossible to tell they had been buried with them for more than a thousand years.

Then the angel trumpeters proceeded to play their silver trumpets, and the drummers to roll timbals and kettle-drums, and the standard-bearers to wave croziers and banners, until silence fell as they gathered together; recording angels proceeded to count the throngs of saints who crowded together by the forests of crosses in the cemeteries, who swarmed in the cloisters of monasteries and atriums of churches, treading on the slabs beneath which they had lain only moments before, who waited, lying on the green grass of battle-fields or floated, drifting, on waves by shipwrecked shores.

Now they were all dressed in white, with palms in their hands and ready to shout aloud 'Hail to our God, who is seated upon the throne, and hail to the Lamb,' and room had been made for the old men, with goblets in their hands, around the banquet table, and the musical instruments were about to be played, when they realized the young Squire was missing.

No one could account for his absence, for they all knew that for centuries the young Squire had been patiently awaiting the Resurrection in his tomb of Italian marble barely visible through the black inlay of the renaissance grille of the most beautiful chapel in the cathedral of his native town. They had seen him century after century clothed in a coat of mail meticulously carved in marble, a cape of white alabaster, its pink veins just visible, around him—on his breast the red cross of Santiago standing out like an open wound, his brocatelle hat on his head—always ready to stand up and leave for eternal glory (earthly he had already gained as a figure in stone) the moment he should be called.

He was waiting so serenely and was so sure of his resurrection that he had not even bothered to take up the attitude of one in prayer, or to lie down face upward with eyes piously closed, as the old knights had done, overwhelmed by the burden of their sins or knowing that the wait might be long and it was better to face it in a posture of serene repose. Instead, the young Squire had taken the precaution of bringing with him to the tomb a book of carrara marble, so as to overcome the boredom of the long wait with the pleasure of a centuries-long read.

That is how the four angels found him when they went to look for him: reclining lazily on his own tomb, his relaxed body was resting on his right arm and in his marmoreal hands he held a half-open book of stone. He was so absorbed in the book that it was very difficult to rouse him from his reverie and persuade him to close the book, to stand up, to take in his hands the palm of glory and to start singing praises to the Lord, because the day of the Resurrection of the Flesh had come.

(*Translated by Dinny Thorold.*)

Pedro García Montalvo

Angela, the Countess of Yeste

The servant showed them into a sitting room on the first floor. There he repeated to the two visitors what he had already told them at length on their arrival: the master of the house was not at home and nor was the lady, but they would surely not be gone long. Would they care to await their return? In which case they could do so in this small sitting room, the orientation of which ensured that at midday it retained all the coolness of the morning and it would also afford them an excellent view of the garden. Should they wish to admire it, they had only to walk over to the French windows and could even start to make their choice of flowers. If the master and lady did not arrive soon, Juliana, the maid, could always take them down to view the plants at close quarters and, of course, they need not worry about the sun as the girl would get out the parasol and they could make a tour of the garden in perfect comfort, concluding it in the glasshouse. But perhaps Sir and Her Ladyship preferred to return to their vehicle and come back at lunchtime . . .

Consulting Pierre with a glance, the Countess replied that they would gladly wait for the master and lady of the house to return. She was much amused by that servant, so nervous in the absence of his employers, but above all over the presence of a beautiful aristocrat under his roof and in his hands. The fellow excused himself with reverential gestures, endeavouring not to turn his back on them even for a moment until he had left the room, brushing past the heavy velvet curtains that flanked the doorway. But he reappeared a moment later wearing the crestfallen expression of a man who has committed an unpardonable offence.

'Would you,' he stammered, 'care for any light refreshment, a cold drink, perhaps?'

Angela declined with a shake of the head and her charming smile, while Pedro Sanjinés raised his fingers a fraction and said nothing. Unable to interpret this as indicative of a yes or a no, his gesture dismayed the servant still more. He eventually vanished, resolving not to reemerge until the owners of the house had returned.

Pierre had known them for years. The Mambrú Gardens were already famous in those days, just after the proclamation of the Republic, and owed their name to the original proprietor of the place, a Frenchman, who had laid the foundations of the present gardens. The name of Mambrú had stuck although it did not do justice to Don Fernando, the old owner's successor and the real architect of that almost impenetrable landscape. The Countess of Yeste had wanted to visit it for some time and wished to make one of her relatives from Murcia a gift of a rather special bunch of flowers. Pedro, or Pierre, Sanjinés had accompanied her faithfully as was his pleasure or, as Angela would say, his 'duty'.

They both left the comfortable armchairs almost immediately to go over to the French windows which gave onto a small balcony, still bathed in pleasant shadow. Angela found the handmade lace curtains enchanting but when Pierre drew them aside to reveal the image of the Gardens under the late morning sun, all other thoughts left her. Overcoming the violent contrast between the cool, dark drawing room and the omnipotent realm of light outside, the eyes slowly adjusted to the richness and began to make out infinite hues of colour amidst that green and splendid scene.

The Countess looked at Pierre with a smile which, with a slight softening of the proud lips, expressed her gratitude and friendship. The smile then broadened without apparent reason while her slender hand swung open one of the double panes right out to the handrail to discover the full panorama beyond.

Pierre produced a silver case and offered her a cigarette.

'Don't you think,' said the Countess, 'we should always have a spectacle of this beauty and plenitude before our eyes, to bind us forcefully to the present?'

'Perhaps. But such sights are often also conducive to memory and retrospection.'

'Memory? Who wants to remember?'

Pierre smiled. The eyes of the Countess returned the smile and then shifted back to admire the garden. Her companion felt a recondite pleasure stir in him as he watched her make this movement but he was unable to put his finger on its precise nature. He therefore chose to savour the view as she was doing and soon forgot that fleeting but intense sensation. From the French windows they could indeed see, as they had been promised, the whole landscape of jumbled trees and nurseries, from the poplars and cypresses growing alongside the north wing of the house, the high Majorcan windows which could only just be discerned through the foliage, to the dark and impenetrable mulberry trees which defined the portion opposite. Profuse flowerbeds luxuriated in the foreground, encircled by a rose garden which seemed ablaze under the dazzling sun and which contrasted with and accentuated that impression of the damp shadiness that characterized the Gardens in spite of the brilliance of all their flowers. Shining at the edge of this tempting half light was one of the jewels that maintained the price of the house, the lilies: purple martagon, purest white arum and lily of the valley. At their centre the Mambrú Gardens boasted their famous carnations, of a white and ochre reminiscent of Zurbarán. But it was not such detail that stood out most powerfully in the image thus contemplated, but rather the sensation of balance discernible within that dense and mottled umbrage of vegetation. The precision and regularity with which the sun crossed the heavens above the flowers seemed reflected in the harmonious lines and rhythms of that lower realm which had been wrought by man from the luminous shadows of the dark, intertwined trees, just as its golden gleam seemed mimicked by the calm water in the sunken culverts.

'Another wonderful thing about the Gardens is that they are not enclosed,' said the Countess after a long pause.

'But they are enclosed, and by the most ruthless of barriers,' replied Pierre, pointing toward the elegant line of mulberry trees from within which reflections emanated darkly.

'A watercourse?' asked the Countess.

Pierre nodded. Before going on he extended his hand towards a silver ashtray, depositing the ash in its shadow.

'Precisely, a watercourse it is.'

'And has no one ever tried to cross it to steal flowers?'

'Almost certainly, but years ago a child drowned in it and the current acquired a sinister notoriety. If anyone has tried again since, it would have been through ignorance of that sad death.'

Angela became pensive.

In the garden a subtle shift of the sun's rays had reddened the gorgeous backdrop of casuarina, their myriad leaves highlighted in black. The fragile threads of water which ran amongst the flowers glittered in unison like gold. A soft breeze stroked the dense, morning-borne fragrance towards the window.

'I remember,' said the Countess, 'when I was a girl my nanny and the servants—who were nearly all from the farms—used to talk in mysterious tones about people who drowned in watercourses. Every year they claimed at least one victim, usually it was several, and they were often children. The day I first saw one I regarded it in awed terror as if I myself were bound to die in its gush. And then there was that impetuous red colour to it, its dark opacity, its murkiness. It was like watching a wild beast in a flimsy cage with the bars about to burst apart at any moment. I remember that sensation of giddiness when my brother stood on the edge, and the nanny shouting. I'll never forget that feeling.'

'You were right earlier, Angela,' said Pierre. 'Perhaps memory is in essence bitter and turbulent like the water in those channels, and we try to tame it in our minds. But you see, it emerges in spite of ourselves, and I was saying, even in this place which should not remind us of anything.'

The Countess smiled and lit another cigarette. As always, her face suggested the idea of plenitude; the big, dark eyes, framed by those light, beautiful lines.

'I smoke too much, I know, but I enjoy that excess. Perhaps

that is why I also enjoy the exuberance of this garden.'

'Everything in excess?'

'Are you making fun of me, Pierre? Still, I don't mind answering your question; no, not everything in excess, but some things, certainly. Because such things would not exist without that excess. Don't you agree?'

Her companion remained in thoughtful silence. He then smiled at her wickedly as if inviting her to guess his reply. Finally he said,

'The Countess of Yeste, for example, would not exist.'

'No, but neither would you, my dear Pierre.'

This time they both smiled. The best proof of the fondness and friendship the Countess felt for Pierre was, as the envious rightly pointed out, that only with him did her dark eyes drop that disarming look of irony, shedding the remoteness bequeathed by not only a select lineage but also her own intense past, lived to the precious limit. Only before him did the Countess of Yeste reveal herself with her doubts and weaknesses, and not the proud, disdainful, self-assured woman she otherwise appeared to be.

Angela restored her gaze to the profusion outside and Pierre admired her solemn, serene features.

'It's like a little paradise,' she said.

And then Pierre knew what the feeling that had taken hold of him minutes before had been. He had seen the inaccessible Countess of Yeste looking at the wonder of the Gardens. He had seen the beauty contemplating beauty, and in that mysterious symmetry lay the hidden charm. Of course, what was beautiful in both beauties was distinct in each, and referred to different aspects of nature. The Countess possessed an elegance and refinement born of pleasure, the denial of suffering, passionate desire, the nights up till dawn and the filter of alcohol. The cast of her mouth and eyes could never be so deep and irremediable without all the dawn hours of her past and without the ecstasy. The wisdom of her aristocratic clan combined with the wisdom of feverish nights, all in the grain of her eyes, so very full of life. Goethe once said that Nature loves luxury, and the Countess was, in human form, that very aspect of Nature. But luxury of the emotions is dangerous and marks the eyes with its luminous stamp. Thus was the beauty of Angela of Yeste.

The Countess pinned back the brooch of fine emeralds which had shifted slightly on the lapel of her black jacket. Then, with a small movement of the hand, she tapped the ash from her cigarette into the silver shadow and once more turned to rest her eyes on the garden and her thoughts, perhaps, on Pierre. And he, in silence, contemplated beauty watching beauty, recovering that sensation through which he had caught a peculiar glimpse of the infinite and beautiful depth of the world.

(Translated by David M. Lambert.)

Antonio Muñoz Molina

The ghost's bedroom

Lorencito Quesada, that dynamic young man who so assiduously waves our town's flag in the provincial paper, will recall the night when, most unusually, our little group at the Café Royal stayed beyond midnight. This could not be blamed on drink, as none of us was given to such sterile bohemianism. It was because someone—perhaps Lorencito himself, a friend (as he himself says) of investigating supernatural phenomena—started to tell ghost stories. Immediately, we all remembered one; and when Plácido Salcedo, who teaches Physics in the local grammar school, tried to clip Imagination's wings and to restore the authority of Science, it was already too late: young Quesada was giving us an exhaustive lecture about I don't know what magnetic properties of the Egyptian pyramids and about the well-documented visits of extra-terrestial spacecraft to our planet. For instance, he said that the chariot of fire, which carried off Elijah, was no such thing: it was a flying saucer, as was the star of Bethlehem ... At that point, my cousin Simón, who is very sensitive when it comes to matters of dogma, asked him not to talk about things he knew nothing of, and said that neither he, Quesada, nor anyone who wasn't authorized to do so, should interpret the Scriptures just as he pleased. Salcedo, trying to smooth things over, made matters worse. While he enlisted Lorencito's support in that, as a scientist, he should be accorded absolute belief, he also wanted to mollify my cousin; but he talked about free inquiry, which was like invoking the devil. My cousin got angry and called him a Lutheran; Salcedo countered with Torquemada; and Lorencito, who was very voluble that night, asked us defiantly if we believed that the Redemption affected the inhabitants of other planets. I restrained my cousin and Salcedo, and forced them to sit down, but it was Don Palmiro Sejayán, to whose white hairs we all bowed, who put an end to the argument. 'Gentlemen,' he said, 'let's be serious!' Immediately we calmed down. Jacob Bustamante, the poet, recently honoured by the Provincial Council, took advantage of the silence to cast a poisoned dart at my cousin and me.

'There are some,' he said, 'who insist on ignoring Vatican Two.'

My cousin exploded like a shot: 'I've got the complete conciliar proceedings at home, and I can assure you that flying saucers are not mentioned anywhere.'

'Don't carry on like that with me, my dear Simón,' Lorencito Quesada said disconsolately, 'you and I have never divagated in questions of faith.'

Everybody knows that young Quesada is a good soul, with a heart of gold; self-taught, the permanent vice-secretary of Evening Worship, an employee of twelve years' standing at the Metric System Department Store. How could anybody reproach him for saying divagated instead of diverged or parental instead of prenatal? No, the real rebel in our *petit comité* was Jacob Bustamante. He sported a thick beard and flowing hair which covered his ears; and he was an ardent devotee of free verse and Mass with guitar accompaniment. Success had made him vain. After his prize in the Provincial Council's competition, it was persistently rumoured that his name was among the finalists in the competition organized annually by the Admiralty . . .

'Gentlemen!' Once again, Don Palmiro Sejayán had to restore order. 'If you promise not to start arguing again, I'll tell you a ghost story.'

'Some folk legend from your country?' asked Salcedo, always an advocate of scepticism and cold reason.

'Nothing to do with legends, my dear Professor. What I want to recount actually happened to me. Well, then . . .'

'Wait a minute, Don Palmiro,' Quesada said, rising, 'if you'll let me, I'll record your story on my tape-recorder.'

With his usual generosity, Don Palmiro agreed. Lorencito Quesada had already recorded several interviews in which Don Palmiro had told him about his long, hazardous life, from the day on which, still a child, he had left Armenia, rolled up in a carpet. Quesada was always assuring us that the interviews were going to be published in *The Nautical Times*, a daily for which he was a correspondent in our town. But time passed without Don Palmiro's adventures being perpetuated in print. 'Patience,' Quesada would plead, 'the editorial department tell me they're overloaded with articles at present.' Salcedo sarcastically suggested that the reason for the delay was the possibility of diplomatic conflict in the Ottoman Empire, and Bustamante, in an undertone, said that Lorencito Quesada was a nobody at *The Nautical Times*. Only Don Palmiro acted as if he were unaware of the pointlessness of so many interviews and he went on submitting to them with an affability that vividly exemplified his ancestral bonhomie, in deference to Lorencito's journalistic vocation.

Who does not remember Don Palmiro? Who has forgotten his bearing, gallantly defying old age; his rattan walking sticks; his suits of strict mourning; the simplicity of his behaviour towards his inferiors, which we all were, because Don Palmiro had the most substantial fortune in our town, if not in the entire province? I can see him now, in his corner of our little group, as strong as an oak, his hands joined on top of his stick, with his aquiline nose and his snow-white moustache, emblems of the Armenian race, unjustly condemned—'unlike others', said my cousin Simon—to an everlasting diaspora. When Don Palmiro was twelve or thirteen, some relatives saved him from the Turks' cruel sword, stowing him away on a steamer, which bore him to Valparaiso. He had no sooner reached land after a year's voyage, when there was an earthquake of such magnitude on the Richter scale that Don Palmiro thought the end of the world had come. He experienced helplessness and hunger; he endured floods; he survived an avalanche in the passes of the Andes; he was shipwrecked in the Caribbean; he was twice on the point of being shot—a danger by no means unusual in those turbulent South American republics. Finally, he carved out a fortune for himself selling sewing machines in Peru's jungles and mountain ranges, and, subsequently, manufacturing them in the highly-regarded assembly-line factory he established in Lima—the pearl of the Pacific, as he used to say. At the age of seventy, he advantageously wound up his overseas business and, as he was unable to return to his captive homeland, he chose to retire to his wife's (he was married to a Spanish woman). And so he came to Spain and to our city, her birthplace, and here he was made a widower. To cure his melancholy and to distract his vigorous old age, he opened the Monte Ararat Electrobazaar, which, standing on the best corner of the Plaza del General Orduña, still today reminds one of Don Palmiro. Respected by all—all and Sunday young Quesada used to say—Don Palmiro punctually attended our little gathering at the Royal, establishing himself as the patron of every coffee, bun and yoghurt there consumed, a habit that particularly pleased the soured Bustamante, not because he was poor, but because he was miserly: he didn't invite us to a round of drinks even when they gave him that much discussed Provincial Council prize!

But I was telling how Lorencito Quesada had got up to fetch his tape-recorder, a miracle of Japanese technology, small enough to fit into his overcoat pocket where he always kept it in case he was given the chance of 'capturing news, the live document'. With reverence and pride, he put it on the table, facing Don Palmiro, and to test the tape, because he was very precise in everything he did, he said, in an announcer's voice: 'Testing, testing', and only when he was completely sure about the sound's perfect clarity, did he invite Don Palmiro to tell us his ghost story.

'But it's after half past twelve, my friends,' Don Palmiro said, consulting his opulent watch chain. 'You must all be dying to go to sleep.'

'Give us an abridged version,' Quesada encouraged him, '*a grosso modo*, without going into details . . .'

'A promise is a debt,' not even Salcedo could disguise his impatience behind his professional gravity. 'You're not going to leave us with our mouths watering, are you?'

'If you stay silent now, Don Palmiro,' my cousin Simón said, 'you're going to upset us.'

Don Palmiro, manoeuvred by our curiosity into having *his back to the wall*—as poor Lorencito might also have said—ordered yoghurt for all (Bustamante quickly requested that a bun for each be added); he took a sip of yoghurt, wiped his lips with an immaculate handkerchief, placed both his hands on the carved handle of his walking stick and began to speak in that calm, deep voice, which we all drank in. We did not notice the passage of time as, clustered around him, we listened, like disciples, to his slow delivery. Thanks to his words at that table in the Royal, we learnt the names of regions and cities which, otherwise, we should never have known existed, not to mention the names of animals and fruits, and of aboriginal tribes who were unaware of even rudimentary civilization. Then we would go home, thinking about yams or the Guarani Indians; and, while cutting through the arcades of the Plaza del General Orduña, well wrapped up, we were amazed to realize how large the world must be.

This story, Don Palmiro told us, took place at the end of the twenties in a village lost in the foothills of the Andes. Don Palmiro, still a young man, travelled through that wilderness on the back of hired mules, selling ladies and gents' underwear and cheap costume jewellery on a commission basis. He reached this particular village as night was falling on a winter's day that threatened snow; he was almost fainting from tiredness after so many hours riding on a mule through ravines and mountain passes. There were no lights in the streets, Don Palmiro recalled, there were no streets almost, only muddy ditches between adobe houses. He saw paraffin lamps in the windows and the inscrutable faces of Indians wearing bowler hats, who closed their shutters when he tried to approach them.

'Do Indian women wear bowler hats, like the English?' queried Lorencito, ever eager for knowledge. But Don Palmiro, who always became a little deaf when telling a story of his youth, did not hear him, and the rest of us, with imperative gestures, demanded silence.

It was as if Don Palmiro's voice had infected us with that village's sepuchral quiet. We were the only ones left in the Royal's lounge, and not even the tinkle of a spoon was heard.

Tired and hungry, Don Palmiro sought accommodation in the village's only hotel, postponing until the following day the visit he'd thought of making that night to the haberdasher's. The hotel was in the square, facing a church, which stood in darkness. As soon as he entered, he told us, he noticed a strange smell: 'that smell of dampness houses always have when they've been shut up for a long time, you know what I mean.' In the very low ceilinged entrance hall were a man and a woman, who were talking in whispers in the light of an oil lamp yellowed by smoke. The woman was dressed in mourning and seemed ill. The man, unshaven and wearing only a vest and looking feverish or drunk, spoke to Don Palmiro, leaning his elbows on the counter. He told him wearily that they couldn't give him supper; they had no free rooms; there was neither stable nor fodder for the mule. Half asleep with fatigue and hunger, Don Palmiro insisted: anything would do, a straw mattress in the barn, a crust of stale bread. The woman looked at the innkeeper out of the corner of her eye and spoke in a low voice, with her hands joined as if praying (the good thing about Don Palmiro's stories was that they made you see every detail). 'Tell him to go away,' murmured the woman, sighing, Don Palmiro said, as if she were at a wake (another word we learnt from him). 'For God's sake, madam,' he almost begged her, 'it's going to snow. I'll freeze like a dog . . .' Youth is vehement. Shrugging his shoulders, like someone declining all responsibility, the innkeeper—a *mestizo*—scratched his matted hair, took up the oil lamp in one hand and a huge key in the other, and told Don Palmiro to accompany him. Turned towards the wall, the woman was holding her mouth and sobbing.

They went up a gloomy staircase with worn steps to a small passage, black and slanting, in which there were three doors. Don Palmiro saw light coming from beneath two of them, and he heard the noises of sleeping bodies. The innkeeper opened the last door and, lifting up the oil lamp, inspected the room's interior without crossing its threshold. He turned away so quickly that he didn't notice the coin Don Palmiro was offering him.

The room, with an adobe floor, had only a very narrow bed, a bedside table with a blue candlestick and a bulrush chair. Don Palmiro heard the window banging because of the wind and, with a heavy heart, he thought of his mule having to spend the night tied to a street railing. Then he removed his trousers and knee-length coat and laid them carefully on the chair. When he was already in bed, he heard, very close in the darkness, some careful knocking, repetitive and constant. 'Some little knocks like this: click, click, click,' he told us, rapping gently with his knuckles on the table's marble top. 'Mice or cockroaches,' he thought, and he snuggled down deeper under the covers, closing his eyes. But, hearing the sound of falling clothes, he realized that he was not going to get to sleep, and he lit the candle.

'Tired as I was, sleep vanished,' Don Palmiro said. 'And so, not to waste my time, I took out my book-keeping book, deciding to study a while. Then I saw that my trousers had fallen off the chair. I got out of bed and picked them up, because they were the only ones I then had and I looked after them as if they were the apple of my eye. I had lain down again when I heard the same slight knocking. It was beginning to wear me out. The knocking wasn't coming from the door, but from very close by, as if someone on the floor below were tapping on the ceiling with a stick. 'If that crook of an innkeeper wants to frighten me, he's going to be disappointed,' I thought, and wrapping myself up once more I determinedly settled down to study the mysteries of the double-entry system. And then there were more short knocks, so: 'click, click'. I looked at the chair and saw that my trousers were beginning to fall very slowly, as if they were tied to a small thread and and were being pulled by it. It didn't take me long to notice that the chair was gently rocking. Was there going to be another earthquake, like the one in Valparaiso? No, only the chair was moving, not the bed and not the candlestick. Then I noticed its legs: one of them was slightly rising and then falling—that was where the knocking was coming from. Then the two left legs rose a little higher and my jacket, which was on the back of the chair, began to slip off; the chair then leaned towards the other side and my jacket and trousers fell on the floor. The chair went something like a minute without moving. Then it was balancing again, very slowly at first and it seemed as if it were going to fall over, but it didn't lose its balance. I got out of bed and it began to move away from me, with short skips, like those people who walk with a stiff leg. When it reached the far side of the room, it again stood still, facing me, as if it suspected something; one of the legs gave three knocks, click, click, click, and then was still.'

'What did you do, Don Palmiro?' Quesada asked.

'Will you believe me if I reply that I felt sleepy again? I turned down the edge of the page I was reading and left the book on the bedside table. I picked up my trousers and jacket and, instead of replacing them on the chair, I put them on top of my suitcase, well folded, so they wouldn't be wrinkled next day. A good appearance is indispensable in business life—that was always my motto. I lay down, extinguished the candle and went to sleep.'

Don Palmiro stopped speaking. He drained his yoghurt, wiped his lips and moustache, and called Sebastián, the waiter who always served our little group. He paid, leaving a handsome tip in the saucer, and told us that it was time to end the session. Only Bustamante dared to ask what all of us were thinking.

'You went to sleep, Don Palmiro? As if nothing was wrong? As if the chair hadn't moved?'

'My dear friend,' Don Palmiro smiled on all of us, like a kind-hearted father. He was already standing up and putting his silver watch into his waistcoat pocket. 'I saw a Turkish soldier slit my father's throat. I thought the whole world was going to be swallowed by the sea during the earthquake in Valparaiso. In the hold of that steamer where I spent two months hidden among carpets, I was woken up by rats biting my ears . . . Do you think that a chair would deprive me of sleep, just because it was jumping about?'

Still without getting up from the table, we looked at Don Palmiro, speechless, overwhelmed by his stature and long life. At that moment, the reel reached its end and, amid the silence, the tape recorder stopped automatically with a click so sudden and sharp that all of us, except for Don Palmiro Sejayán, were startled.

(Translated by Anthony Edkins.)

Sergi Pàmies

Losing face

This morning he told his family of his decision: he was going to give up drinking. His wife hugged him and the children applauded. Then he phoned his friends and asked them never again to offer him a drink or ask him out.

'Not even on Lola's birthday?' one of them asked.

'Not even on Lola's birthday,' he answered.

On his way out, he met the caretaker's wife and told her what an important day it was, because he had given up drinking. The caretaker's wife was very pleased and congratulated him from the bottom of her heart.

When he got to the office he spoke to the managing director and apologized for recent events. He also swore to him—on his mother's life—that from now on he would be on his best behaviour. The boss thanked him for his frankness and confessed that for some days now he had been turning over the idea of sacking him. Nevertheless, and in view of his abilities, he had preferred to give him a vote of confidence; time, as usual, had proved him right in the end.

'We've all been through bad times,' he said, as he saw him to the door.

He set to work with a vengeance, so as to get up to date again and also to kill the thirst that had been tarring his throat since he'd arrived. The others watched and wondered. They didn't know whether this was part of a new show, the result of his excessive drinking, or if the human sponge had really decided to reform and give up alcohol for good. He didn't know either. By this time he should already have had two or three drinks, that way he wouldn't feel as though he'd had a ton of mustard poured over his tongue.

He went down for breakfast. As soon as he went in through the door, the waiter picked up the bottle of gin, but, in a loud voice, he asked for a mineral water and a ham sandwich.

'With or without tomato?' asked the waiter.

'Without.'

When he took his first sip of fizzy mineral water, the waiter looked at him, expecting some kind of volcanic reaction, but nothing happened.

By twelve o'clock he still hadn't tasted a drop of alcohol. His wife rang twice. The first time to find out if everything was all right and the second to remind him that he had to take their son to the dentist's tomorrow to have his brace changed.

He tried the whole time to be pleasant with people. He vaguely remembered having gone too far, in words and actions, and he wanted this new period to be nice and peaceful. He wanted to inspire confidence, and to show it, he phoned the doctor to ask for a check-up.

'I've given up drinking,' he said, loud enough for everyone to hear.

After that they started talking to him again, instead of avoiding him, accepting with resignation his return to normality. One girl even asked after the family.

Later he had a meeting in the boardroom. Everyone was very friendly to him, and he assumed the boss had made a point of letting them all know about his new, abstemious personality.

They discussed future exports, and he said that as long as they stuck to this idea of imitating their rivals, the company wasn't going to get anywhere. He spoke clearly, without the excessive figures people normally use to cover up a shortage of ideas. On his way out, the managing director congratulated him and promised to take his suggestions into account.

At lunch time he went back to the bar. The waiter served him a mineral water and a mixed dish of fried potatoes, fried eggs and sausages. He was going to eat at the bar, but a group of people from the office asked him to sit with them, and he was forced to say yes out of courtesy and to show good will. They talked about money. About the price of cars, about houses in the country, about schools, about membership cards and about the tits on the girl who worked the photocopying machine. Someone advised him, now that he didn't drink, to buy himself a car, and he answered that he couldn't drive.

'Well then, take lessons,' insisted another.

'No, thanks,' he answered.

'That means you still don't feel too sure.'

They said goodbye and he thought to himself that he didn't feel at all sure, that he was very thirsty and that he was dying to hear the noise a gin and tonic makes as it pours down your gullet. But he resisted. He bought a bottle of orange juice at the wine shop, walked up the four flights of stairs and sat listening to boring sales reports.

The receptionist handed him a message from a friend who had phoned while he was at lunch. The message said, 'I'm pleased to hear you've given up drinking, but we could at least celebrate. We'll be at the Brasil at nine. If you don't come there'll be trouble.' He tore the piece of paper up. He knew that if he went to the Brasil again they'd force him to drink a toast, and then another, and he'd end up dragging himself around the bars like a wounded elephant.

He spent the rest of the afternoon sipping orange juice that tasted like medicine and going through his mail. When it was time to pack up he didn't know what to do. He put his jacket on and followed the others. At the door, some were going off to play a game of indoor football, others were going home in a shared car, others disappeared down the steps of the underground. He decided to wait and follow the first person to leave. To pass the time, he thought. The girl who did the photocopies went out and he hid at the corner. He was going to let the matter drop, but if that was a day of decisions he had to be strict and consistent. The girl was standing still, as though she were waiting for someone. The managing director walked past her. She followed him. They walked for a quarter of an hour at a discreet distance from one another. Near the park they turned into a bar with a complicated English name.

'Even they drink,' he said to himself.

He waited outside until it got dark. White clouds scudded across a bluer sky. Cold. When he'd had enough he stopped a taxi and gave his home address.

'Which way do you want to go?' asked the taxi driver.

'As you like.'

The taxi driver explained that bearing in mind the rush-hour traffic they'd be best cutting across from the north. They went along streets he didn't know, dodging traffic jams of trucks and cars that hooted and insulted each other. It was just his luck that they should have to turn into the street where the Brasil was. He did nothing to avoid it. Sometimes, he thought, it's no use fighting destiny. As they drew level with the bar, he said,

'Drop me here.'

'We're not there yet,' the taxi driver said.

'I know, but I want to walk.'

He paid and got out. He took a deep breath, as though he were about to dive into a swimming-pool, and opened the door of the Brasil.

The waiter greeted him and poured him a stiff gin and tonic. He didn't answer. He looked at the tall glass, the ice cubes, the slice of lemon and the bubbles of tonic fizzing onto the bar. Then he took a long, slow drink, letting the liquid go right to the tips of his toes. By nine o'clock, he was drunk. His friends arrived, and when they saw him they were relieved to find that it had all been a false alarm.

'Don't you ever do that again,' someone said. 'You had us worried.'

They drank until closing time. As usual. They didn't want to go, and while they clamoured for another drink, the landlord had to come and give them the story about how they'd close the premises because the local authorities were very strict. As usual. They damned the mayor and left. Someone dropped him off at home and when he opened the door he found his wife waiting for him. She didn't say anything. She helped him off with his jacket and took him to the bathroom. He knelt down and was sick as a pig. She asked him to keep quiet and not wake the children. He had a steaming hot shower and she helped him get into bed. She didn't seem very pleased. He wanted to explain to her that he was very sorry and that it wasn't his fault, but she stopped his mouth with an icy kiss:

'Now go to sleep,' she said.

When he woke up she was gone. He got up and went into the children's room. There was no one there. In the kitchen, he found a note stuck on the fridge that said, 'You ought to be ashamed of yourself. Goodbye.' His face dropped. He washed at the sink and thought how unfair and cruel life was. He sat down. He read the note again, three or four times. First, he felt the strange way his cheeks pulled at his skin. It could be the pain. Or the anger. Or the hangover. He rubbed his face, trying to stop the twitching. He couldn't. He got a fright when he felt his face come away in his hands, it was flabby-looking, repugnantly deformed. He couldn't cry out because he didn't have lips, or a nose, or a forehead. He dropped whatever it was he had in his hands and the mask flopped onto the floor like a plasticine pizza. It wasn't exactly a photograph, nor even anything like a portrait, but he recognized a familiar twitch in the viscous mass. His eyes dropped out. He struggled to his feet and groped his way towards the dining room. He felt the objects in his way and bumped into the furniture until he got used to the dark. His mind was made up. Even if he had to turn the whole place inside out, inch by inch, he'd find out where they'd hidden the gin bottle.

(*Translated by Andrew Langdon-Davies.*)

Pedro Zarraluki

The gallant ghost

Miss Diana never used the peep hole in her front door. Had she used it that first winter night she might not have met Isancient, but Miss Diana was a lively spinster who had come to terms with her loneliness. In the hardened manner of those who deny themselves what they want she considered that fear was the emotional luxury of young, timid women. Forty years of boredom had taught her that in the end the world was not so dangerous. Because of this, on that first winter night, she wasted no time checking who had rung the doorbell. When she opened the front door she was only momentarily surprised that there was nobody on the landing. But an ice-cold draught, followed by a muffled sound, slipped past her into her flat. Miss Diana, who loathed practical jokes, cursed aloud and slammed the door shut. She had no idea that Isancient had entered her home, but he was soon going to introduce himself. Back in her dining room Diana noticed that the flower vase decorating her table was empty, and made a mental note to buy a bunch of flowers the next day. She sat down at the piano and for a while played 'The Man I Love'.

Moved by a pang of hunger, she turned round and saw that the vase was bursting with flowers. Miss Diana remained absolutely still next to the cumbersome John Spencer. She took longer to react this time because she couldn't blame anybody for what she was seeing. She stared around the room, went out into the hall to make sure the front door was properly shut, and then went to the kitchen, bewildered by indefinable doubts. As she lit her oven, a sound of glass breaking made her jump.

Frightened, but curious, she rushed to the dining room. The flower vase now stood on the piano. Through faint candle light she could just make out that the table had been exquisitely laid for two. A wine glass, however, lay in smithereens on the floor tiles. Miss Diana, though flattered by this mysterious admirer's romantic gesture, let fly a string of insults while she picked up the pieces and chucked them in the dustbin. When she returned to the dining room a dish gleamed in the middle of the table. Genuinely impressed, Diana sat in her usual place and lifted the silver lid. A sweet-smelling cloud rose from the soft folds of a cooked pheasant, scenting the room. Miss Diana's skilled sense of smell alerted her that the sauce had been made with raspberries. She sat silently for a few minutes, looked about her, and stared again at the pheasant. Realizing that she was too puzzled, Isancient decided to pour the wine. When she saw the bottle move about in the air she let out a little shriek, but more in admiration than in panic. The effort to make sense of what was happening showed on her face. But she was not scared, for women do not fear gallant ghosts.

Moments later she was helping herself to the pheasant. Before she could taste it, the wine glass opposite her rose in the air, toasting her. Miss Diana decided to follow suit, blaming her excitable nerves for what was happening to her. The wine glasses tinkled when they touched, and Miss Diana raised her glass to her lips. However, she nearly choked when she saw her invisible admirer's glass pour its wine into empty space. She dug into the pheasant and said 'Wonderfully cooked' to the vacant chair opposite. She then suddenly blushed, and finished eating without uttering another word.

Not knowing what to do, and not able to reproach that astounding presence, she withdrew to her bedroom without bothering to bolt the door. She had decided to put everything down to a trick of her senses and took no further precautions. While she was undressing in front of the great moon-shaped mirror on her cupboard, as she did regularly every night, she was struck by a confusion of absurd shame and thrilling lust. Isancient, at the risk of spoiling his conquest, chose to reveal himself the way all ghosts do. He passed three times between

Miss Diana and the mirror, and three times she lost her reflection in the mirror. This proved that there was a ghost about, but Isancient couldn't take any further advantage of his condition to violate a lady's privacies. And she reacted as he had predicted. Modesty had at first frozen her fingers on the first button of her dress, but then she undid them all. She had resolved not to be frightened by her own fantasies, though the excited way she moved her hands betrayed her secret longings. Isancient watched first Miss Diana's dress, then her underwear, drop to the floor. The charming lady admired her nakedness in the mirror. The ghost's invisibility made it all the easier for her to give in. Her sensual pleasure was obvious by the way she avoided fetching her nightie on the pillow. She crossed the room with the elegance that only women display to walk about naked. She sought the most trivial pretexts to show herself off completely to someone who didn't exist. Secret desires gave her the courage to accept what was now inevitable. In that slow, marvellous way in which a woman in love surrenders to a man for the first time, she lay back on her bed and turned out the light. Immediately she felt an ice-cold draught waft over her belly. After a moment's indecision, she tried to pull a sheet over herself, but her desire was too obvious for the ghost to be put off. A weight pressed heavily on to her body, and something amazingly soft, though freezing, caressed her. She began to react, but the gentleness of her gallant lover ensured her total surrender to his embraces. Her muscles relaxed while her breathing became agitated. When a burning fire brushed her lips she moaned prayers and protested, without a struggle.

In this way Isancient made his presence known in the local community. Miss Diana, who could boast of a stainless reputation, hurried to the parish priest to confess her passionate meetings with the ghost, as well as her inability to resist the temptation. The priest, understandably, told her to stop fantasizing, and recommended pious reading matter to overcome her insomnia. However, his prudent measures had no effect at all. Miss Diana had given in, the way all satisfied women do, and not content with flaunting her Christian duties, she walked about every evening on the arm of her non-existent man, arousing all kinds of gossip. People quickly called her that 'wanton woman'. A group of indignant women visited the priest to beg him to put an end to Diana's delirious affair. The priest, a sensible man, called on Miss Diana to see if he could find signs in her house of such improper behaviour. His inspection was fruitless, although Miss Diana, provoked when this topic was raised, discreetly boasted of her sin. The priest was livid with her raving actions, and the combined sin of lust and stubbornness. In spite of everything, his innate patience and an understandable bewilderment warned him to give her more time. He wanted to offer her a second chance, without realizing that only Isancient would benefit from this deferment.

Listening to confessions brought further surprises to the parish priest. A young but decent woman married to a well respected member of the community confessed in tears that she was tossed about in bed by an invisible force whenever her husband was away, and couldn't help feeling intense pleasure in her private parts. One of the women who had led the protest against the enamoured spinster Diana, and who was the respectable owner of a pharmacy, explained how something excitingly snakey slipped between her thighs whenever she perched on a stool to fetch something from the shelves, and how, to her own surprise, and her voice grew faint, she found herself arranging things on these shelves in order to feel that 'thing'.

The priest decided that matters had gone far enough, and checked as discreetly as possible with several doctors that no deadly virus could have spread like the plague inducing these odd outbursts of lust among women. He then wrote a report to his superiors. They ordered him to open a formal investigation, and to be prepared, if necessary, to carry out an exorcism with a specialist in such matters sent out by the archbishopric. Meanwhile, without the priest once betraying the secrecy of confession, the gallant ghost became known to all. The women he seduced, who when it comes to fidelity share something with the praying mantis, flocked to confession to claim their conqueror's head. Even Miss Diana when she got wind of her lover's flirtations paid a call on the parish priest and begged him to put an end to such scandals.

The good priest, who still did not believe in the ghost, found himself under such pressures that he was obliged to call in an exorcist who promptly announced his arrival. On the same day that he awaited the archbishopric's envoy, the perplexed priest put a finishing touch to his report in the parish office. Exhausted by this new strenuous work, he decided to take a rest. He was reading some passages from the Bible, and regretted, as he always did when opening this book, that he didn't own a more venerable edition. When it was near the time for the exorcist to arrive, the priest decided to clear his head by taking a shower. He locked himself in the bathroom, and stripped naked with his back to the mirror, hanging his clothes on a peg behind the door. Although he tried to relax he could not stop thinking about this bizarre and obscene plague.

Isancient, standing by the toilet, was excited by the innocent priest's fleshy bum, as white as a seagull's underside. Isancient was a respectful ghost, but his good intentions were undermined and he knew he could not resist this temptation. At the very moment when the priest walked towards the shower Isancient materialized a rare treasure of a sixteenth-century Bible on the bathroom floor. The priest, pleasurably surprised, stooped down to pick it up.

(Translated by Jason Wilson.)

Javier Cercas

Lola

Morales parked his VW next to the iron gate which led into the forecourt of the faded building of the railway station. From the inside pocket of his mac he took a 9mm Browning automatic; he glanced to check that the magazine was full, and spun it. Then he murmured: 'Son of a bitch.'

He walked slowly over to the building. Over the door hung a sign which read 'Station Hotel'. Some kids were playing with a tyre on the pavement.

Morales went into the empty vestibule of the hotel. There was a bell on the counter in reception, and he rang it, twice, but there was no reply. He looked around, and decided to venture into the cubby hole between the counter and the board announcing the names of the hotel's guests.

'Hey you,' came a voice from behind him. 'Whadya want?'

He turned round, and saw a fat, bald character stalking towards the counter, buttoning his black waistcoat as he came. This challenge was repeated.

'Yeah, you—what d'you think you're doing there?'

'I rang the bell, and nobody came.' Morales paused for a moment. 'I'm looking for a character by name of Sardano, Pablo Sardano. I believe he's staying here.'

'Is he a friend of yours?' asked the fat man, with what Morales took to be a curious mixture of suspicion and expectation.

'Let's say I know him,' he replied, emerging slowly from the cubby hole behind the counter.

The fat man went into the space which Morales had vacated,

opened a drawer and took out a book which he proceeded to peruse minutely, peering closely and tracing through with his forefinger.

'Seventeen days,' he said, raising his head. 'Your friend owes me for seventeen days. Now, you tell me what I'm supposed to do,' he added, looking him in the eye.

Morales pulled a wallet from the inside pocket of his mac and laid a couple of notes on the counter.

'Just tell me what room he's in.'

'Room thirteen,' the fat man murmured, checking the money.

Morales gestured vaguely with his left hand as he advanced to the other end of the corridor.

'By the way,' said the fat man, looking up from the banknotes, 'Mind how you go . . . Your pal's in bed with the heaviest tart on the block.' He let out a raucous guffaw. As Morales disappeared into the dark of the stairwell, he shouted after him: 'Do me a favour . . . see if you can persuade him to leave and never come back?'

Morales went up to the first floor and picked his way down a dimly lit corridor. The wooden floorboards creaked beneath his feet.

The door of Room 13 was ajar. Morales pushed it gently open and entered. Inside the silence was disturbed only by the rasping noise of somebody breathing and by the faint sound of a radio playing. Its pilot light blinked in the dark. The room smelt of urine, of old wine and of dead meat.

Morales drew the curtains and hauled on the shutters. The harsh noon light flooded into the room.

'Damn the son of a bitch and the whore who bore him,' the heap of bedding grunted in a voice that was heavy with sleep and alcohol, whereupon the heap curled up in bed to protect itself from the fierceness of the light.

The furniture in the room consisted of two chipped, dark-wood chairs; a lopsided pine table; a double bed; and a wall mirror that had lost its silvering at the edges and which hung over a small wash basin whose plughole was clogged with hairs. There were empty wine bottles all over the place, wineglasses full of cigarette ends, and the revolting half-finished remnants of somebody's meal. Next to the bed a woman sat, motionless, wrapped in yellowing bedsheets and leaning against the bare wall. At her side lay pieces of crinkled baking foil, greasy bread and a half-empty bottle of white wine.

Morales gathered up the female clothing scattered at the foot of the bed and flung it at the woman, who peered round from behind her sheet, gave him a sleepy look, and turned back to the wall, studiously indifferent to his presence.

Morales went over to her, took her by one arm, and shook her roughly.

'I want you out of here, and pronto,' he said.

'Tato Morales, you always were a son of a bitch,' the man groaned from under the bedclothes. 'Forever you've been a son of a bitch.'

'You shut up,' said Morales. 'I'm not talking to you.'

'What the hell's this all about?' the woman asked, finally stirring into consciousness. She sounded decidedly rough.

'Someone's waiting for you outside, doll,' said Morales, tossing four crumpled banknotes onto the pile of clothing. 'And you wouldn't want to keep them waiting, would you?'

'Who's waiting outside?'

'It doesn't matter really; the fact is, it's time for you to leave. Understand? Because if you don't, I'll start getting impatient, and you wouldn't want to see me annoyed now, would you?'

'Who's waiting outside for me?' the woman asked again.

'Your fucking mother!' Morales shouted.

He grabbed her by one arm and dragged her out into the corridor. Then he picked up every item of female clothing that he found in the room, threw it after her, and shut the door with a slam that shook the whole building.

'You have such a charming way with women, Tato,' said the man in the bed.

'Whores aren't women, they're merchandise.'

'True,' agreed the other. 'But they tend not to work out as expensive as the other sort.'

Morales walked over to the window and leaned against the frame, looking out into the street. The man was still sprawled in bed, but he eventually sat up, took a swig at the bottle of white wine, which shone with the bright midday light, and spat to one side of the bed; then he searched to find a cigarette in one of the various packets strewn around the bed; he didn't find one. He said:

'Give me a cigarette, Tato.'

Morales reached him a cigarette. The man lit it, inhaled deeply and breathed out the smoke with an air of gratitude. Then he said:

'I presume you've not come to talk to me about women.'

'In a manner of speaking,' Morales replied. 'Now, get yourself dressed, Sardano.'

'Coffee?' asked the waitress, a blonde whose opulent shape was concealed behind a blue striped uniform.

Morales nodded.

'Two coffees,' Sardano interjected, looking her in the eye and smiling.

The waitress removed their dessert plates and disappeared. Sardano's eyes followed the blonde's wiggling hips as she went between the tables towards the swing doors leading to the kitchen.

'Not bad, the blonde, eh?' he said, lighting a cigarette.

'You've got women on the brain, Sardano.'

'Haven't you?'

'In moderation.'

Sardano smiled and breathed out a cloud of smoke.

'How's Lola?' he asked.

'The same as ever.'

'I'd say better than ever,' Sardano laughed. 'At the party the other night we were talking about the old days. You know, the *barrio*, and all that. When we were just starting up. You remember all that, Tato?'

Morales nodded. Sardano sighed, smiled, and said:

'Those were the days!'

The blonde arrived with their coffees, and Sardano gave her another smile; then he downed his unsweetened coffee in one go and lit another cigarette.

'OK, Tato, what's it all about?'

'I want you to help me on a job.'

'What kind of job?'

'Killing someone.'

Sardano smiled and shook his head.

'Don't even think about it. I already told you, I'm not getting involved in anything like that again. I had enough of all that with the Bastida business.'

'This is different,' Morales stressed.

'It's all the same to me. Count me out.' He shook his head again. 'Why don't you ask Tico Medina, or Salcedo, or any of the others. Like I say, count me out.'

Morales finished his coffee, and crossed his hands over the cup and rested his lips on his fingers. Then he called the waitress over.

'Do you want a brandy?' he asked.

Sardano nodded.

'Two cognacs, please,' Morales asked.

The restaurant had already been deserted for a while. Behind the swing doors of the kitchen the staff were still busy at work.

'Look, Sardano,' Morales said, relaxing his facial muscles. 'How long have we known each other? Twenty years? Twenty-five? Maybe more. You and Max are the only family I've ever had. My only friends. And Lola too, of course. Friends since way back . . .'

He paused, and sat watching the static flaps of the door to the kitchen. Then he added, almost angrily: 'Since way back, damn it.'

Sardano stubbed out his cigarette in the ashtray, and looked at Morales. Then he thought of Max: the curious way he looked like a stork, with his round glasses, the beginnings of a receding hairline, and his eternal grey gaberdine mac.

'You're the only ones I can trust,' Morales continued, in a tone that suggested he was asking for something. 'The rest of them are rubbish. When they find someone who'll pay them better than me, they'll pump me full of lead and off they'll go.'

The blonde arrived with the two brandies and the bill.

'I'm sorry, gents,' she said. 'We're just about to close.'

Morales nodded, without looking at her. Sardano didn't look up either. The blonde shrugged and withdrew to the kitchen.

'How much?' asked Sardano.

'Half a million.'

'Must be a big fish, eh?'

'Just a son of a bitch.'

'If every son of a bitch was worth even half what you're offering for this one, you'd be a rich man by now.'

'Forget the wisecracks. Are you with me, or not?'

'When?'

'This afternoon.'

'When!!?'

'You heard. He comes out every afternoon to walk his dog on a patch of wasteland. That's where we come in.'

'But I haven't even got a . . .'

'Don't worry. I've taken care of that.'

Sardano stared at him, wide-eyed. Then he slapped the side of the table with the palm of his hand, and said:

'OK, let's go.'

'Yes,' said Morales. 'It'll be a piece of cake.'

They parked the VW on the gravel parking lot in front of a ramshackle bar on the outskirts of town. The place had white, peeling walls and an asbestos roof. Away in the distance evening was settling on the chaotic and murky city. They went in.

Morales ordered two beers and they leaned up against the grimy brass counter. The walls of the place were covered with posters featuring the line-ups of various football teams, and autographed photos of famous bullfighters.

'I presume we're not going to have to wait long,' said Sardano, as he sized up an impressive bull's head which presided over the empty bar.

'Not long,' Morales said. 'Just time enough to down a beer.'

Morales drank his in one long swig, and smacked his lips. Then, having checked that the bony type who had served them was out in the backroom of the bar, he said:

'Don't you want to know who's the target for tonight?'

Sardano shrugged his shoulders and took another swig at his beer.

'You know I never ask questions,' he said.

Morales offered him a cigarette: he lit Sardano's first and then his own.

'The bastard was screwing Lola.'

Sardano thought: 'You're the one who's a bastard; that's no kind of a reason to be killing a man.' But he didn't move a muscle of his face as he said:

'You're talking like he's dead already.'

They paid and left.

They drove back in the direction they had come from. After a while the VW took a right turn down an earthy track running parallel to a small stream that was full of muddy water. They parked down by the stream-bed.

'Hey, Tato . . . Are you sure this is the place?' Sardano asked, surveying the stretch of wasteland that met his eye. The only sign of human habitation was a number of tower blocks picked out in the distance, against the evening sky.

'Who the hell's going to come out to a place like this, at this time of night?'

'Nobody,' said Morales, calmly, taking his Browning from the inside pocket of his mac. 'That's exactly why we're here.'

Sardano turned round. Morales avoided his eyes.

'I don't know why you had to go and do it,' he said, as if talking to himself. 'I don't know why you had to go and do it.' He paused for a moment, shaking his head. Then, seeming to recover, he raised his gaze, looked Sardano in the eye and said: 'For God's sake—as if there weren't plenty of other women in the world.'

A slight twitch took control of Sardano's upper lip and he had to bite his lip to stop it. The only thing that broke the silence of approaching night was the sound of the water in the muddy stream.

'You know I've always liked Lola, Tato.' Sardano's voice sounded resigned, almost ironic, and with a barely perceptible tremor. 'We've always fancied Lola—all of us—why deny it?

You just happened to be the one who came up lucky. You got her. End of story.'

Sardano fell silent, half smiling, with his head bowed. The tremor had disappeared from his lip and his voice was steady. He raised his head and looked down the barrel of the Browning.

'OK, if you're going to do it, then do it, you son of a bitch.'

It was already dark by the time Morales got home, He parked the Volkswagen in the garage, and when he saw the green Volvo round the back of the house, next to the lawnmower, he thought: 'Lola's home.'

He crossed the garden and went in through the back door. The ground floor was in darkness. As he went up the stairs he heard Lola humming to herself. He saw her form silently silhouetted against the bedroom door. Lola was sitting in front of the mirror on the dressing table, putting on lipstick. She turned to greet him.

'How are you, Tato? You're late.'

'Are you going out?' Morales asked.

Lola continued applying the lipstick.

'Queta rang to invite me over for a game of cards at her place,' Lola said. 'You know how she is,' she added, shrugging her shoulders in the direction of the mirror. 'Impossible to say no.'

She got up, picked up her handbag from the dressing table, said 'I won't give you a kiss, I've just done my lips,' and out she went.

Morales went down to the dining room and heard the sound of the Volvo starting. He peered through the curtains at the garden window. Lola closed the garage door and got into her car.

He climbed into his VW, started it, and followed the Volvo at a distance through the mid-evening traffic.

After about half an hour, the Volvo stopped in front of a fancy apartment block in the centre of town. Morales parked the Volkswagen on the other side of the street, and as he cut the engine he saw Lola get out of the car and head for the building. He settled down to wait.

He was no more than halfway through his cigarette when he saw Lola coming out of the building again, on the arm of a man who was wearing a grey mac and had the air of a stork, with round glasses and the beginnings of a receding hairline.

Morales thought to himself: 'Son of a bitch.'

(*Translated by Ed Emery.*)

José Antonio Millán

The little footbridge

Few will remember (if, that is, anyone even got to hear of its existence), the epidemic that invaded six successive girls' schools on Padre Damián Street in Madrid one year at the end of the sixties.

Our school, the only one for boys in the area, was the first in a long rosary of religious institutions that snaked its way up the street. From the playground we had a good view of the school next door. It was clear to us, however, that there was no point in looking that way too much; at the end of the day there was little that might be of interest to us. Between cement and sky, patrolled by figures in black, experts at detecting dangerous conversations (at a distance and without hearing a word!), our playground was an absorbing enough space. The fact was that the girls' yells were barely worth a glance. Until the plague started. One thing was the noise of play, the clamour when a ball went over the fence between the yards, but quite another was the rhythmic chanting which started up one day from a choir of hundreds of throats and was to accompany us, break time after break time, for a long period.

First we identified the tune, a brief musical phrase constantly repeated. Then we half made out the words, which we finally confirmed in a rapid exchange of information: '. . . and a little footbridge?' or perhaps, 'And a little footbridge . . .' or 'And a little footbridge.' And a little footbridge!

At that time, as the eldest, it was my job to collect the other three at the school gates and take them home. I generally had a shortish time to wait which I could spend scrapping or playing on the machines. On the second day of the chanting (not on the first), covered in dust on the way home, I deigned to question my sisters about the curious phenomenon. As pupils of the school next door they should have some knowledge of it, if not an active part in the proceedings. The older one answered me excitedly.

'It's a new game. We all get together and hold hands, in circles. We sing "and a little footbridge", taking one step forward and raising our arms. Then one step back and it starts all over again.'

The truth is that this explanation did not satisfy me. I had found out the how but not the why. What did they get out of it? What remote mechanisms were being put into play? For I had the feeling that in all this there was something brutal, atavistic; that something was amiss.

One day over lunch with the family the subject came up again. I pricked my ears and kept quiet. I was hoping my sisters would give something away. But not even my mother, always on the lookout for whatever might rub, the slightest little thing, did not pick up on anything suspicious. She went, 'Oh, really?' in a distracted sort of way and paid no more attention to it. But of course she had not heard the massed chanting of a thousand throats, her spine had not had the shivers sent running down it.

Fresh facts confirmed my fears. All the girls' schools on Padre Damián street were a hotbed of 'little footbridges': the Worshippers, the Consolation, the Sacred Hearts, the Daughters of Jesus (wrongly called the Jesuitinas), at all of them the flame had caught hold.

How had it all started? Good question. Would it not be better to ask who the first person was to make two words rhyme, or where the first joke was born? I do not think we shall ever know. I did ascertain that it had begun with 'the seniors'. The seniors! Even now the name evokes a faint tremor. But they were no more than fifteen years old and they all had to wear a uniform. I later found out that the juniors, taking up the macabre game almost immediately, poor little things, had tried to break away in that manner that today, having learnt a thing or two and contemplated so many impotent forms of servitude, I can only describe as astonishing; they tried to broaden the paradigm. Their timid protest, soon stifled by mockery and a little hurly-burly, manifested itself as a minor variation in the words; every now and then they interposed, 'and a little hilltop.'

Unfortunate creatures! The chant was not a catalogue of geographical features. The isolated footbridge, as head or tail of God knows what warped series, had more venom in it than any sequential system. Years later, wandering round the lanes of the city centre, I noticed on a sign outside a bar, 'Speciality: rabbit with garlic, etc, etc.' The grave dislocation this produced in my spirits took me back to the 'era of the little footbridge'. There are things in this world that press a deep nerve.

But I carried on with the academic year, a good habit I maintained until I finished college, and the peculiar (for want of a better word) sensation of days passing, alternately immersed in fascinating subjects dealt with by idiots and idiotic subjects dealt with by them too, almost distracted me from what was happening two hundred yards outside the window. But the thing continued, as evidenced by the distant swell of arms alternately raised and lowered.

I wondered how the nuns, whose rigorous discipline was notorious, could permit such slackness. I can now see clearly, and it merely reinforces the feeling that I was witness to something abominable, that 'the seniors' had found, perhaps by chance, the gap, the (outwardly) semiotic and (inwardly) impulsional interspace where pleasure was optimized at minimum risk. Who could ban the girls from singing and dancing at break time? And if anyone reported the danger that lurked behind, would they not be giving in to the vertigo themselves? Hey you! scowling censor, you! old fool (in my dreams I still cross-examine the nuns), how do you know it's evil? where do you perceive it? And even then, even if, in a sacrifice for which at the end of the day they were professionally prepared, some of them had raised their voices in admonition, what would they say? 'Don't sing'? 'Sing different things, not always the same'? 'You can't repeat a word a thousand times . . .'? Useless.

Regrettably my interests at that time did not remain fixed on any subject for long. We had managed to get the philosophy master fired; every time he looked at a pupil he would see on his lips the mouthed words, 'son-of-a-bitch', clearly pronounced, until he ended up with a nervous breakdown. At the 'El Alce' arcade they had installed a new machine (I was seeing, without knowing it, the introduction of the third generation of pinball machines: only one ball, with electronic game count). Also, my explorations of the city had extended to cover a wide radius and I had a lot to see.

And one day there were no more little footbridges.

At first it was a simple absence; everything carried on the same as ever: the noise of the playground, father Turrado warning that he could identify boys who 'played with themselves' just by looking at their hands, Antonia the Mummy pacing the corridors (and a new question that I thought about for a long time: did the priests acknowledge each other every time they passed in the corridor? A nod or fleeting gesture? Not even that?) But not a sign of any chanting. I did not want to ask my sister about it. What for? To see, perhaps, while she feigned a great effort to remember, her little eyes shining for a second as she recalled a pleasure she would now have to seek elsewhere.

Luckily for myself at that time (the memory would stay with me after all), there was always another subject to reflect upon, another mystery to explore. It must have been around then that I first wondered why there are only five vowels in Spanish.

And I trod the articulatory pathways, slowly, carefully, closing A's and opening E's until, all of a sudden, ping!, I had passed from the one to the other without realizing it, with no memory of the moment of the miracle.

(*Translated by David M. Lambert.*)

Laura Freixas

The clyptoderm

'The clyptoderm won't scare you,' the mistress of the house said, rather than asked, as we went by the animal pen. I thought, of course, that I hadn't understood rightly, but out of shyness all I did was smile politely.

If the strange phrase had aroused an anxiety in me, the arrival at what was going to be my bedroom, soon made me forget it. Not even in my most beautiful dreams—the ones whose supernatural sweetness counteracts the terrors of the day for a few hours—had I ever reached the point of imagining so perfect a retreat: a spacious room with a wooden floor and beams, austere furniture, and Vermeer-like light. The windows opened out onto the garden, onto the peaceful golden afternoon. A landscape drawn by a child, an innocent paradise, an ideal of harmony . . . Was it possible that fate, so unjust up until then to me, would allow me to regard exhaustion, uncertainty, sudden frights as over and done with? Was it possible that I had reached the end of my anguished journey at last? I had an urge to kneel down, to weep, to thank God, in whom I do not believe.

Not only the cordiality of the family—made up of the owners of the house and their adolescent son—but also the little rituals of the evening meal, the silence round about, and even the banality of the conversation, confirmed my happiness. The air smelled of home cooking, of pure soap, of a summer night in the country. I hadn't been mistaken, I thought: this was the cool oasis, the maternal shore, the compassionate congregation of the faithful, that the man parched with thirst, the shipwreck victim, the lost sheep yearn for.

As we were getting up from the table, I heard the husband ask his wife:

'Is the clyptoderm . . .?'

'It's quite all right,' she interrupted him: 'it's sleeping.'

I looked at them questioningly for the space of a second, but the explanation I was waiting for wasn't forthcoming, and I didn't dare ask for one.

We said goodnight to each other, and I went up to my room. I spent a long time gazing out at the stars, listening to the sedative chorus of cicadas, absorbing that peace I was so badly in need of. But even so I was unable to silence the internal screeching, the discordant note scratching hope. 'The clyptoderm . . .?' 'It's sleeping.' I was unable to fall asleep, no matter how hard I tried, with growing agitation, to reduce to its just proportions what, I told myself, was no doubt a misunderstanding . . . Before plunging into a sleep confused and inhabited by echoes, I heard, stabbing the monotonous and disciplined chorus of cicadas the sudden scream of a bird in the distance.

All was serenity when I awoke. With my easel and my paints, I went out into a sunny, singing morning. Silhouettes of mountains, black and sharply outlined at first, then violet and vaguer, and after that blue—a transparent, miraculous blue— finally dissolving into an immensity of dust and light; soft almond trees in bloom, pink and white; gray stretches of stony ground; the wind prattling like a child . . . Everything welcomed me.

Forming part of the world and being, oneself, almost nothing . . . I realized that I ought not to see my existence, my task, either as something intolerably absurd, or as a transcendent and grandiose mission either, but simply as the modest, but useful, role that had been assigned me; recreating within the narrow limits of a canvas an infinitesimal part of infinite beauty, and extracting from it a humble satisfaction. Not the stupid, animal one of Sisyphus, nor the stupid, arrogant one of the national heroes whose bronze statues would be torn down in due time; but rather, the simple, ordinary one of a bricklayer, of a blacksmith, of a cook. In that spirit, I painted joyfully and diligently the whole day, and came back at nightfall feeling at peace with myself and with the world.

I was still sailing in the gentle waters of serenity, when my anxiety was again aroused with a jolt; after supper, the inexplicable dialogue was repeated:

'Is the clyptoderm . . .?'

'Yes, yes; don't worry, it's sleeping.'

The perverse seed stirred in my insides, as husband and wife smiled naïvely at me, as though to excuse themselves for going on with a private conversation in my presence. After bidding me goodnight, they went off to bed; I did likewise.

I tried in vain to convince myself that the enigma was ridiculous, that its solution, when I found out what it was, would make me feel ashamed because it was so easy and obvious. I sought in vain to calm myself down by recalling the unhurried way in which the day had gone by, my limpid certainty, as I faced the landscape bathed in sunlight, that that, and nothing else, was the world: ordered, solid, without mystery . . .

A few minutes later, I went downstairs, with a flashlight in my pocket.

It startled me to see a line of light around the edge of the kitchen door. Torn between the wish to see and the fear of what I might see, I hesitated for a long time; when I finally knocked on the door, uneasiness, like a bird, fluttered in my throat.

'Come in,' a voice bade me. I entered the room.

Sitting at the table, with a notebook open on the oilcloth covering it, was the son of the owners of the house. He had left his raised hand suspended in the air, holding a bit of eraser: perched on top of the chair opposite, the pet black cat of the household was watching his every move attentively.

I couldn't say which was greater: my disappointment or my relief. The youngster looked at me in surprise awaiting an explanation. Making one up on the spot, I told him I'd come downstairs to get myself a glass of water, and drank one down immediately. I was about to leave, when it occurred to me that this was a good opportunity to put an end to my doubts, before my impatience and my stupidity caused a catastrophe. So I took out my pack of cigarettes and offered him one. As a bribe, it was a rather feeble one, but it did the trick: after a cautious glance in the direction of the door, the adolescent accepted the cigarette, thanking me with a smile. As I lit it for him, I asked him, with feigned offhandedness:

'Incidentally . . . what's this business about the clyptoderm?'

He burst into hearty laughter:

'Don't tell me—is that honestly worrying you? Well, don't be afraid, we really keep it tied down tight.'

A chorus of bells deafened me; violent peals of ridicule, peals of annoyance as keen as spurs, sarcastic peals that were a slap in the face to me. I muttered something, I don't remember what, and left the kitchen and the house in a fury. I lit the flashlight, sought out the path leading to the animal pen; and once there, resolutely shined its beam inside.

A second later, the flashlight had fallen out of my hands and I was running, screaming in spasms, through the vast, absolute darkness. I had seen the clyptoderm.

(*Translated by Helen Lane.*)

Agustín Cerezales

Last judgement (Aldo Pertucci)

A ldo Pertucci disembarked in Barcelona without apparent reason. Nothing about him betrayed that he might be running away from something, or pursuing anything either. In reality, the reasons for his arrival in Barcelona—which in time would constitute an obsession—he was to discover later, little by little, though he always believed that at every moment he had acted in the full knowledge of what he was doing.

'My story is very simple, but God knows only too well how much I'd like to be able to tell it.' At least that was what was understood by Pedro Arenillas, the man who had found him alone on the breakwater, looking with fragile awe at the petroleum iridescence on the water. And with these words, Aldo considered that he had told Pedro the whole truth: his story was summed up precisely in his powerlessness to tell it.

Pedro Arenillas was a man of lacerating impulses: he had caressed the beauty of the furtive green eyes at the mere sight of the fragility of the shadow on the asphalt, and with these naked words, he was already caressing the depths of a beautiful, bitter and unquenchable passion.

Pedro was squat, hairy, fat. He wore plaited sandals and a checked shirt. One might have said that his figure screamed out for a noble peasant-style sash to girdle the lolling, rounded lasciviousness of his belly. His entire being shivered at the beauty: it was only available in inverse proportion to his longing, and to make Aldo yield, to take possession of his virginal indifference, to trample it in the mire of his lechery, he would have given his all, from the first moment he saw him, with his leg dangling, his pensive countenance, empty as a god, hollow as a snailshell polished by the wind.

And yet, this same impulse paradoxically created its own restraint, elevating before him, before his blind and vehement desires, the burnished sword of a strange compassion.

From the start, then, the clumsy Arenillas was to know that love had set upon his neck a yoke more powerful than that of the flesh, that from the precise instant that Aldo had raised his eyes to look at him—guileless, without a shadow of rebuff—a new life, with new suffering, had begun for him.

Once Arenillas had submitted himself to this savage toll, Aldo's life in Spain could not have initiated under better auspices, or worse, if one looks at it differently; the fact is, that under this patronage, his past, his motives, and the mystical gleam in his eyes remained safe from any inquiry.

In effect, Aldo knew how to drive trucks. He possessed a brand-new licence and although, as Arenillas suspected, he only knew the instructions of hydraulic systems, he appeared willing and able to carry anything. His new boss offered him the Rome-Bilbao route, one of the best, flouting agreements with his staff. But Pertucci showed no enthusiasm about going to Italy. Reading a shadow of mistrust in Pedro's eye, he hastened to tell him, with a bitter look, that he had no problems with the law. Which turned out to be true.

So Aldo renounced driving a magnificent Saab Turbo, which glided along like silk, and took over a grumbling old Barreiros which covered the Murcia tomato run twice a week.

In time, Arenillas was able to confirm that Aldo not only did not aspire to any improvement in his working conditions, or tire of his monotonous mission (Monday soap, the return trip on Tuesday with tomatoes, the same Thursday and Friday), but that nothing seemed to change in him, neither in his physical state—if perhaps rather more tanned—nor in his state of mind, of apparent apathy.

Aldo did not seek distraction. He was up to date in paying the pension where he lodged and slept at night, frequenting the same eating houses, and if anything declared his tastes, it was his roaming around the port area, the solitude of the sheds.

Arenillas trusted that he would open up a little in the end. He stayed on in the depot office in order to see him come in on Tuesday and Friday nights, trying to read some sign in him, an indication of any pain or happiness: but Aldo always had the same confused look, of effaced dreams, the same phlegmatic steadiness of hand, the same minimally cordial pressure in his handshake, and the smile he seemed to scrape together when he said goodbye.

Nonetheless, Aldo's life was not short of emotions. On all his trips, he was in the habit of stopping the truck near the Cornellá cliffs, or at La Roseta heights, and whether it was cold or hot, night or day, he scaled the rocks from which he could best see the sea. He would remain then as if enraptured in his contemplation of the winey surge. If anyone had been able to approach him in these moments of deep projection before the abyss, this person would have verified that his eyes slightly changed colour, that the wincing of his mouth recalled the diffuse semblance of a prayer.

Was he returning, perhaps, to his origins. Was this the sea of Sicily? Was he thinking of his mother back there in Camueso, taking flowers to the saint every day to ask an intercession for him? Or was his mother now just a memory, one more memory, unleashed and absolved in the swell?

From these presumed excursions to the infinite, Aldo returned as if drunk, his legs trembling, and having difficulty climbing into the cabin of the truck.

He usually drove then to the nearest bar where he had a milky coffee, or rested before getting on with the trip, reassembling his imperturbable mask, concealing his expression and reining in his heart.

His ambiguous air of a heroin addict and his raw-boned beauty easily aroused affection, or a maternal instinct, in women, when it was not abruptly declared fever, like that of Arenillas.

In summer, he would often stop in the province of Valencia. He had a weakness for it, especially the zones near the capital: foul, touching places that preyed on souls. On the beach at

Calafat, five hundred metres from the effluent channel of the industrial estate, he got to know a girl whose looks had caught his eye at once: her name was Nieves, and she was not Italian as he had mistakenly assumed.

The girl died, almost without surprise on her face, sweetly, not relinquishing the slightly silly expression that had first captivated him.

That night, Arenillas detected something akin to happiness in Aldo, a subterranean tension that mellowed his voice and calmed his eyes, and he wondered what could have happened. He could not escape a stab of jealousy. The next trip, he followed him at a distance on the Kawasaki, but noticed nothing special.

He thought he was beginning to understand something when he found under the truck seat a notebook of watercolours. There were several sketches, clumsy, but not devoid of genius, which moved him. He fancied that these almost child-like sketches showed, without prevarication, the personality of his beloved.

In fact, he did not begin to understand a thing until he saw in a newspaper the photo of the girl who had died, strangled. Her eyes, round as chestnuts, were unequivocally those repeated time and again—with strange fidelity for such seeming inexpertness—in Aldo's sketchbook.

Arenillas' imagination took off: he saw with conviction how Aldo, sketchbook in hand, had fooled the young woman who appeared with a group of girlfriends—somewhat apart from the others—her head resting on her knees which she clasped with crossed arms, dreamily looking at the sea, or perhaps the sand; then he represented them together, heading off for some deserted spot, under the envious gaze of some of her companions.

Aldo was in danger; it was essential to change his route to avoid any risk that he might be recognized. But he testily rejected the proposal and insisted on continuing with the tomato run in the Barreiros. Arenillas ended up wondering if it wasn't all a product of his imagination, and gave up the idea of hinting at a confession: he had had obscure dreams of blackmailing him, obtaining thus his body, dreaming crazy things that he would never have been able to carry out, subjugated as he was to his incomprehensible love. All his dreams evaporated in the presence of an unshaken Aldo, in whom there no longer remained any trace of the happiness or internal combustion that Pedro had once thought he divined.

Patricia was a mature woman who would never have set foot in that discotheque unless she had not suddenly decided to free herself from the past, at least for a few hours, in approaching a different present, a strange one to her eyes, which would not leave any chinks open to her worst fears. Life had not been kindly to her and now circumstances had finally stranded her in the big old family house where only an elderly maid and a still-older aunt survived the hurricane of the years. Feeling that she was dead to love and buried alive, she wanted to commit the extravagance of contemplating for those few hours the illusion of the world before surrendering herself definitively to the irremediable desolation that promised her peace for the rest of her senseless days.

Aldo had gone in there by mistake, believing it was a normal bar. He had no need of anyone to report to him such a peculiar state of mind to gauge in a split second, just as he was turning to leave, the depth and velocity of the current in which Patricia— of small veiled eyes—was submerged.

Arenillas, who kept an eye on him whenever he could, was, on this occasion, on the point of being the witness to its denouement: the truck was pulled over near the Payés bend, and he stopped the motorbike some fifty metres before. All he could see was how Aldo came back from the edge of the cliff, emerging from the shadows with the noncommital face of someone who has just relieved his bladder. He was returning alone.

Patricia's corpse was found the next day by an underwater fisherman seeking rest on the shore. It was stamped onto a rock and at first they said it had been an accident.

Soon the murders multiplied in the region. All were attributed to the 'Madman of *El Pasillo*'.[1] *El Pasillo* is a typical under-ground commercial centre in the typical greasy tourist village, and it seems that several of the victims were recruited there.

Arenillas was sure that Aldo had only killed two women. When he saw the robot-portrait circulated in the newspapers, just after the last crime, perpetrated on the person of a buxom refreshment stall assistant, he thought that Aldo was not as handsome as he had imagined him; there was something about him that was dissimulated in real life, which the robot-portrait accurately caricatured, perhaps some excess in the nose, or a kind of clownishness about the fanning ears. An observation that only transported him to a sentiment which added to that of love, where Aldo was more helpless child than coveted god.

When the police came to arrest him, Aldo put up no resistance, but neither did he confess. In fact, he did not even protest his innocence, confining himself rather to declaring absolutely nothing.

Pedro went to visit him as soon as the judge authorized it. Despite the bruising from his interrogation, Aldo was the same as ever, and once again, Pedro's indescribable ambition, the agreeable heartache with which he had imagined seeing him face-to-face, the taste of his tears, the weight of the head on his shoulder, had to evaporate in exchange for a practical appraisal of the situation.

Determined to defend him, come what may, he engaged the services of the best lawyer and had a tremendous row with his wife, in the ravings of which he went so far as to confess to her that he felt secret envy over the fate of the women murdered at the hands of his truck driver.

Nothing deterred him. He had several alibis worked out and was prepared to give perjured evidence on his behalf, when, before the judge, Pertucci came out with an odd proposal: he would tell all if he were guaranteed the presence of a priest in a session open to the public.

Aldo's childhood had entirely run its course in the little Sicilian

---

[1] Literally, 'The Passage' (trans.).

village of Camueso where his mother had been employed as a washerwoman on being widowed and finding herself alone in the world with a child of only a few months.

Aldo had grown up between the skirts of his mother, the sacristan and the local Virgin: from the very beginning his devotion had flowed undeviating, clear and sweet-smelling as thyme sending up its fragrance to the clouds, which are God's frown.

Aldo asked nothing special of life. He would have liked to have spent it all near his mother, in his village, watching the days go by like someone telling rosary beads, and maybe not growing up, being the eternal altar boy at the parish church, with no other objective, no other music than the routine cadence of peace.

As an adolescent, he was confronted with the need to learn a trade. He had grown too big and the altar boy's smock no longer concealed his hefty calves. When he rang the bell, the diminutive Don Cósimo found it being agitated almost at the level of his nose. The nuns found him successive employment with a shoe-repairer, a housepainter and in a granary; but nowhere did he land on his feet, and although no one could have branded him as a loafer, they rejected him as slow, as a jinx, and as a hindrance: the shoe-repairer's leather curled, the painter's paint cracked, and the granary owner's grain rotted. All coincided in discharging their wrath onto Aldo.

It was a young and spirited nun, *sor* Valona, who began to show him the rudiments of sketching and watercolours. They spent long, agreeable afternoons together, but eventually she had to go off to another convent and Aldo was once again left up in the air. In the end, the nuns, who were now committed to his training, decided to pay for his getting a licence and to employ him themselves, driving the van, but not without vexing sister Plácida who was a demon at the wheel.

As if bad luck were pursuing him, he had hardly been two weeks at the job, when coming out of a curve in the port of Racciolo (it was night and he was returning from Palermo after unloading a consignment of sponges and cup-cakes), he felt a hard bump on the nose of the DKW, which had him on the point of overturning and almost going over the cliff.

He braked, jumped out of the van, ran and found the cause of the blow: he had killed a man. Or maybe he had not killed him yet because later he believed that the bloodied face, which seemed to be grimacing in the orange light of the indicators, had murmured something after he had dragged him in a frenzy to the clifftop, and before he let him drop into the distant sombre sea.

He had acted blindly, prey to an impulse of terror, but managed to pull himself together, return to the van, start it, and get to his mother's house as if nothing had happened except that he was tired and preferred to go straight to bed, without dinner.

In the course of that sleepless night, he resolved to confess to father Cósimo, and went to put it into practice next morning. But the deafness of the old priest generally promoted a long line of faithful at the confessional box, and after waiting a while, Aldo left, telling himself that he would have to shout if Don Cósimo was to absolve him in any positive way, and then everyone in the church would know about it.

Besides, though he knew he was most certainly in a state of mortal sin, he did not succeed in feeling repentance: only fear. This absence of repentance slowly became a torture because, as far as he knew, he would never thus be able to obtain divine pardon. As for the idea of turning himself over to justice, that terrified him too but he contrived to believe that, in any case, human courts were unable to resolve anything that was essential.

From the night of the accident until the day he killed Nieves González, he was unable to sleep peacefully.

Though he reasoned it all out rigorously and with conviction, it is not easy to believe that he decided to flee Camueso precisely so as not to sully the maternal home, and out of respect for the hospitality of the convent. It would be more logical to think that every time he took the Racciolo bend, he was assailed by the same vertigo that so often had him pulling up on the Barcelona-Murcia run.

Another of his explanations was that he had decided to come to Spain because this was a Catholic country, in the hope of having a church to hand if at some moment the longed-for contrition should come to him.

It never came after all, and as long as he was condemned to hell—and there was no doubt that he was—his life made no sense. Thus, the three crimes committed in Spain had a justification: he had surprised those three souls, by chance, perhaps, in a moment of unwonted purity. In killing them, he was sending his victims straight to paradise, removing them from any subsequent peril. Unable to save himself, at least it was good he could save others. After all the hell that awaited him would always burn with the same intensity. It must be said that, having come to this point, the public and the bench remained perplexed, and the entire courtroom shivered in a ripple of silence.

Equally perplexed was Arenillas, for whom the general incredulity only reinforced the truth of what his protégé said. It was evident that Aldo had come to Spain suffering from an emotional shock, and it was only later that he had been able to elaborate his theory, fashioning it so admirably that he convinced himself, as was demonstrated by the fact that he had requested the presence of a priest, hoping that, in the absence of knowing how to repent honestly, this would earn him some kind of indulgence in heaven.

The judge did not believe a word of what the olive-skinned altar boy came out with in his awkward Castilian and monotonous accent, and was even toying with the idea of an adjournment to study possible proceedings against Pedro as an accessory after the fact. But in the end, the duodenal ulcer pronounced sentence in some haste: Aldo was condemned to the three hundred and forty-nine years that the public prosecutor requested.

Aldo Pertucci went into prison with the same singular attitude of manifest indifference with which he had disembarked in Barcelona. There is little chance that any other inmate divined or ever would divine, in the three hundred and forty-nine years he had ahead of him, the depth and the tumult of the pain concealed behind his unflinching appearance.

They say that Pedro Arenillas was overcome by desperation on seeing him led away by the escort to the police van, and that, at that instant, his love, however human it had been, had to be sublimated abruptly into freestone, a crystal of a thousand facets that now shone with unexpected light.

This would explain his selling off the trucks and winding up the business, leaving his family a passable income deducted from what he put aside to defray the prisoner's costs. The rest he gave to works of charity. As for himself, he crept in ardent humiliation to the doors of a cloistered order where the brother doorkeeper received him somewhat harshly owing to the hour at which he arrived.

No doubt he thought that, with the years, his prayers, doubly persuasive in coming from the lips of a redeemed atheist, might end up tipping the balance and presenting a final argument to Pertucci, the possibility of being able to tell at last his story, and who knows, maybe in his own presence, on the Day of Judgement.

(Translated by Julie Flanagan.)

Bernardo Atxaga

The torch

I wanted to find a word to finish the book with. I mean I wanted to find one word, but it couldn't be just any word, it had to be a word that was both definitive and all-encompassing. I mean, to put it another way, that I wanted to be another Joubert, that he and I shared the same goal: 's'il est un homme tourmenté par la maudite ambition de mettre tout un livre dans une page, toute une page dans une phrase, cette phrase dans un mot, c'est moi.' Yes, that man was Joubert and, as I have just said, I wanted to be another Joubert.

I felt tired and disillusioned, old before my time, and when I sat down in front of a blank sheet of paper, I would weep. I mean that I found the invention and putting together of sentences was becoming ever more difficult, a torment, the cause of great suffering, which is why, as I said before, I kept dreaming about Joubert.

But I couldn't find that last word. I would look out of the window, I would watch the waves of the sea rising and breaking and I would ask the waves for an answer, but it was no use. Then I asked the stars in the sky and it was the same. I asked other people and that was even worse. I mean they were no help at all, they always ended up leaving me alone in front of the blank page. And then I would ask myself: Why don't you tell the story of the journey you made to Obaba? Maybe in recounting the events of that weekend you'll find the wretched word. I mean that I screwed up my courage and set off in search of the word, since it clearly had no intention of coming to me. That's what I mean, more or less.

But the task I had set myself turned out to take longer than I thought. I mean recounting what happened on my journey was not the brief, pleasant pastime I had at first supposed, quite the contrary. The days passed and I made no progress. The last word was nowhere to be found. And I would say to myself: All right, it hasn't turned up today, but maybe it will tomorrow. Don't worry about it. Instead of worrying, why not write down that story about Baghdad? And so I did. I mean I devoted all my time to recording the things that had happened on that journey and, in the process, months and even years went by. And what I really wanted kept being left to one side, kept being left farther and farther behind. Some nights Joubert would appear to me in my bedroom and call me to account. Why do you turn away from your true work like a sick dog from a bone? I do not spurn it, master, but there is another story I have to write down first, the one an old man told me at a village fiesta; Laura Sligo, that was the name, the character's name I mean, not the old man's. No, no, no! Joubert would say to me, don't deceive yourself, the problem is that you can't do it, the problem is that you're just like a lot of other writers of today, you're just the same as them, you're identical or similar or comparable. And with that, Joubert would go, leaving me sad. I mean no one enjoys hearing the truth.

For the fact is that I did keep putting off my real work until the next day, again and again, and that was my downfall. Because now it's too late, because now I never will find the final, definitive, all-encompassing word. And that's why I could be likened to those pilgrims who went off in the hope of seeing the sea but died without even setting foot on the beach. For I too am dead, at least according to my uncle. Dead without ever having found the final word. That's why I mentioned the story about the pilgrimage and the beach. I'm not sure if I made myself clear.

But perhaps I'm going too fast, which is utterly ridiculous. I mean it makes me laugh to think that the reason I have to go fast now is that I went too slowly before. I have very little time, in other words, and I'm going much too fast. Or at least that's what they tell me, my friend and my uncle that is. I don't really know why they say that, but they're probably right. We mustn't forget that my friend is a doctor, which is important. But, anyway, as I was saying, I go much too fast and get confused. But now I'll explain properly. I'll explain the reasons for my impotence, the reason why I never will find the last word and all that.

Well, what happened was that, some months after my visit to Obaba, the people at home said to me: You're deaf, aren't you? Me, deaf? I don't think so, I said, going on with my work. Because at that time, as I said before, I was engaged on writing down all the things that had happened on the journey to Obaba. But they didn't agree: You *are* going deaf. If anyone talks to you on your right side, you don't hear a thing. You should go to the doctor. And so I went. You've got a pierced eardrum said my friend, the doctor. I mean that the doctor is my friend and it was he who told me that.

My friend—the doctor, right?—looked at me hard and said: Has your head felt strange at all? Any headaches? Do you sleep well? Of course I do. Why do you ask? I asked. And my friend looked away, embarrassed.

I did feel a little worried that day, but not much. I went on with my work. I mean I was translating a story entitled *Wie Lie Deshang* and had no time to think about anything else. And anyway, to tell the truth, I didn't really understand my friend's question. After all what did it matter if I was a little deaf?

My worries, my real worries, began later, a month later. I mean my friends began to hate me, not much, but a little. What happened was that we were all eating and drinking in a restaurant, when they suddenly burst out laughing. What are you laughing at? I asked. And they replied: What's wrong, 'Mr I-mean'? Didn't you enjoy the joke? What joke? I said, getting angry. And anyway why have you started calling me 'Mr I-mean'? Don't you know my real name? That was no way to talk to one's friends, of course, and it was then that they began to hate me, not much, but a little, as I said before.

Then, since my friends didn't want me around any more, I decided to leave for Obaba and go to my uncle's house. And I spent hours and hours there reading and reading. One day my uncle asked: Why are you reading so many children's books? Are you thinking of writing an essay on children's literature? No, not at all, I replied, I'm reading them because I like them. Children's books are really fantastic, uncle. Are they? he asked, looking puzzled. Yes, they are, I said. For example, this one I'm reading at the moment is all about a mouse. It seems that this mouse, whose name is Timmy Willie, lives in a vegetable garden in a little village and what do you think happens? Well, one day he climbs into a basket to eat some peas and he goes to sleep there. I mean he just sort of drops off. And the owner of the vegetable garden comes along, lifts the basket on to his shoulder and goes off to the city to sell the peas. And all this time Timmy Willie is inside oblivious to everything and then, I'm sorry, uncle, but I have to laugh. And I burst out laughing. But I stopped at once when I saw the tears in my uncle's eyes. I mean it's not nice to laugh in front of someone when they're feeling sad, not nice at all.

Even so, though he was sad, my uncle looked after me well, very well, I've absolutely no complaints on that score. He brought me orange juice in bed every morning and even a newspaper. I didn't fancy it though. I mean I'd drink the orange juice at once, but I didn't touch the newspaper. I preferred to continue the adventures of Timmy Willie. Put that book down now, nephew, and read the articles in the paper, he'd beg me. And because I love my uncle very much, I made an effort to please him. But it was all in vain. It was a real struggle for me to understand what was in the newspaper, especially the sports pages, that was the hardest bit, much harder than the political reports.

And that's why I started going out. You see, my uncle wouldn't give up, he kept going on about the newspaper, which I found both objectionable and in bad taste. So I'd go out instead and meet up with Albino María, spend all day with him and go back to his house to sleep, because there are lots of beds in Albino María's house, at least ten.

Then one day my uncle got really angry with me and he phoned my friend, the doctor I mean, and the two of them got hold of me and bundled me into a car. Then we drove and drove until at last we came to a big house, and all the people there were dressed in white. In fact everything in the house was very white, it was almost frightening. And then they led me to a room lined with cork and my uncle said: Forgive me, nephew, but it's for your own good. Putting it in terms that you can understand, what's happened is that a lizard has got inside your head. And we have to get rid of that lizard, because it's making you very ill.

A lizard making me ill? I replied. That's not possible, uncle. Lizards are so lovely and green. But I regretted my words the moment they were out of my mouth. I mean I saw the tears in my uncle's eyes.

Then my friend said to my uncle: I'm more to blame than you are. I didn't realize he was being serious, I thought the business about Ismael was just another of his literary games, a bit like playing at being detectives. And, like a fool, I went along with it.

My dear friend, I said, you're not a fool. Anyway, as far as I'm concerned, you can leave the lizard where it is. It doesn't bother me. And we chatted on like that for a while and then they shaved off my hair and they hurt me, hurt me really badly. I mean they clamped some iron things on my head and I screamed blue murder.

That was five days ago, I think, yes, five days and the three of us were happy as larks afterwards. I mean the pain stopped and we all felt really glad, especially my uncle. You're your old self again, he cried. And then, even more loudly, he said: The torch burns as long as the flame lives! The fact is he was behaving like a madman.

But now we're back again to how it was before. My uncle isn't happy any more. Yesterday he came to me and said: 'Nephew, write down what you told me about Joubert, make that your final text. And do it as soon as possible, because you're dying.'

'Me? Dying?' I replied. 'What do you mean? I think you're wrong about that, uncle.'

'What I mean is that before, your head was like a flaming torch,' explained my uncle, 'but that torch is burning lower by the minute.'

I didn't say anything at the time but I really think my uncle is going mad. My head has always been round, it's never been anything like a torch. And anyway I can't remember a thing about this Joubert person and I don't know what to write. I get bored sitting here in the library. Just as well there are some flies in here. I mean later on I can go fishing with Albino María and they'll come in really handy then, these flies I'm catching now.

(*Translated by Margaret Jull Costa.*)

About the Authors

ATXAGA, Bernardo Pseudonym for José Irazu. Born in Asteasu (Guipúzcoa) in 1951; he is a graduate in Economics and writes in Basque. Author of poetry books, children's and adolescents' books. In 1989 he received the Critics' Award and the National Literary Award for *Obabakoak* (tr. Hutchinson, 1992), a collection of short stories.

CERCAS, Javier Born in Ibahernando (Cáceres) in 1962. At the end of 1966 his family moved to Gerona. He is a graduate in Spanish Philology from the Autonomous University of Barcelona, and since 1987 he has lectured at the University of Urbana-Champaigne in Illinois. He has published a book of short stories, *El móvil* (1987), and a novel, *El inquilino*.

CEREZALES, Agustín Born in Madrid in 1957, he graduated in French Philology. He has translated Chrétien de Troyes, Balzac, Fénelon and Louise Labé. He is an occasional contributor to newspapers and magazines, and has published *Lucrecia Borgia, máscara de sombras*, a fictionalized biography, and two books of short stories, *Perros verdes* (1989) and *Escaleras en el limbo* (1991).

DIAZ-MAS, Paloma Born in Madrid in 1954 she now lives in Vitoria. She lectures in Spanish (Golden Age) and Sephardic Literature in the University of the Basque Country. She has written scholarly papers on Sephardic literature and 'Los sefardíes: historia, lengua y cultura', for which she was shortlisted for the 1986 National Essay Prize. Her play *La informante* received the 1983 Theatre Award from the City of Toledo. She has published three novels, *El rapto del Santo Grial*, *Tras las huellas de Artorius* (1984 Cáceres Prize for Fiction), and *El sueño de Venecia*, for which she received the 1992 Herralde Prize. She has also written a 'travel book': *Una ciudad llamada Eugenio* on her experiences in the United States, and a book of short stories, *Nuestro milenio* (1987).

DIEZ, Luis Mateo Born in Villablino (León) in 1942, he has lived in Madrid for more than twenty years. He is the author of three novels, *Las estaciones provinciales* (1982), *La fuente de la Edad* (1986), for which he obtained the National Literary Award and the Critics' Award, and *El expediente del náufrago* (1992) and two books of short stories, *Memorial de hierbas* (1973) and *Brasas de agosto* (1989).

FERNANDEZ CUBAS, Cristina Born in Arenys de Mar (Barcelona) in 1945, she is a graduate in Law and Journalism, has lived for two years in Latin America and spent one winter studying in Cairo. Her novel *El año de Gracia* was published in 1985, and she has published three books of short stories: *Mi hermana Elba* (1980), *Los altillos de Brumal* (1983) (on which Cristina Andreu's film with Lucía Bosé and Paola Dominguín was based) and *El ángulo del horror* (1990).

FREIXAS, Laura Born in Barcelona in 1958, she graduated in Law and studied at the Ecole des hautes Etudes in Paris. She was Assistant Lecturer in Spanish in two British universities. She works as an essayist and literary critic in Madrid, and she directs Editorial Mondadori's series 'El espejo de tinta'. She is the author of the collection of short stories *El asesino en la muñeca* (1988).

GARCIA MONTALVO, Pedro Born in Murcia in 1951, he graduated in Philosophy and Letters. He spent 1973–6 studying Anglo-Saxon culture, and travelled extensively in Britain, Canada and the United States. He has translated a volume of Malcolm Lowry's previously unpublished writings, and a collection of essays by Joseph Conrad. *La imaginación natural* (1977) is a book of essays on American classics, and he has published a collection of texts on *Las villas de Roma* (1984). He has also written several novels, among them *El intermediario* (1983) and *Una historia madrileña* (1988), and two books of short stories: *La primavera en viaje hacia el invierno* (1981) and *Los amores y las vidas* (1983).

GARCIA SANCHEZ, Javier Born in Barcelona in 1955, he studied Journalism in Madrid's Complutense University. He was chief editor of the literary magazine *Quimera* and coordinated the cultural section of the San Sebastián newspaper *La Voz de Euskadi*. He has published essays (*Conocer a Hölderlin y su obra*), poetry (*La ira de la luz*), a collection of interviews (*Conversaciones con la joven filosofía española*), books of short stories: *Teoría de la eternidad* (1984), *Mutantes de invierno* (1984), *Los amores secretos* (1987) and *Crítica de la razón impura* (1992). He has also published several novels: *Continúa el misterio de los ojos verdes* (1984), *La dama del viento sur* (1985), *Ultima carta de amor de Carolina von Günderrode a Bettina Brentano* (1986), *El mecanógrafo* (1989) and *La historia más triste*, which won the Herralde Prize for 1991.

MARIAS, Javier Born in Madrid in 1951, he lectured at the University of Oxford for two years. He has published several translations, and he received the National Translation Prize in 1979 for Laurence Sterne's *Tristam Shandy*. His novels include *Los dominios del lobo* (1971), *Travesía del horizonte* (1972), *El monarco del tiempo* (1978), *El siglo* (1983), *El hombre sentimental* (1986 Herralde Prize), *Todas las almas* (1989 City of Barcelona Prize; tr. as *All Souls*, Harvill, an imprint of HarperCollins Publishers, 1992), and *Corazón tan blanco* (1992). He is the author of a collection of short stories, *Mientras ellas duermen* (1990) and two compilations of essays, *Pasiones pasadas* (1991) and *Vidas escritas* (1992).

MARTINEZ DE PISON, Ignacio Born in Zaragoza in 1960, he now lives in Barcelona. He graduated in Spanish and Italian Philology, and contributes regularly in newspapers and magazines and occasionally translates Italian fiction. He has published two novels: *La ternura del dragón* (1984 Casino de Mieres Prize) and *Nuevo plano de la ciudad secreta* (1992 Torrente Ballester Prize), and two books of short stories: *Alguien te observa en secreto* (1985) and *Antofagasta* (1987).

MERINO, José María Born in La Coruña in 1941, he lived in León for many years before settling in Madrid. He has published several books of poems, a chronicle of a voyage in collaboration with Juan Pedro Aparicio: *Los caminos de Esla* (1980), a trilogy for young people ending with *Las lágrimas del sol* (1989) and four novels: *Novela de Andrés Choz* (1976 Fiction and Short Story Award), *El caldero de oro* (1981), *La orilla oscura* (1985 Critics' Award) and *El centro del aire* (1991). He has also published two books of short stories: *Cuentos del reino secreto* (1982) and *El viajero perdido* (1990).

MILLAN, José Antonio Born in Madrid in 1954, he is a graduate in Linguistics, and in 1973 he supervised research on Latin metrics with computers. He has translated Henry James and Noam Chomsky, among others. He is the author of two books of short stories: *Sobre las brasas* (1988) and *La memoria (y otras extremidades)* (1990) and a novel, *El día intermitente* (1990).

MILLAS, Juan José Born in Valencia in 1946, he has lived in Madrid since the beginning of the 1950s. He studied Philosophy and Letters at the Complutense University and writes regularly in newspapers and magazines. He is the author of *Cerbero son las sombras* (1974 Sésamo

Award), *Visión del ahogado* (1977), *El jardín vacío* (1981), *Papel mojado* (1983), *Letra muerta* (1983), *El desorden de tu nombre* (1988), *La soledad era esto* (1990 Nadal Prize) and *Volver a casa* (1990), and a book of short stories, *Primavera de luto* (1992).

MOIX, Ana María   Born in Barcelona in 1947, she graduated in Philosophy and Letters. She was included in Josep Maria Castellet's *Nueve novísimos poetas españoles* (1990). Her poems written between 1969 and 1972 ('Baladas del dulce Jim', 'Call me Stone' and 'No time for flowers') have been published in *A imagen y semejanza* (1984). She is the author of two novels: *Julia* (1969) and *Walter ¿ por qué te fuiste?* (1973) and of two books of short stories: *Ese chico pelirrojo a quien veo cada día* (1972) and *Las virtudes peligrosas* (1985).

MONZO, Quim   Born in Barcelona in 1952. He has been a cartoonist, script-writer for films, radio and television, lyricist, graphic designer and war correspondent. He is a Catalan writer, and all his work has been translated into Castilian. He has published books of short stories, *Uf, va dir ell* (1978) and *Olivetti, Moulinex, Chaffoteaux et Maury* (1981), published in Castilian as *Melocotón de manzana* (1981), *L'illa de Maians* (1985) and *El perquè de tot plegat* (1992), and novels *Benzina* (1983) and *La magnitud de la tragedia* (1989). *La maleta turca* (1990) is a selection of his best articles published in 1987–9 in the Barcelona press.

MUNOZ MOLINA, Antonio   Born in Ubeda (Jaén) in 1956, he graduated in Art History from the University of Granada, where he now lives. He writes regularly for the daily press and in several weeklies and literary magazines. He has published some of his newspaper articles in *El Robinson urbano* (1984) and *Diario de Nautilus* (1985). His short stories have not been published in one volume, although they have been included in several anthologies. He is the author of *Beatus Illae* (1986 Icarus Literary Award), *El invierno en Lisboa* (1987), *Beltenebros* (1989, tr. as *Prince of Shadows*, Quartet, 1993), which was made into a film by Pilar Miró, *El jinete polaco* (Planeta Prize 1991), and *Los misterios de Madrid* (1992).

MURILLO, Enrique   Born in Barcelona in 1944, he studied Journalism in Spain and obtained an M. Phil. from the University of London, a city where he lived for many years. He has edited *El Europeo* and Spanish *Vogue*, and was the literary editor of *El País*. He has translated Coleridge, Pound, Nabokov, Truman Capote, Djuna

Barnes, Sam Shepard and Martin Amis, as well as published a book of short stories, *El secreto arte* (1984) and a novel, *El centro del mundo* (1988).

PAMIES, Sergi   Born in Paris in 1960, he has lived in Barcelona since 1971. He writes regularly for the Barcelona press. He has published two books of short stories: *T'auria de caure la cara de vergonya* (1986) and *Infecció* (1987) and the novels *La primera pedra* (1990) and *L'instint* (1992). He writes in Catalan and his work has been translated into Castilian.

POMBO, Alvaro   Born in Santander in 1939, he read Philosophy at Madrid's Complutense University and has a BA in Philosophy from the University of London. He lived in London from 1966 to 1977, and now lives in Madrid. He has published three books of poems, and for *Variaciones* he received the 1977 El Bardo Poetry Award. He has published a book of short stories: *Relatos sobre la falta de sustancia* (1977), a short novel: *El hijo adoptivo* (1984) and several novels: *El parecido* (1979; tr. *The Resemblance*, Chatto & Windus, 1989), *El héroe de las mansardas de Mansard* (1983 Herralde Prize; tr. *The Hero of the Big House*, Chatto & Windus, 1988), *Los delitos insignificantes* (1986), *El metro de platino iridiado* (1990 Critics' Award), and *Aparición del eterno femenino contada por S.M. el Rey* (1993).

PUERTOLAS, Soledad   Born in Zaragoza in 1947, she now lives in Madrid. She studied Journalism and has an MA in Spanish and Portuguese Language and Literature from the University of California at Santa Barbara. She has published short stories: *Una enfermedad moral* (1983) and *La corriente del golfo* (1993), and the novels: *El bandido doblemente armado* (1979 Sésamo Award), *Burdeos* (1986), *Todos mienten* (1988), *Queda la noche* (1989 Planeta Prize) and *Días del arenal* (1991).

PUIG, Valentí   Born in Majorca in 1949, he graduated in Philosophy and Letters from the University of Barcelona. Poet and essayist, he has written travel books on Dublin and Palma, a book of notes extracted from a diary (*Bosc endins*, 1982), a book of memoirs (*Matèria obscura*, 1991), a book of short stories (*Dones que fumen*, 1983) and the novels *Complot* (1986) and *Somni Delta* (1987 Ramon Llull Prize). He writes in Majorcan and is translated into Castilian. He is currently London correspondent for the *ABC* newspaper.

RIERA, Carme   Born in Majorca in 1948, she graduated in Philosophy and Letters from the University of Barcelona. She is a lecturer in Spanish Literature at the Barcelona Autonomous University. In 1988 she won the Anagrama Essay Prize with 'La Escuela de Barcelona'. She has written several works of fiction, all in Majorcan and most have been translated into Castilian. Among her novels are *Te deix, amor, la mar com a penyora* (1975), *Jo pos per testimoni les gavines* (1977), *Una primavera per Domenico Guarini* (1980 Prudenci Bertrana Fiction Award), *Questió d'amor propi* (1987), *Joc de miralls* (1989 Ramon Llull Prize) and *Contra l'amor en companyia i altres relats* (1991).

SALADRIGAS, Robert   Born in Barcelona in 1940, he studied Economics and went into journalism when he was very young. He is a literary critic and literary editor of *La Vanguardia*, Barcelona. He has written many books, amongst them six volumes for young people (*El viatge prodigiós d'en Ferran Pinyol*, published between 1971 and 1978), books of short stories (*Boires*, 1969 Victor Catalá Prize), *Néixer de nou, cada dia* (1979), *Sota la volta del temps* (1980), and *Imatges del meu mirall* (1983), and novels: *El cau* (1967), *52 hores a través de la pell* (1970), *Aquell gust agre de l'estel* (1976 La Dida Award), *Pel cami ral del nord* (1980), *Sóc Ema* (1983), *Memorial de Claudi M.Broch* (1986 Critics' Award), *Claris* (1990), and *El sol de la tarda* (1991 Sant Jordi Prize). His work, written in Catalan, has been translated into Castilian.

TOMEO, Javier   Born in Quicena (Huesca) in 1932, he studied Law and Criminology at the University of Barcelona. He has published books of short stories (*Historias mínimas*, 1988, and *Problemas oculares*, 1990) and several novels: *El Unicornio* (1971 Ciudad de Basbastro Award), *El castillo de la carta cifrada* (1979) and *Amado monstruo* (1985) these two titles tr. as *The Coded Letter and Dear Monster*, Carcanet, 1992, *El cazador de leones* (1987), *El mayordomo miope* (1990) and *El gallitigre* (1990).

TUSQUETS, Esther   Born in Barcelona in 1936, she read History at the Universities of Barcelona and Madrid. Since the early 1960s she has directed Editorial Lumen. She has published a book of short stories, *Siete miradas en un mismo paisaje* (1981), and the novels: *El mismo mar todos los veranos* (1978), *El amor es un juego solitario* (1979 Ciudad de Barcelona Award; tr. as *Love is a Solitary Game*, John Calder

(Publishers) Ltd., 1985), *Varada tras el último naufragio* (1980) and *Para no volver* (1985).

VAZQUEZ MONTALBAN, Manuel   Born in Barcelona in 1939, he graduated from the Faculties of Philosophy and Letters and of Journalism. He was included in Castellet's *novísimos* anthology. As essayist and journalist he has published *Manifiesto subnormal* (1970), *Crónica sentimental de España* (1971) and *Mis almuerzos con gente importante* (1984). He has published a series of detective novels which feature the well-known detective Pepe Carvalho: among them *Yo maté a Kennedy* (1972), *La soledad del manager* (1977; tr. as *The Angst-Ridden Executive*, Serpent's Tail, 1990), *Los mares del sur* (1979 Planeta Prize and the 1981 Grand Prix de Littérature Policière Etrangère; tr. as *Southern Seas*, Serpent's Tail), which was made into a film by Manuel Esteban, *Asesinato en el Comité Central* (1981; tr. as *Murder in the Central Committee*, Serpent's Tail), filmed by Vicente Aranda, and *El balneario* (1986). He has also written *El pianista* (1985; tr. as *The Pianist*, Quartet, 1989), *Los alegres muchachos de Atzavara* (1987), *Galíndez* (1990) and *Autobiografía del general Franco*. A selection of his short stories has been published under the title *Pigmalión y otros relatos* (1987).

VILA-MATAS, Enrique   Born in Barcelona in 1948, he has published books of short stories (*Nunca voy al cine*, 1982, *Suicidios ejemplares*, 1991, and *Hijos sin hijos*, 1993) and several novels: *Mujer en el espejo contemplando el paisaje* (1977), *Al sur de los párpados* (1980), *Impostura*, *Historia abreviada de la literatura portátil* (1985) and *Una casa para siempre* (1988), which can also be considered as a book of short stories. He has also published a compilation of essays and articles: *El viajero más lento* (1992).

ZARRALUKI, Pedro   Born in Barcelona in 1954, he received the Margarita Xirgu Prize for the radio play *Retrato sobre una barca*. He has published two novels (*La noche del tramoyista*, 1987, and *El responsable de las ranas*, 1990) and the books of short stories *Galería de enormidades* (1983) and *Retrato de familia con catástrofe* (1989).

Founded in 1986, Serpent's Tail publishes the innovative and the challenging.

If you would like to receive a catalogue of our current publications please write to:

FREEPOST
Serpent's Tail
4 Blackstock Mews
LONDON N4 2BR

(No stamp necessary if your letter is posted in the United Kingdom.)

Also published by Serpent's Tail

The Lonely Hearts Club
Raul Nuñez

'Magnificent.'   *Blitz*

'The singles scene of Barcelona's lonely low life.
Sweet and seedy.'   *Elle*

'A celebration of the wit and squalor of Barcelona's
mean streets.'   *City Limits*

'This tough and funny story of low life in Barcelona
manages to convey the immense charm of that city
without once mentioning Gaudi. . . . A story of
striking freshness, all the fresher for being so casually
conveyed.'   *The Independent*

'A sardonic view of human relations . . .'
                                                   The Guardian

'Threatens to do for Barcelona what *No Mean City*
once did for Glasgow.'   *Glasgow Herald*

'A funny low life novel of Barcelona.'   *The Times*

Murder in the Central Committee
The Angst-Ridden Executive
An Olympic Death
Southern Seas

Pepe Carvalho thrillers by
Manuel Vázquez Montalbán

Also published by Serpent's Tail

Landscapes After the Battle
Juan Goytisolo

'Juan Goytisolo is one of the most rigorous and original contemporary writers. His books are a strange mixture of pitiless autobiography, the debunking of mythologies and conformist fetishes, passionate exploration of the periphery of the West – in particular of the Arab world which he knows intimately – and audacious linguistic experiment. All these qualities feature in *Landscapes After the Battle*, an unsettling, apocalyptic work, splendidly translated by Helen Lane.'   MARIO VARGAS LLOSA

'*Landscapes After the Battle* . . . a cratered terrain littered with obscenities and linguistic violence, an assault on "good taste" and the reader's notions of what a novel should be.'   *The Observer*

'Fierce, highly unpleasant and very funny.'
The Guardian

'A short, exhilarating tour of the emergence of pop culture, sexual liberation and ethnic militancy.'
New Statesman

'Helen Lane's rendering reads beautifully, capturing the whimsicality and rhythms of the Spanish without sacrificing accuracy, but rightly branching out where literal translation simply does not work.'
Times Literary Supplement

Also published by Serpent's Tail

Marks of Identity
Juan Goytisolo

'For me *Marks of Identity* was my first novel. It was
forbidden publication in Spain. For twelve years
after that everything I wrote was forbidden in Spain.
So I realized that my decision to attack the Spanish
language through its culture was correct. But what
was most important for me was that I no longer
exercised censorship on myself, I was a free writer.
This search for and conquest of freedom was the
most important thing to me.'

Juan Goytisolo, in an interview with *City Limits*

'Juan Goytisolo is by some distance the most
important living novelist from Spain ... and *Marks of
Identity* is undoubtedly his most important novel,
some would say the most significant work by a
Spanish writer since 1939, a truly historic milestone.'

The Guardian

'A masterpiece which should whet the appetites of
British readers for the rest of the trilogy.'

Times Literary Supplement